THE
REVELATIONS
OF
CAREY
RAVINE

DEBRA DALEY

Quercus

First published in Great Britain in 2016
This edition published in 2017 by

Quercus Publishing Ltd
Carmelite House
50 Victoria Embankment
London EC4Y 0DZ

An Hachette UK company

A CIP catalogue record for this book is available
from the British Library

PB ISBN 978 1 78206 996 6
EBOOK ISBN 978 1 78429 186 0

This book is a work of fiction. Names, characters,
businesses, organizations, places and events are
either the product of the author's imagination
or used fictitiously. Any resemblance to

THE
REVELATIONS
OF
CAREY
RAVINE

Chapter 1

A Case of Human Poisoning

May the 3rd, 1776

The servants finally roused themselves to mutiny this afternoon. It was the cook that gave voice to their demands. She threatened to expose the truth of our rickety situation to the tradesmen on whom we depend unless the unpaid wages were imminently forthcoming. I was suitably frighted. Once a supplier suspects that one's prospects have dimmed, he will press like a hound on a fox for liquidation of his account – I could already hear the horrible howls of our credit being torn apart. I knew where Nash kept the key to his locking box. It was under a pot on the middle tier of the plant theatre that I maintain in our bedchamber. There was nothing for it but to go to his closet, haul the box from beneath the skirts of his hanging coats and extract most of the guineas we keep for such emergencies as paying the wine merchant or ordering a wheel of Parmesan from Modena. Once I had distributed the coins between the housekeeper, the footman and the cook, and order was once again established at Hood Street, I returned to the closet and consulted the box again. I am not in the habit of nosing about in Nash's belongings, but it seemed timely to steel myself to know the number of promissory notes that remained. They are issued under my husband's name, of course, but it was I who had earned them – and earned them hard.

The banknotes were kept in their own velvet case. I cannot say that I was surprised by its meagre contents, since Nash and I had burned through the money like wildfire. I knew that very well and yet at the same time I kept up a pretence of ignorance as to the truth of our situation. But now there was no avoiding it. Of the five hundred pounds that I had brought to my marriage, only twenty lonely pounds had survived the rout of the preceding three years. I crouched on the floor in front of the box like someone in an attitude of supplication. One rather had the sense of coming towards the end of a road.

I dragged the box on its little wheels out into the bed-chamber. I did not think that Nash would mind if I ferreted through its contents. He is generally frank and hospitable in most of his doings, and in fact, no one would be more jubilant than he if I should discover some overlooked banknote lurking in the recesses of the box like a pheasant in the undergrowth. I shuffled through the papers of consequence that Nash keeps in a Manilla sheath – his passport, his credentials and letters of introduction; in another sheath I found the rental agreements for the house, the furniture, the plate and all the items one hires in order to make a show of being comfortable, since everybody knows that success only visits those who seem already to be in possession of it. Our certificate of marriage was tucked into one of the pockets on the walls of the box along with a letter from the Duke of Larchmont's secretary warning Nash of possible legal action in regard to a dust-up between Nash and one of the younger Larchmonts. The threat had turned out to be no more than bluster, but I supposed that Nash had kept the letter for the sake of the crested ducal stationery. It is a little vanity of his to bask in any association with the nobility and he will count a hostile response as gratifying as any other. At any rate, there was not a single stray banknote anywhere in the box.

I almost failed to notice an additional pocket in the lid. I only saw it as I went to close the box. Slipping my hand into the pocket, I touched something weighty, and my heart lifted for a second at the prospect of discovering an item of worth, but when I eased the object out of its niche, I saw it was only a dossier in the form of an oilskin pouch. It contained *Reports*, according to an inscription in a cartouche pasted to the front of the pouch. I upended it in the vain hope that something valuable might fall into my lap, but there seemed to be nothing within but papers. Yet, as I turned the pouch right way up again and fixed my gaze on the stamp in the bottom right-hand corner of the cartouche, a ripple of interest ran through me. The stamp showed a crest of two lions holding a regal crown above the initials E.I.C. The East India Company.

I am captivated by any mention of India. I read everything I can of its history and customs and it especially frustrates me that Nash has had so little to say about the time he spent there. Oh, he has sketched a few scenes for me of life in Calcutta – Nash at his law firm; Nash dining on incendiary curries; Nash going about in a fringed palanquin – but he insists that Bengal is a tiresome place (I can't imagine how! I would say) and it bores him to bring it up. In his view, there is nowhere in the world that can ever be an adequate substitute for London.

I pulled the papers from the pouch and rifled through them, still in the hope that I might discover a banknote within. I was disappointed in that regard, but my curiosity was roused by the documents. I wondered if they might throw light on the work that my husband had undertaken in Calcutta. I do rather wish that he would return to practise law. We cannot go on pretending that the assignments he accepts at present are worthy of his talents.

There were two reports. They were both addressed to Major-General the Honourable Sir John Lambert at the Dinapore Cantonment, Patna, and they were marked *CONFIDENTIAL [to be sent to the District Magistrate, Patna]*. The author of the reports was an A. J. Martenson, M.D., Former Surgeon, 37th Infantry, Bengal Artillery and Engineers. Currently Naturalist, Bankipore Research Station. I assumed that these documents were germane to cases that had retained Nash's services, perhaps, in Bengal. In any case, the titles were sufficiently dramatic that I at once felt an inclination to read them: *A Case of Human Poisoning* and *A Case of Collective Poisoning*. Each of them *By Agents Unknown*.

I brought the documents into the light by the window next to the plant theatre. As I was about to sit in the easy chair, I saw a damaged leaf tip on one of the American woundworts and I pinched it off. People do not think them a very attractive plant, but they are dependable and hardy and do not mind our winter dankness; and just when summer flowers have gone over to their deaths, the woundwort blossoms into a cloud of golden yellow. The bloodroots, on the other hand, were already in bloom, the flowers a virgin white, although I noticed that their fleshy palmate leaves were already beginning to senesce. The pathos of these spring ephemerals always touches me so.

As I took up the *Human Poisoning* report, my attention was caught at once by an asterisk in the second line of the introduction: *On the 11th of February 1772, the Author of this report was asked by the Defence Research Committee* of the Bengal Army to attend a medical trial at the hospital in the Dinapore cantonment.*

The asterisk referred me to a footnote. I am instinctively drawn to notes and parentheses and marginalia. I always think that such annotation goes beyond the merely bibliographic. It strikes me more as a recess off the great room of information, where the author may take the reader into confidence and direct her, by means of a clueful footnote, to the meanings buried in the text. Therefore, I was disposed to notice in the report a feature shared by five of the asterisked members of the Defence Research Committee.

* Consisting of Lt-Col. S. Long, Officiating Representative of the Board of Ordance, since retired from the service.

Rollo Hayle, Bart., Lalatola Research Station, Patna.

Dr C. Gibbon, Officiating Secretary to the Medical Board, soon after appointed Civil Surgeon to the Persian Gulf.

Dr Pugh, Principal of the Medical Corps, since dead.

Maj. J. Skipwith, Bengal Engineers, Dinapore, soon after appointed Lt-Col. in the North-West Provinces.

Mr V. Archer, Senior Clerk in the Civil and Military Pay Department, soon after went to England.

Retired, transferred, dead, transferred, sent home. I wondered if it were a coincidence that these committee members had removed from Bengal after the poisoning took place.

As I explained the stand-off with the servants over their wages and the sacrifice of the guineas, Nash inspected his ensemble in the glass, and turned the cuffs of his new suit. The marvellous shimmering blue of the shot silk favoured him to perfection. 'I am afraid I had to pay them,' I said. 'They were awfully bullish.'

'It can't be helped,' Nash replied, unconcerned. 'We held out for as long as we could.'

He is a good-looking man with thick brown hair falling to his shoulders, high cheekbones in a broad-planed face and sensual features that are nearly excitingly brutish. He put his hand on his hip to show off his paisley waistcoat. Its pattern was very, very intricate. 'Too much, do you think?' he asked. He was smiling, his lips drawn back over his teeth in that way he has that is rather wolf-like and always quickens my passion. Isn't it amazing the way you can feel desire gather in your secret parts just by the way a man smiles? The sliding of the lips on the teeth. 'But what do you know, my underbred darling.'

He teases me about my lack of breeding only because he despises his own. His brawny physique made me wonder, when I first met him, if he came from stock that had performed physical labour in recent generations. The possibility appealed to me. But, actually, he was sired by a clothier in Clerkenwell, whom he refers to as 'the deceased draper'.

'Even at this remove of time and distance,' Nash will say, 'I can still see the old man prowling that damned shop, fingering his bolts of coarse cloth and half-worsteds.'

I stood before the glass with my box of kajal and outlined my eyes. Then I pressed rouge on my lips. My looks are those of an outsider – dark, olive-skinned, with eyes and hair a sooty hue courtesy of French forebears – but that is not the reason I am drawn to transform my features. I do not care whether I might pass for a conventional blue-eyed beauty or not. I like to paint my face in order to render it a mask. I am fond, as well, of the shielding accessory, an intercession between me and others: the mantilla worn low on the forehead, the raised fan, the wide brim of a hat. Veils, too. Why do I shrink in this manner from human exchange? Why, to avoid judgement, obviously – although I freely admit the ambiguity of this impulse given that Nash and I are so very much upon the town and flash with it. I began to dress, drawing my shift over my head, and then I said, 'Do you know, Nash, I read the dossier that was in your locking box. I came across it when I was grubbing around to pay the servants.'

'A dossier?'

'Two cases of poisoning. Did they come to trial in Calcutta?'

'I cannot recall.' He did not look up. He was fitting a ring on his finger.

I tied a petticoat around my waist and smoothed it. I said, 'There was a medical experiment at the army cantonment and a young man died, a gunner named James Kinch. He was only twenty-two.'

Nash was not satisfied with the ring he wore. He removed it and sat down to fasten the buckles on his shoes.

I said, 'He only volunteered for the trial because he was a prisoner at the cantonment. The report did not explain what crime he had committed.'

'Probably done for drunkenness or desertion. They are the most popular misdemeanours in the ranks.'

'The trial concerned a new variety of *Ammannia Vesicatoria*. That piqued my interest because it is a plant that my father used to raise. Apothecaries value it as a remedy for skin parasites.'

Nash straightened and peered downwards to inspect his buckles for symmetry.

'The leaves were applied to the bare arms of the volunteers,' I said, 'but, oddly enough, according to the attending medical officer, who wrote the report, the victim, James Kinch, was administered to in a room that was separate from the others and without the medical officer being present. When the officer looked for poor Kinch, he found him in spasms, frothing at the mouth. I thought perhaps you might have worked on the case.'

'It does not ring any bells. I wonder why I kept the dossier.'

'Perhaps because the cases are so intriguing, especially the one that concerns a mass poisoning.'

Nash's face was blank.

I said, 'Fifty bandits were found dead at a campsite in the jungle, at a place called Rajmahal. Can you imagine? Fifty men felled all at once in their bivouacs.'

'An accidental food poisoning, no doubt. It is a common occurrence in Bengal.'

'Is that so? They were discovered with contorted limbs and blue faces, just like the gunner at the cantonment.'

Nash said, 'Nothing about India surprises me. One very quickly becomes used to events there that would seem extraordinary at home. Now, lovely, will you please make haste. The Mango awaits and we must catch our bird while she remains at roost.'

The bird in question was Lady Celia Malet and her roost was a club called the Mango Tree on the south side of St James's

Park, near Great Queen Street. It is frequented by some of London's choicest spirits, men and women of wit, as well as the usual squanderous nobles. How disappointing it is that Nash and I are not of sufficient standing to be recommended as members. We were not even sure that we could enter the club on this occasion, but we had conceived a plan to linger until a diversion presented itself – as soon it did when a cluster of macaronis arrived lit up with booze. Dressed in coats smothered with cartloads of sequins, they looned about in the throng at the entrance, until presently one or two of them made an attack on some of the waiting chairs for a jape, and then they all joined in, beating on the leather walls with their fists and attracting the ire of the chairmen. As soon as the stewards at the portal of the club left their posts to inspect the scene on the stairs, Nash and I ducked into the reception hall, where a clerk was checking members' cards of admission. Nash approached the clerk in a furore, announcing that a general engagement had ensued outside, and insisted that he should call the watchmen to save the stewards. The clerk jumped up and edged towards the door, and while he and a couple of footmen were consternating themselves, Nash and I slipped by them. None of the footmen standing sentinel at the entrance to the cloakrooms or the saloons gave us a second glance. We passed for quality, I in my spangled sleeves and Nash in his unctious suit. The topography of the Mango Tree is familiar to anyone who reads the many accounts in the papers of the club's zesty goings-on and we easily found our way into the first of a series of saloons, with tall, arched windows, silver-fringed curtains and crystal chandeliers. There was a banqueting hall somewhere, we knew, and drawing rooms above reserved for dancing, and a slew of little side-rooms, where I expect members retired to contemplate the disaster of their vanished fortunes, before going home to break the bad news to their spouses and heirs. The Mango Tree, famously, sets no limit on its wagers.

We proceeded with a jaunty step, looking for the object of Nash's business among the crowds of fashionable specimens gaming at the tables. As one saloon succeeded another, the play grew deeper and I was transfixed by the hundreds of pounds in specie that lay upon the baize. I stayed Nash to watch with me at a hazard table as a dapperling threw his dice. A shout went up and then a groan, but who the loser was it was hard to say, since no person of merit would be so vulgar as to make a spectacle of his calamity. When someone threw in a gold bracelet upon the coins, I murmured to Nash, 'There is a sign of desperation.'

'This is a twenty-guinea table. Each player must keep that amount before him to stay in the game.' He turned to look towards the far saloon. 'I am certain that the lady I am after will find this small beer. Let us walk on, my pretty.'

Arm in arm, we strolled onwards until we reached the furthest saloon, which Nash knew to be a fifty-guinea room, and in short order he spotted his quarry. Lady Celia was dressed extravagantly in flowered silk, with a gold net on her petticoat. Her hair was powdered and arranged in a *pouffe*. She was among a dozen stylish ladies crammed around a faro table. They were surrounded in turn by many loud danglers and admirers, whose shouts and cheers contributed to the frantic atmosphere. Lady Celia was laying down her money with a great deal of perseverance. She had used to host a faro table at her townhouse, Nash told me, until her husband put a stop to it. Now she was constantly at the Mango Tree, where she nightly liquefied at cards an allowance she received from her brother. With her eye still on the play, she groped behind her for the hand of the young man hanging at her shoulder. He had crimson clocks on his stockings and flounces on his sleeves.

But it was Nash who seized her hand and pulled her away from the table. Her companion blanched. He had a smooth blonde face and a weak jaw.

'How dare you!' Lady Celia cried, but there was such a din around the tables, no one heeded her protest.

Nash pulled her close to him as if they were walking in intimacy like old acquaintances and forced her along towards one of the side-rooms. I had never witnessed Nash at this work before. I followed, fascinated to see what he would do next. I was also, I will admit, a little uneasy about this new career as an enforcer.

There was no one else in the room but we three. I closed the door behind me. Lady Celia threw herself into an armchair, but Nash clasped her arms and hauled her to her feet.

'You must give me your serious attention, madam,' he said.

The door opened at that moment to show the young man

in his high heels, but Nash gave him such a look that he immediately withdrew. Nash returned his gaze to the lady. He said, 'You have a bill of one hundred pounds outstanding that is owed to a jeweller.'

'Oh, that.' Lady Celia forced a laugh. 'Such insolence from these tradesmen.' The two vertical lines between her eyebrows deepened. She was about fifty years of age, I guessed.

Nash said, 'He has presented the bill numerous times, but the exchange is always the same. You refuse to honour it.'

Her chin went up. 'I am offended at the prospect of having to pay, since I do not believe that the bill has been accurately cast up.'

They can be slippery customers, the high and mighty; too elevated in rank to fear the threat of a debtors' prison, yet too careless to meet their obligations. Recently, Nash thought to settle his own debts with genteel tradesmen by offering to try and recoup larger sums owed them by recalcitrant lords and ladies – and so, here we were. I acknowledge the irony of depending on debt collection for our income, when we ourselves are so overdrawn, but such work has never been more than a stopgap while we manoeuvre into a more favourable position. As an attorney by profession, it is not what Nash was destined to do, of course.

He was saying, 'If you do not give me the money, you will be very sorry.'

'Shall I? I do not think so.' Lady Celia examined the state of the nails on her jewelled fingers with apparent nonchalance, but I saw that her hand shook slightly.

Nash said, 'Lord Dexter will be sorry, too.'

Lady Celia looked at Nash through narrowed eyes. 'I suppose you are one of the spies that my husband sets on me to watch my actions. It is not my fault if Lord Dexter chooses to play at the same table as I.'

In a swift movement, Nash slid his arm tight around Lady Celia's shoulders and chivvied her towards a corner. She struggled, but he held her fast. He bent to her ear and, with an expression on his face that was dark and menacing, he spoke in a low, urgent tone. I could not make out what he said, but it greatly perturbed the lady, because as soon as Nash let her go, she hissed at him, 'This is blackmail, sir.'

'I do not care what you call it, but I will tell you that I will stoop as low as I must to get my way.' Nash's voice, as a rule, has a lazy quality that is awfully attractive. I had never heard him use this cold, stony tone before. It gave me a shiver.

'I have had a run of ill luck, you know.' Lady Celia's voice trembled. 'You can ask anyone here. I can scarcely raise five pounds.'

'Then you must draw upon your brother, the earl,' Nash said.

'That I cannot do.'

'In which case you must take the consequences.'

'I won't be coerced like this! I shall tell my friends that the jeweller is a pesterer and he will lose all our custom.'

'I think you will decide not to do that. Otherwise, I shall only have to find another way to hurt you, which will be a nuisance for me and painful for you. So, come now, madam, out with your pocketbook.'

Lady Celia, who had not given me a glance, now looked in my direction. Her complexion was waxy, as if all the life had drained from it.

Nash said, 'It is pointless to apply to that lady. She is not here on your behalf.'

Oddly enough, though, I felt a little stab of pity for the woman. Her husband was a brute, everyone knew that, and I certainly understood what it was like to spend recklessly on bright things as a recompense for sadness. But, as Nash often observes, usually in relation to the letting go of a servant, sometimes strength of purpose requires a hard heart – and so I suppressed my feelings of sympathy.

Nash said smoothly, 'Shall I call for pen and ink so that you may write a draft upon your banker?'

After another fierce glance to the right and left, and finding there was no way out of her predicament, Lady Celia was obliged to capitulate.

Chapter 2

The Mango Tree

May the 3rd, 1776

The settling of Lady Celia's account meant that Nash was in a position to claim fifteen per cent of the jeweller's bill as a recovery fee, and so it was with effervescent spirits that he and I made our way upstairs towards the music and laughter drifting from the drawing room. As we passed along a hall where expensive tapers burned in towering candelabra, I said, 'You are quite the persuader. I was ready to write you a banker's draft myself. What did you say to the lady?'

'Oh, this and that.'

'You would not have hurt her though.'

'Who knows? I am an awful brute, you know.'

With his wicked smile, he took me tightly by the arm and drew me away into a corner. The fragrance of beeswax was heavy in the air and I could hear strings playing a minuet in a high, complicated style. Nash caressed the swell of my breasts. 'Your ladyship looks ravishing tonight.' He smiled. 'How can your husband be indifferent to such charms?'

I did not hesitate to join Nash's game. 'And yet he employs spies to watch me.'

'They cannot see you here.'

'I fear that they do.'

'In that case, come with me.' Nash took my hand and led me to a small, plain door that gave way to a low corridor and the back stairs of the house. We crept up to the next floor and pushed our way into a mean room, lit only by the moon. There were two narrow cots on either side of a stingy fireplace and a line pegged with washing. We could hear the distant thud of footsteps on the stairs as servants went back and forth, and, far away, the rise and fall of the music like the soughing of leaves and branches in a woodland. I fell on to the bed and Nash leaned over me and I kissed him deeply. He unbuttoned his breeches, excited at the possibility that someone might come in and discover us. To be sexual conspirators, that is one of our favourite frolics. He kissed me again with a growing urgency, the sense of haste, the fumbling, fuelling our desire. I arched my back and melted against him, my arms tight about his neck, my thighs pressed against his hips. As he entered me, I sighed with pleasure.

Ah, my Nash. He has all the answers.

As he got to his feet to pull up his breeches, and as I was smoothing my skirts, the door suddenly opened and a wench stood gaping at us with an apron bunched in her hand. Nash glanced down at his expended member and quipped, 'Alas, my dear, you're too late.'

She retorted with a chuckle, 'They're serving supper downstairs, sir. I suppose you and the lady might have an appetite.'

Nash coolly handed me to my feet and set himself to

rights. The maid walked with a casual air to the washing line, set aside her spoiled apron and took down a fresh one. She cocked her head at us and Nash brought a shilling out of his pocket and tossed it to her. The coin flashed in the moonlight and the maid expertly caught it. She said, 'For a guinea, I will tumble with you, if you like.'

'Much obliged,' Nash said with a smile, 'but I find I can resist.'

'Suit yourself.'

Nash and I laughed about the incident all the way down the stairs. There was a crowd outside the banqueting hall and we joined them, lolling against one another, and amused ourselves by comparing notes concerning the elegance and the behaviour of the persons around us. Then, all of a sudden, Nash drew in a breath, his attention captured by a sight near the top of the grand flight of stairs that led to the ground floor.

He squeezed my arm and said absently that he would return in a minute, and, leaving my side, he made off at a scurry. How unlike Nash that movement was, I thought. It made him seem small and anxious, which is not at all his style. I watched as he apprehended a gentleman in a coat of watered silk laced with silver, who was strolling with a swagger towards the stairs. He had a comely lady on his arm. There was something about this personage, perhaps it was the way faces turned in his direction as they passed by, that suggested the centre of the universe. With a deep bow, hinging at the waist, Nash engaged the gentleman in what appeared to be a conversation of a somewhat importuning nature, judging by the way that he leaned towards his auditor and raised his hands as if in appeal. After some minutes and an exchange of salutations, Nash returned to me with his face alight. It crossed my mind, foolishly, that he seemed rather more on fire than he had been after our romp upstairs.

As he assisted us both to glasses of wine from the salver of a circulating footman, I said, 'I am very inquisitive to learn the identity of that gentleman.'

'He is Sir Rollo Hayle, a name that is very much on the ascent. He made his fortune in India. Diamonds at first, then shipping. Now his interest is opium. The firm I worked for in Calcutta did some work for him.'

'Sir Rollo Hayle! How extraordinary. That is a name writ large in the report I read this afternoon.'

'Is it?' Nash said, looking towards the spot where Sir Rollo had stood.

'He was in charge of the medical trial at the cantonment.'

'He's in charge of everything in his part of Bengal. He is one of those white nabobs that you so despise.' Nash's arched eyebrow indicated that a degree of forbearance was required concerning my views. Well, hang me for it, but I do despise them. Everyone knows those brazen East India men have ransacked Bengal to line their own pockets, and put the Company in arrears at the same time. Nash is less outraged than I am about it. I believe in a just partition of the world, even if that seems an impossible ideal. He is more flexible in his beliefs. Indeed, he said at that moment, 'There is no injury in taking from others what they do not care to defend.'

I opened my mouth to make a retort, but Nash placed a finger against my lip. 'Hush now, my little critic. Do not spoil the evening with talk of politics.'

I said instead, 'So, Sir Rollo has a genius for money.'

'Indeed. It is a great stroke of luck to have encountered him. I had heard of his return home and it was on my mind to make him an approach. Now he has given me leave to call on him at his townhouse.'

'For what purpose?'

Nash swigged his wine and did not answer my question. I tapped his arm with my fan.

'Wait and see.'

'What are you up to?'

But Nash only smiled to himself. It was an archaic smile that gave nothing away.

'Perhaps he will employ you to do some conveyancing for him.'

'Good God, my sweet, did you utter the word *conveyancing*?'

I burst into laughter. 'I don't know what came over me.'

Nash laughed too. 'This glass of wine will come over you if you ever refer to such an odious occupation again.'

In the banqueting hall we nibbled on roast beef from the supper table, and sweetmeats, then settled down on a comfortable couch with a bumper of champagne. Nash had signed a fictitious name on the chit we were given for the food and drink. We had the feeling of living dangerously and it filled us with fizz – and yet, despite the many distractions of our surroundings, I found myself thinking about the young man who had died during Sir Rollo's medical trial. Martenson, the surgeon who had written the report, had found the gunner paralysed, his face turning blue. I could imagine vividly the lad's convulsions and his struggle to breathe. Dr Martenson had tried to save Kinch's life by performing a tracheotomy, but Sir Rollo Hayle had ordered the gunner to be taken away to an operating room under the care of another surgeon. Martenson's attempt to gain admission to the operating room was prevented by sentries. Then he was informed that the patient had expired due to a fatal antipathy to the test plant that could not have been foreseen. Martenson's report, however, said there is no evidence that the *Ammannia* leaves were ever applied to Kinch's skin and that the poisoning must be attributed to some other agent – one that had not been identified.

'I am curious, Nash,' I said. 'What did you speak to Sir Rollo about?'

'He has an associate in business by the name of Fenton Gifford. They met through their mutual interest in East India and formed a partnership in vessels trading there. You must have heard of Gifford, surely, on your travels around the printers' yards.'

'I have! He does not go upon the town very visibly, but he is awfully connected. Doesn't he own *Town's Weekly Post*?'

'And *The Discoverer*.'

The Discoverer is the sort of paper that will print the latest about the rebellion in America cheek by jowl with some heated story about a beast roaming the courts off Tyburn Road or cannibals living the high life in Cripplegate.

'Why does Mr Gifford interest you?' I asked.

'I rather have an ambition to be brought into print.'

My surprise must have showed on my face, because Nash said, 'I am a keen man for the buzz of events and the badinage of the town.'

'I don't dispute it, but you always say that the wits who go into print never make any money.' In fact, it seems to me that people in society do not hold any person of wit in esteem unless he is in the act of entertaining them or unless he belongs to their class. In this world, the wit and the poet are little more than jesters, despite their fine words, and woe betide them when they fall out of fashion. 'How shall you advance yourself, then, if Mr Gifford should publish you?'

'By acting as his mouthpiece. He will honour me for it with favours and influence. His fortune is fuelled by government contracts, you know.'

'So he leans to the side of whoever is in power. He is a man who adjusts his loyalties according to the times.'

'He is also a conduit to the corridors of power where real fortunes are to be made. It is a question of crocheting myself into the gilded network.' Nash offered me his hand. 'Shall we show these clodhoppers how to cut a caper?'

As we danced, I noticed that Nash was a little preoccupied,

in spite of his smile. He did not keep time in the cotillion, although it is not like him at all to miss a beat.

At length, around two in the morning, we left the club and came out into the street. It was noisy with the sound of lackeys yelling for their masters' carriages, and of altercations, the shouts of watchmen trying to get the jam of vehicles to proceed in a more orderly fashion, and link boys with flaming torches, calling for customers.

Nash hailed a hackney coach and we drove away towards Holborn. He put his arm around me and I rested my head on his shoulder. After a little while he said, 'Fenton Gifford is the way forward, by Jove. I intend to get a splendid sinecure out of him, damn my blood if I don't.' He made this statement with steely certainty – and I was glad to hear it, because I did not like to see my husband practise blackmail and intimidation, no matter how barren we were of funds.

I said, 'Sir Rollo is clearly a gentleman whose enterprises run to the large scale, is that right?'

There was a creaking of leather as Nash shifted heavily in his seat and turned to look at me. 'Yes, expansion is very much his game.'

'I am interested to know what fortune he hoped to get out of those *Ammannia* leaves.'

'Which leaves are they?'

'The leaves of *Ammannia Vesicatoria* that killed the gunner. I wonder why a notable such as Sir Rollo would involve himself personally in testing such a limited and lowly plant.'

'Obviously, I have no idea.'

'Unless he had developed an amazing hybrid. But such a discovery has not been noted in the recent botanical literature.'

'It astonishes me the way your mind works, Carey. Haven't we had an outstanding time at the marvellous Mango?'

'We have.'

'Lady Celia bested, a tumble upstairs, a free supper and a lure dangled in the waters of opportunity.'

'It was an evening of superbness, without a doubt.'

'And yet, instead of dwelling on the many sweet things that you might do to express your thanks to your obliging husband –' he twined his fingers in mine and raised my hand to his lips and kissed it lightly – 'you squander your thoughts on some extraordinarily irrelevant event that has no bearing on either of us whatsoever.' He nuzzled into my neck. 'I look forward to seeing what you can do to ingratiate yourself into my good opinion.'

Chapter 3

Running with a Heavy Load

May the 26th, 1776

As I pushed my way through the throng on Drury Lane, I caught sight of a woman wearing one of those preposterous elongated hats known as a ziggurat. It was Fanny Abington, I was thrilled to see, a favourite actress of mine. Nosegay Fan, the papers call her, because she used to sell flowers at Covent Garden when she was a girl, or so the story goes. Everyone knows she has suffered her share of knocks and has not been always in the full swing of cash. I like that about her. She is one of life's survivors and I think you can see that in her performances. Even when she is playing in a laughing comedy, you feel that there is something tough and invincible in the core of her that anchors the flightiest of lines. I followed her for a little way, curious to see what she did, but just as I reached Long Acre, I heard the bells of the actors' church sound the hour of five and I cursed myself for my tardiness. Our guest of honour was to arrive at eight o'clock. There was nothing for it but to risk a dash through the alleys and courts that lie between the northern end of Drury Lane and High Holborn, where Nash and I live.

I plunged into a dark warren of sickly dwelling-houses

and dens, their broken windows stopped up with rags. It is an odious quarter, where purse-cutters and bone-pickers ply their trades. The way before me was clogged by a party of saunterers and I could not get by them. I was forced to turn up one of the lanes, and then wished I hadn't. It was haunted by wild-eyed women in tatters, shouting things that were not quite language. As I lowered the brim of my bonnet to avoid their gaze, I happened to catch sight of a biggish man dressed in black, who was propelling himself among the potholes by means of a tall walking stick – or was it a stave? I had the disturbing feeling that he had noticed me, too. I was laden with stealable items – a box from Hillier's in Covent Garden, a bunch of roses and a fat parcel tied with ribbon. It contained a ready-made petticoat of a gorgeous coral hue that I had snapped up at a dressmaker's in Earl Street after fretting about the ensemble that I would wear in the evening. Like so many things in this world, I felt that I had to have it, even though everything I buy buries me further in debt and its ever-expanding arrears of interest. I don't know how to extinguish the longing to purchase. It smoulders always within and just when I feel I have beaten it down to ash it flares up again, more hot and intense than ever. But I try, I am always trying, to fight the fire.

I turned into an alley in an attempt to cut a diagonal towards Holborn, but I came out into a fetid court instead. It was dominated by a dilapidated drinking house with peeling shutters. A pewter measure dangled from a fixture over one of the windows and below the sign a handful of tipplers congregated with mugs in hand. They perked up when they saw me mincing across the court like the idiot I was for taking such a sinister shortcut. Then, as I looked around for a route out of the court, who should I see but the man in black – and my uneasiness increased tenfold. Convinced that he was following me, I bolted towards a sliver of passageway beside the drinking den in a bid to escape him. I ran on as best I could, stumbling on broken stones that were unkind to my feet, with my stupid parcels and my stupid roses impeding my pace. I thought I heard footsteps behind me, but I arrived at another court before my pursuer caught up to me. It was filled with scrawny urchins rushing at one another, whether in play or combat I could not tell. There was a man in shirtsleeves and apron, thumping at something in an open-fronted structure I at first took for a stable. As I passed by, I realised that he was banging at a case of type. He was one of those ruffian printers that abound these days, turning out illegal ephemera. I rushed onward, weighed down by my burdens, and yet kept looking over my shoulder, apparently spellbound to the man who continued to advance on me.

I flung myself at an opening in the court and there ahead was a glimpse of Lincoln's Inn Fields. As I reached the thoroughfare, a sedan chair pulled up to disgorge its passenger and although the sanctuary of my home was barely five minutes away and a journey of such brevity constituted a mad waste of a shilling, I leaped into the chair and pulled down the blind. We set off for Hood Street with my heart pounding as loudly as the thump of the chairmen's footfalls.

I let myself into the house, lurched into the front room that Nash uses as an office and dropped my parcels onto a divan that was already strewn with broadsheets and pamphlets. There was a decanter of brandy on a shelf in one of the bookcases. I poured a measure into a sticky glass I found on the desk and drank it down. Then I sidled to the window and peered through the gauze curtain. There was no sign of the man in black. I felt a mixture of relief and foolishness at having got so worked up about him, but I could not help it. The combination of his white face, his thin but threatening shape, and his pitch-dark clothes, provoked a fearful memory of the day I had been sent out to service at a household in Chelsea. I was sixteen years old. I can see that grim mansion still – I will always see it – standing on the edge of desolate fields. I gazed up with foreboding at its high, sharp gables, my arms straining under the weight of my valise and my writing box. I stood there, frozen, as the door opened and a pale, black-suited butler loomed at me. The expression on his face turned my knees to jelly and sickened my stomach.

Just as I was struggling with that image in my mind, a shadowy, hunched figure passed before the window at Hood Street. I could almost believe that I had summoned it. Seconds later, someone lifted the knocker and struck the plate on our door with a resounding bang. I became very still, hardly daring to breathe, but it was useless to pretend that no one was at home. There were already footsteps in the hall, followed by a muffled utterance from Jane, our housekeeper, as she opened the front door. I felt a chilly waft of air enter the house and then Jane flung open the door of the office and announced in her irritated way, 'There is a person wanting the master.'

I drew myself up to confront the visitor, but as soon as I stepped into the hall I saw that I had no need to be afraid of him. His height and wide shoulders suggested a man who had once been imposing, but the wretch before me was a man who was much reduced in figure and spirit. His face was gaunt and he had legs like cat-sticks. He removed his tall buckled hat to show hacked-about hair that looked as though someone had cut it to suppress a case of lice.

'Good evening,' he said with a clumsy bow, 'Felix Spencer at your service, ma'am. I am here to see Mr Oliver Nash. He is expecting me.'

I was reassured to hear the suppliant tone of his voice. It gave me leave to treat him with hauteur. 'I am sorry to disappoint you, sir,' I said, 'but Mr Nash is not at home. Can he really have made an appointment with you? He is away in Hertfordshire on business and I do not expect him back for a week at least.'

This was my customary response to any stranger who came to the door in search of Nash, especially one who resembled a wreck, as this one did.

'Confound it!' the man cried. 'I sent him a message two days ago!' He looked around at the street as if expecting a passerby to come to his aid and then turned to me again. He gripped his walking stick tightly and I could see that he was making an effort to control his emotions. 'Mrs Nash, is it? I beg your indulgence; may I come in?' He offered me a frightful smile. 'Let us not discuss business on the doorstep.'

I raised an eyebrow. 'Sir, I cannot be expected to invite into my home a gentleman who is unknown to me.'

'For the love of God, madam, tell Nash I only want him to repay the money he owes me. I have given him every latitude in regard to the matter!' There was desperation in his voice, but I hardened my heart against him, just as I had done with Lady Celia. I moved to close the door, saying, 'I have never seen you before, sir, or heard of you.'

The man, Spencer, leaned a hand against the jamb of the door. 'The debt was incurred years ago when I lent Ollie the money to fit himself out for India!'

I shut the door in his face. You cannot give these pleaders an inch or they will take an ell, in my experience – and I speak as one who has been, in the past, on Spencer's side of the wicket. I expected to hear him pound at the door again, but there was only silence. Glancing at my hands, I saw that they were trembling. I retreated to Nash's office and drank a second brandy to steady them, then I picked up the box from Hillier's and carried it downstairs to the kitchen. Ruth, the cook, was at the hearth inflaming the coals of the stove with a bellows. Thankfully, it being the month of May, eggs and poultry are easy to be had; I had asked her to make a chicken fricassée for our supper party, which she seemed to be doing.

There was lard bubbling in a stew pan on the hob, at any rate.

It is the job of Jane's husband, Ned, to turn the stove's old-fashioned spit, when he is not otherwise engaged as our steward, valet, butler and footman. He was formerly occupied as a hemp-dresser in High Wycombe. The art of service is not in his blood, but Jane refused to take our situation without him, so there we are. Nelly was bent over the sink in the corner, washing a bunch of parsley. She is a scullery maid at the Eclipse tavern, whom I had got in for the evening to assist the preparations.

'Made-dishes is in the larder,' Ruth said. She began tossing chicken pieces into the pan.

I put down the box I was carrying and went to inspect the dishes that I had ordered from a cook shop: buttered rusks with anchovies, fritters, plovers' eggs and a minced lamb's head, and the jellies. I emerged from the larder just as Ned clattered down the stairs with Jane in his wake. He is a balding, buttery-looking fellow. I asked him to chip the ice as soon as it was delivered and to fill the champagne buckets and, before he served upstairs that evening, to please change into the silk stockings and the waistcoat with sleeves that Mr Nash had given him.

I believe that I could happily live a life that was independent of servants. I do not think it such a travail to clean and cook for myself and keep things in order. A messy kitchen is at least a comprehensible chaos that can be controlled by brooms and cloths, by boiling water and vinegar. Obviously,

I speak as someone who is no châteleine. In that event, I should probably sing a different tune.

'What is this, then?' Jane said, pointing at the box that sat on the table. 'A golden crown for Mr Gifford's head, is it? I cannot wait to lay eyes on him, madam, there has been that much fuss about him.'

'There will be no gawping at Mr Gifford,' I said. 'Remember that if the evening goes well for Mr Nash, it will be all the better for you.'

I unlatched the box. The opening of it released a luscious, otherly fragrance and the servants clustered around to gaze at the precious object in its nest of tissue paper.

'That's a pineapple, God strike me,' Ruth said.

'It will be the centrepiece on the sideboard,' I explained.

'Blimey,' Ned said. 'It's smaller than I thought. Will there be enough to go around?'

'It's just for show, you paperskull,' Jane retorted. She shot me one of her sceptical looks again.

'She's only hired it.' Ruth spoke as if I were not in the room.

I have in general done my best to alleviate the gloominess of the house. It was all bottle-green wainscotting and cobwebby tin ceilings when we moved in, but I whited the walls and papered them with Indian prints, and beautified the rooms with paisley drapes and embroidered rugs. Now the place looks much better than it ought to. This morning, I dressed the drawing room with flowers and votive candles from the India Warehouse near Chancery Lane. As I stood back to admire my handiwork, I was satisfied by the *mise en scène*. It gave the impression that Nash and I live in plenty. The sideboard teemed with Staffordshire creamware and, in pride of place, the pineapple lolled on its fruitstand like a little fat potentate of the vegetative realm.

'What a beauty!'

I spun around at the sound of Nash's voice.

'I went to Hillier's to buy roses and saw they had two pineapples just come in. I could not resist.'

'I meant you, little idiot.' Nash approached me at a saunter, his hazel eyes light and lively. He picked up the pineapple and sniffed it.

'We have it for twenty-four hours only, Nash. For the love of God, do not eat it. I shall have to pay a forfeit if it is breached.'

'Fear not, *ananas immaculata* it shall remain.'

I took the pineapple from his hands and set it back on its throne.

'Are you in order?' he asked. 'You seem fretful.'

'So I am. There is a great deal riding on this evening.'

'Let's have a drink to calm the nerves, then. Where's Ned?'

At that moment, he hoved into sight. Bottles of champagne protruded from the ice bucket that he was hefting into the room. 'Well met, Ned!' Nash cried. 'What a devilish fine figure you cut in that waistcoat.'

'Thankee, sir.'

Ned did look slightly less of a rude mechanical in Nash's

old coat and stockings. Nash removed one of the dripping bottles from the ice bucket, winked at Ned, and said, 'Mrs Nash and I are about to dress. You know what to do, old man, don't you? Make sure the lush is all nicely set out.'

We went upstairs, taking the champagne with us.

The atmosphere was close in the bedchamber. The season was not yet warm enough to keep the windows open and a stuffy smell of winter still cloyed the house's interior. I set down my foaming glass and began to untie my gown. Nash flung off his coat and stood looking down into the street while he drank his champagne. His arms were muscular in the sleeves of his white shirt. A sudden shower of rain hissed at the window and I hoped that the unreliable weather would not put off Mr Gifford. Nash turned to me and smiled and said he ought to change. I remember that it rained on our wedding day – heavy rain dashing itself against the windows of the chapel. Afterwards, the sun came out as we drove through Piccadilly and it was so bright I was completely dazzled. In the carriage, Nash kissed me with his champagne mouth and I pressed myself hard against him, the lace of his shirt scratching my bare breasts. As we were then, so are we now. I have no *gravitas*. I am made up of so many panting emotions always running at a full gallop.

'Nash,' I said, 'do you know a gentleman by the name of Felix Spencer?'

Nash drained his glass and said that he did not recall the name.

'An old Indian crony. He came to the house this afternoon looking for you.'

Nash crooked a finger at me. 'Let me handle your laces, lovely.'

'Do not you think I am apt enough to do it myself?' But I was already moving towards him. I let him unknot my sleeves. Nash says there is nothing that captures the affections of women so soon as to be always obliging to them. Then he reached around my waist and untied my stays.

There was a knock at the door. It was Nelly with hot water for my toilette.

I dipped a sponge in the water and passed it across my chest and my shoulders. Rivulets of warm water trickled the length of my arms and dripped on to my belly. Nash wrapped a hank of my hair around his hand, pulled my head towards his and kissed me. The kiss made me think of earthy things, of gardens and damp, shady places where hostas and ferns grow.

'Later, lovely,' he whispered into my neck, and walked away in the direction of his closet.

I put on a wrapping gown and lit the lamps at the sides of the glass. It was still light outdoors, but our windows face north and the chamber falls into shadows very quickly even in summer, and besides, there was the rain, which insisted on falling. I began to make up my face, but my mind kept straying to the thought of Nash's mysterious visitor from India. There was something about Mr Spencer that was not dismissable. Nash returned to the chamber and I watched him through the glass as he secured a brooch to his lapel. He looked up with a smile and asked me to dress his hair, since Ned was too dispersed in his tasks to oblige him.

He sat before the glass and I warmed a little pomade in my hand. As I stroked it through his hair, I said, 'I wonder if Mr Spencer sent you a letter a day or two ago?'

'What? Oh, I do not know. Perhaps he did.'

I smoothed his hair into the palm of my left hand and began to braid it. 'You might give it me to read,' I said, 'so that I know where we stand, should he call again.'

Nash groaned. 'Old Felix is quite a tear-milker. It's all theatre, of course.' I tied the braid and garnished it with a ribbon. Craning his neck to inspect his hair, Nash pronounced himself satisfied and got to his feet. I gazed at him expectantly. He rolled his eyes, but he went to his closet. Some minutes later, he returned with a letter, which he handed to me. It was dated three days earlier.

My Dear Oliver Nash

By the time you receive this, you can be assured that I will shortly follow in order to accept your bond, which will close the business between us. I trust, dear friend, that you will not dishonour me by protesting the debt. My personal freedom depends on it. Child's bank will hound me to Newgate unless it is paid. My dear fellow, if you do not settle our account I shall be thrown into jail and what will happen to my dear Sophy and the children, I do not know. But I have confidence in your high sense of honour.

I beg you to satisfy me in the name of our old friendship.
I depend upon it!
Your wretched friend,
Felix Spencer

'Do you owe him money?'

'Only a fraction of what he demands.'

I scanned the letter again. 'He doesn't say here how much. Have there been other letters?'

'One or two. Spencer is an infamous dissembler, you know, and an awful souse.' Nash stood to face me. 'He did lend me a trifling amount, twenty pounds at the most, but I supposed I had paid him back long ago. No doubt he is in trouble now and thinks to revive a debt and embarrass me into helping him. I don't blame him for it, although it's an inconvenience.'

'When did you incur the debt?'

'It was at a difficult moment. The litigating work had fallen away, my father had just died and I needed to refresh my situation. I hoped to go out to India on the small legacy that I expected, but then I found the old swine had left behind a will that was heavily buttressed against me. My sisters had married servile wretches, mere wearers of trademarks. Can you imagine how it wounded me to find that they were my father's only beneficiaries?' Nash shrugged with a lopsided smile that said, *Such is life.* 'I mean to give Spencer something, of course I do, but I cannot until I have something more than the devil dancing in my pocket. It all depends on Gifford and whether he offers me a situation.

Until that moment comes, Spencer must bark at the moon.'
Nash took the letter from me and went to the chimneypiece
for his snuffbox. He said, 'It pains me to see you ruffle yourself with this matter.'

'It is only that the man seemed so desperate.'

Nash laughed, 'Well, so are we.'

I tore the head from one of the roses that I had got at Hillier's and pinned it into my hair.

'Look at you,' Nash said, 'a nymph on a summer's day.
Gifford is bound to be beguiled.' He opened the snuffbox
and offered me a pinch. It was a good gingery blend that
made the brain effervesce.

How raffish Nash looked with his long silk cravat and ruf-
fles hanging out at his cuffs. His waistcoat was entirely open,
except for one button, in a deliberately careless way. I dusted
the snuff from the crook of my thumb and said, 'Oh, do
please write Mr Spencer a cheque, my love.'

'What a tender heart you have. Any swell-talker may hum
the coin from your purse.'

'It is his wife that I feel sorry for. We can manage twenty
pounds, can't we?' I knew that obliging Spencer would mean
an end to my nest egg, but it was the honourable thing to do.
'Let's pay him,' I urged, 'and be done with it.'

Nash rather reluctantly went to his closet. He returned a
minute later to show me a note signed for twenty pounds,
which he pledged to give to Spencer, should he call again.
So, there it was: the five hundred pounds had run out at last.

'Why the grave expression?' Nash asked.

'I only hope the evening goes well, that is all.'

'Damn my blood, but it will. It will go off like a bomb.'

That is Oliver Nash in a nutshell: the essence of confidence. Is it any wonder that I married him like a shot?

He threw his arm around my shoulder and said, 'And a word in your ear, my love. Do try not to quiz Mr Gifford about your father.'

'What do you mean?'

'Oh, Carey, you know very well. Whenever we meet anyone with the slightest whiff of India about him, you begin the interrogation. "Were you in Calcutta?" "Did you ever encounter a man named Daniel Ravine?" "Are you sure?" "Are you absolutely sure?" "Shall I describe his appearance?" And so forth. A rather squinty look comes upon your face as if you think your poor victim is not telling the truth and in general it very much darkens the mood.' Nash gave me a little shake. 'I want you to give up tormenting yourself about the fate of Mr Ravine. India is a vast place. Anything could have happened to him and no amount of speculation will bring him back. You must accept that he is gone. It has been how many years?'

'Ten.'

'Painful though the loss is, you must let it go for the sake of your own serenity. Haven't I given you such advice countless times? I beg you to heed me.'

'I am sure it is not so strange to ask a person who has been in Bengal if he has encountered another person who was in the same place.'

Nash opened his arms wide in a theatrical gesture of despair. 'There we have it. An obsessive at work.' He looked at me with a reproachful eye. 'It is neither attractive nor useful to mourn the past, Carey. Are we not traders in the future, you and I?'

I nodded and Nash pinched my cheek and grinned. 'That's my girl. That's my little aspirant.'

Chapter 4

Butter Upon Bacon

I received our guests with the warmth of old friends, although most of them were unknown to me. Nash made smooth introductions: a wealthy haberdasher, two newspaper men and their wives or mistresses, two or three men in business with the army, and a man named Stark, who had worked for the East India Company. There was a magistrate's secretary, too. Nash greeted him with an especially extreme bow. When the secretary had passed on, Nash stage-whispered in my ear, 'A precaution. One cannot be too obsequious to the fraternity of justice.' I must confess that these characters were not very typical of the people we entertain and I felt a twinge at finding myself fussing over men whose politics lay very far from my own. I accepted compliments from the ladies present on the standard of my table. The refreshments were presented in the French style of a *buffet*, which makes for congenial mingling and an easy atmosphere. The dishes, with their bright garnishes, were an agreeable sight, the dispersal of candles, jellies and flowers adding to the lustre of the tables, and Nash was very pleased that they had won the confidence of the assembly.

Just before nine o'clock, Ned appeared at the door of the drawing room with our guest of honour, and Nash steered him into the room.

Gifford was a man of rather coarse appearance, with grizzled hair cut short and a furrowed forehead, as if he were peering at something on the horizon. He was really not more sizeable than Nash, but there was a flintiness about him that made my husband look small in comparison. Nelly, having been over-warned about Gifford's importance, panicked and rushed at him straight away with a plate of razored veal in one hand and bread slices in the other. Gifford lifted some of the meat, put it on a slice of bread and ate it effortfully as he scanned the room. His gaze was shrewd. I knew that he had been arrested on occasion and fined for the libels in his newspapers, but his connections and his deep pockets always kept him out of jail.

I came forward to be introduced, Gifford chewing as I sank before him. He was accompanied by a page, a little black boy dressed in nautical livery, who presented me with a velveteen box, a gift of confectionary from his master. I gave it to Jane to put on the sideboard and sprayed Mr Gifford with a scattershot of light, grateful remarks. When he was sufficiently drenched by my cordiality, Nash took him around the room, greeting the guests. Gifford, wiping his veal-greased fingers on his coat, seemed already to know most of them. Then he expressed a desire to engage me in conversation and waved Nash off. Nash gave me an eloquent look as he retreated. I reassured him with a smile – I would not ask Mr Gifford if he had ever come across a horticulture man in Bengal named Daniel Ravine. Nash was right, of course. I needed to give up the desperate flailing about for an answer that would never come. The fact was, my father had disappeared and there was nothing to indicate that he was anything other than dead.

I beckoned Ned to bring a tumbler of brandy. Gifford took the glass and we sat down on a divan in a corner of the room. He asked where I hailed from. When I told him, he gave a scornful laugh and said, 'You do not sound like Bethnal Green.' His manner was faintly confrontational.

'Bethnal Green by way of a boarding school in Kensington.'

'Kensington,' Gifford repeated as if grappling with a difficult concept.

Being curious to know if it were true that he did not favour a particular party, I said, 'I hear that partisans are out of fashion, sir. Will you do me the favour of giving me your opinion?'

Gifford shifted on his haunches. He blinked at me, and said, 'I trust you do not take it upon yourself to be interested in your husband's work.' Then came his mirthless smile. 'But why would you, Mrs Nash, when you are surrounded by the enjoyments of life and the gifts of nature?'

Having absorbed this rebuke, and sensing that Gifford was waiting for me to redeem myself, I asked him to discourse upon the highlights of his career. I sat meekly and listened to him bloviate.

'Well, madam,' he said, 'I will tell you that I have been operating in the India trade since 1762. Master and owner I was of the *Lionheart* and she was three hundred tons, madam. Three hundred!' Gifford's tone was a rumbling one, as if the great Yahweh himself were enumerating the tonnage of his ships. 'I sailed her to Calcutta and found that Rollo Hayle required to have a ship at his disposal for his private trade and that led us into partnership.'

'I should love to go to India,' I said.

'No, you would not,' Gifford countered. 'It is no place for a woman.'

'Mr Nash agrees with you on that point,' I said. 'He believes that the glamour of India is much overrated. Is your interest entirely in the East Indies?'

'I have taken in slaves from the Gold Coast as master of the *Raven*, madam. A vessel, mark you, of one hundred and ten tons.'

'Is it, indeed?'

'On the last voyage from that coast we had a hellish time of it. We took aboard a hundred or so slaves to carry to Jamaica. A passage of eight weeks and nothing but dysentery. It carried off six of our sailors and half of the slaves.'

I could not help glancing at the Negro page, sitting cross-legged at Gifford's feet as if carved in stone, and wondered about the story that was confined behind his still countenance.

Gifford said, 'Are you acquainted with Sir Rollo, madam?'

'I have not yet had the pleasure.' This response caused

Gifford to laugh for some reason. At that moment, I was over-joyed to see my dear friend Selina Colden make her entrance into the drawing room. She caught my eye, pointed her fan in the direction of Gifford and raised her eyebrows inquir-ingly. I nodded with a slight rolling of eyes. She understood my meaning at once. Seconds later, I was introducing her to Mr Gifford and she had made herself comfortable on a chair at his side. She offered Gifford a hand glittering with rings and fluttered her eyelashes at him, and at the same time she complimented my new coral petticoat. She wore a short vel-vet cloak over a shining gown, her dress not more elegant than her person. Selina's face answers my idea of beauty. She has neat, shapely features set in a milky complexion, fine sky-blue eyes and caramel-coloured hair swept into a cloud like spun sugar. We sat like devotees before the idol as Gif-ford explained the many misfortunes that can befall the condition of a merchant ship – leaky hull, rigging all to pieces, toppled mast – until he took out his watch and declared that he would speak with Mr Nash.

Selina and I relinquished Gifford to Nash and took over Nash's group of army contractors and the magistrate's secre-tary. The secretary was three sheets to the wind, but he managed to raise a claw and beckon Ned to fill his glass. One of the contractors had a wife, Mrs Hyland, who abounded in anecdote. While she detailed the way in which Sir Rollo had made a fortune in the diamond trade even before he put his fields into opium, I watched as Gifford drew Nash to one side and they left the drawing room, the page trailing in their wake. Selina and I exchanged significant glances and she lifted up her narrow hand and crossed her fingers.

'He used to be the Company's opium agent in Patna,' Mrs Hyland was saying, apropos of Sir Rollo Hayle's early career.

'And bloody made the most of it!' the secretary bellowed. 'He dwindled the supply through his muddle . . . his muddle . . . his *middle*men.' He sat down suddenly upon a footstool.

'The French and the Dutch could not get their hands on a skerrick of opium to save their lives,' Mrs Hyland said. 'Then he used his profits to go into the shipbuilding business with Mr Gifford.'

The conversation continued upon the paragon Sir Rollo Hayle and accounts of various passages to India and the disagreeable detention of the voyage and the unpleasantness of prickly heat.

Nash and Gifford had been absent for fully half an hour. Selina leaned into my *coiffure* and murmured, 'Are those roses real? What a surprise. They look sumptuous enough to be silk.'

A sudden loud report drew the general attention. It was the rap of Mr Gifford's walking stick, which he had banged hard upon the floorboards. He was framed in the doorway with Nash at his side and I knew at once by the brightness of Nash's face that the outcome of his interview was a happy one.

'A word, ladies and gentlemen,' Gifford boomed. After paying his compliments to me, he clapped Nash on the shoulder and said, 'I have been very much astonished by the rare abilities of this gentleman, here. A more penetrating wordsmith does not live, by God. I at once knew, as soon as I made his acquaintance, that the talents of Oliver Nash must be brought to work on behalf of myself and my esteemed partner, Sir Rollo Hayle, and our companies. It gives me enormous pleasure to tell you that Mr Nash will forthwith write a weekly essay for *The Discoverer* and produce other creations such as we need to advance our cause. I think it is fair to say that everyone in this room is of the same general interest as myself. I commend Mr Nash to you in this public manner, so that you may know, should you encounter him upon the town, that he is one of us. Let us raise a glass now to him, and to his charming wife, and to the promotion of his success.'

After the toast, Nash spoke a few words of gratitude, nicely restrained and appropriately humble, and then accepted individual congratulations. When we at last came face to face, he seized my hands and whispered in my ear, 'Two hundred and fifty pounds per annum for one column per week.'

I gasped. Two hundred and fifty pounds!

'That is only the beginning,' Nash said *sotto voce*. 'Gifford has suggested that there are many other endeavours belonging to him and Sir Rollo in which I might have a stake. The tide of our life is about to turn.'

I hurried to Mr Gifford and, with a deep reverence, expressed my gratitude. I inquired if he would take his ease again on the divan, since I was about to serve coffee, but he announced that he had already ordered his carriage and had sent his page downstairs to await it. With the news of Gifford's going, the party quickly began to wind down. Nash tried to prevent his departure, ferociously opposing so early an end to the evening, but Gifford urged to be allowed to leave, since he had business of importance to transact the following day. Selina smoothed his way downstairs.

Afterwards, when all of the guests had gone, Selina returned and we drank bumper toasts to Nash's success.

'We are connected to a topping network now,' Nash said. 'Gifford's patron is Lord Casserly, who has the ear of the prime minister and the king.'

'Lord Casserly.' Selina whistled, impressed. 'He is quite tentacular, is he not?'

'President of the Honourable Artillery Company and a director of the East India docks. The Casserlys have provisioned the navy since the days of the Armada – His Lordship owns half of Wapping. He is the link that secures government contracts for Hayle's and Gifford's companies.'

'Gifford is a slaver, though,' I said.

'He is not in that business so much any more.' Nash filled our glasses.

'Public opinion begins to go against the Africa trade,' I said.

'That is exactly why Gifford has hired me,' Nash said. 'I will form opinion to his interest.'

'But you would not write in support of slavery in order to help another man's profits.'

Nash stood up to open another bottle. 'I must bang the drum for Sir Rollo as well. This is a big year for him. He is to enter Parliament as the member for Wensum.'

'Where is that?' I asked, while at the same time registering, even in my wine-haze, Nash's evasion of the slavery question.

'In Norfolk. It is a borough under Lord Casserly's control. Casserly's tenants will ballot according to his direction and the by-election in autumn will see Sir Rollo in the Commons.'

'So he has bought himself a parliamentary seat.'

'Naturally. He bought his title, too, and once you have the one, you might as well have the other. Don't make such a face, lovely. Let us revel in the moment.'

'I *am* revelling.'

'It will be all butter upon bacon for us now and we can live as we deserve.'

'You will soon have intolerable airs, the both of you.' Selina laughed.

We made ourselves more comfortable then, Nash reclining on the sofa, Selina squeezing up next to me on a floor cushion as we drank our claret. I lifted my foot and dangled my slipper from my toes and giggled when it fell on the floor.

'Your wife is in need of new slippers,' Selina said, her voice a little slurred. 'It is about time that you earned a decent crust, Nash.' Playfully, she shoved at his shin with her naked foot and caused him to spill his wine on his beautiful blue breeches.

'Confound it, Sel!' Nash was amused.

'It's no more than you deserve.' She returned his laugh. 'Thank God Gifford came through. You are bound to fly very high now.'

'I take Sir Rollo Hayle for my pattern. He started low, but he had the nous to cultivate the right people.' Then Nash murmured almost to himself, 'You need to have something over them, if you want to mix on equal terms with the masters of our systems.'

'What do you mean?' I asked, thinking of the manipulations that had characterised Nash's recent work.

Nash shrugged. 'I am only thinking of Sel and how she gets on mighty well by keeping the secrets of her admirers.'

'You are mistaken, sir.' Selina laughed. 'My expectations have been let down in this last year. I hoped that Woodbridge might settle on me, but his mother scared him off.' She made a face and shrugged. Where romantic love is concerned, Selina is not a believer. No courting ensues until she knows the condition of the suitor's wallet. She has saved herself a great deal of heartbreak in that regard.

She tapped my wrist with her fan. 'Perhaps you shall not need to toil so hard for your pin money now.'

She was referring to the translations that I undertake from the French. For the last few months, I have been rendering into English a volume by the naturalist Marcel-Ange Degoutte. *Botany Explained: Dialogues Between Flora and Her Professor* is a work of natural philosophy calculated for young ladies. Monsieur Degoutte plays the part of a professor who must initiate a maiden into the mysteries of Carl Linnaeus's system of botanical classification. Linnaeus orders plants according to their sexual identities and, to explain him in a way that Flora can understand, Degoutte presents the flower as a marriage bed and fertilisation as a form of seduction between stamens and pistils. He stretches out this metaphor over four hundred pages.

'Professor, my arse. A lecher by any other name,' Selina scoffed. 'Send this little minx Flora around to Golden Square. I can show her in one hour enough about stamens and pistils to serve her for a lifetime of romping. And, speaking of lechers, I suppose that Sir Rollo might invite you to the summer masquerade that his Soma Club is putting on, now that you have an entrée to his world.'

'What is the Soma Club?' I asked.

'Sir Rollo and some gentlemen of the same turn of thinking as himself, with a connection to India, meet occasionally at his seat at Epping to entertain one another and discuss politics and make back-room deals,' Selina replied.

'How do you know of it?'

'Well, Newington is a member.' Lord Newington was Selina's latest beau. In his heyday he had been a military paymaster-general at Madras and was afterwards created a peer for his sins. These days he was simply ancient and rich.

'I daresay you have heard of this club,' I said to Nash.

'I have. It's a powerful coterie. The treasurer of the Admiralty is a member, and men belonging to the East India Company. The Earl of Worsley, too, and Lord Casserly, of course. Fret not, my sweet, I shall be angling for an invitation to the masquerade.'

I turned to Selina. 'You must ask Newington to get you a ticket. It would be amusing if we could all go together.'

'I do have a penchant for being pleasured in fancy dress, but don't we all?'

'I suppose that Newington will be able to pull strings so that you can see Garrick, too.'

'Oh, he is not in the habit of the theatre. It sends him to sleep.'

'Well, I am mad to see Garrick one last time.'

The great actor was to perform a final round of his best characters before he retired and I very much wished to see him play the part of the rakish Ranger to Mrs Abington's Clarinda. Nash is a follower of the playwrights and knows their best *bons mots* by heart, but I am fascinated by the actors themselves. I wonder about the life behind the stage and the precariousness of it. The thought of it gives me a shiver. Perhaps my interest stems from the apprehension that actors, whose calling depends on looks and voices and bodies that cannot last, must confront the same hard laws of life that women do. When the brightness of our beauty dies, we are plunged into the dark.

Nash, I realised, was offering me something on a plate. It was a wedge of pineapple.

'Oh, Nash,' I sighed.

He grinned. 'The urge came over me. Besides, we can afford it.'

I gave a start when I bit into the pale green flesh. Instead of the sweet, exotic taste that I expected, the pineapple's astringency set my teeth on edge. No amount of sugaring the slices made any difference and we could not overcome the disappointment of the fruit. Selina tossed her half-eaten piece to one side and yawned.

Ned knocked at the door then and announced it was half past one o'clock and he begged leave to retire. Nash ordered him out to hail a cab for Selina and we climbed creakily to our feet. I was so tipsy I hardly minded the destroyed pineapple, fallen from its throne.

There was a dirty dark-yellow moon shining in the window of our bedchamber. I had forgotten to draw the curtains. Nash was stretched out on the bed like a marvellous big animal, his torso bare above the sheet, his eyes closed; a creature that had padded through the dark and lay at rest now in its lair. I lay my cheek against the silky hair on his chest. He said something that I did not catch and when I asked him what it was, he said, 'I am jealous of them all.' I pulled the sheet from his body. He placed my head in the vice of his hands and pushed the fullness of his tongue inside my mouth, our tongues wrapping, the wet muscular kiss making me feel sticky and reeling. He liked that, my squeezing him in my hand, jerking that hot heaviness. We were grappling now, slipping and sliding. He lifted up my hips and fitted his sex into mine and I put my arms around his neck. We were drunk and too relaxed and I wanted something that rolled out of reach like a skein of thread that falls to the floor. Being too slow to retrieve it, you must watch as it tips over the edge of the staircase and tumbles over and over itself, unravelling. None of these observations were in my mind while Nash was making love to me. I had no thoughts at all. He pulled out of me, panting, then his cock filled me again. I urged myself into a hot spasm of ecstasy that was too brief, a flash, a shower of falling sparks. He rolled over on to his back with a groan and we lay side by side, our skin burning. My hand reached for his, our fingers entwined, my head was spinning.

Chapter 5

The Harbinger

June the 9th, 1776

I awoke in a state of confusion, uncertain of the time. I levered myself from the bed and stumbled to the window. Through a gap in the curtains, I expected to see the usual shrouded forms appearing out of the mist, milk sellers and pie girls and the like, but it was too early even for them. I lay down again, with a dry mouth and heavy head. Oh Lord, I know that I am living too hard. It is a course of life that has settled into a habit which I cannot seem to break, no matter how horrible I feel. What had we done exactly to make me feel so terribly baked? Had we stayed up late, drinking with Selina? No, that was days ago. I gazed at Nash, his curls tousled on the pillow, his face empty of care. He was sleeping like a baby. A recollection of the theatre gradually formed in my mind. We had tried to obtain tokens for a performance of Garrick in *The Suspicious Husband*, but there was such a crush of people on the same mission we hadn't a chance. The whole of London wants a last glimpse of Mr Garrick. We were terribly disappointed and ended up – ah, yes, it is all coming back in shameful detail – we ended up roistering at Vauxhall Gardens. I touched Nash's cheek, willing him to wake and speak to me with tenderness, but he turned over and lay with his back to me. I resigned myself to beginning the day then, although I was expiring with a headache.

As I tiptoed down the stairs, I remembered that we had kept the servants up late. Their moods would be murderous if they were not permitted to stretch out their slumber, and so I descended to the kitchen and prepared my own coffee. Then I came up to the breakfast parlour on the first floor, where I keep my writing box. The box sits on a narrow table that contains two slim drawers. I opened one of the drawers to look for ink powder and saw a commonplace book, which had lain undisturbed since I bought it more than a year ago. I picked it up and found an inscription on the first page. I do not recall writing it, but the hand is mine, so I must have done it in a first flush of enthusiasm after bringing the book home. It is a quote from Horace: *Dare to know!* Dare to know nothing, evidently, for the remainder of the pages lie blank. Well, that is my way – to buy and then to abandon. I suffer to pay the price of a thing, yet once it is in my ownership it seems depleted and not worth the bother of acquisition. I returned the book to its repose and shut the drawer and sat for several moments under a burden of self-dislike.

I drank my coffee and then prepared to leave the house in order to convey the last chapter of Degoutte to its printer, Mr Wheeler. As I squared the chapter's pages, my eye lingered on the top page and I felt a twinge of misgiving at the number of footnotes I had added. In the cold light of day, it occurred to me that I might have gone too far, but I had been irked by many assertions in Monsieur Degoutte's work: his opinion, for instance, that botany is the only arm of science that is acceptable for women to study, since we are naturally disposed to understand the world of plants. Like nature, we are sensuous and fluctuate and breed; and, it follows, we must be tamed. Monsieur Degoutte's book left out many practicalities that it seemed to me women should like to know – descriptions of the tools, for example, that are required for botanising and the methods of using and maintaining them. I had added footnotes in the translation to address these omissions, but I will admit that in regard to the deluge of amendments, there had been some urge at work on my part that was not altogether about clarifying the text. I saw on this rather sickening morning a good deal of conceit in the magnitude of the annotations. There was sincerity and earnestness in the motivation for them, but I wondered if at the heart of it lay an effort to bring myself to prominence.

I opened the drawer of the table again and looked at the commonplace book. I could redeem the purchase – paper was expensive, after all – by actually writing in its pages. But what I should write, I did not know.

I closed the drawer and tied the Degoutte chapter into a neat parcel. Then I went downstairs again to find some morsel to eat before I went out. There were half a dozen stale pikelets in the larder and I had just gnawed on one of them when a knock sounded at the front door. Were Jane or Ned up yet to answer it? Apparently not, for the minutes passed with no sign of life in the house. The knock came again and so I went upstairs and opened the door myself.

Felix Spencer stood before me, stooped in an attitude of supplication with his buckled hat in his hands. He looked more haggard, if such a thing were possible. I said at once, 'Mr Nash has written you a promissory, Mr Spencer. I will fetch it for you, if you will wait here.'

He cried, 'Ah, madam, I rejoice at this news! My wife and I have been in great suspense about the matter. May I have the pleasure of thanking Ollie in person? Is he here?'

Despite his appearing to be a disreputable person, I could not bring myself to lie to Mr Spencer for a second time – or, at least, I only slightly lied. I said that Mr Nash was in a deep sleep after having returned from an arduous journey and that I preferred not to wake him. Spencer nodded as if he understood the truth of the situation. I found myself in a dilemma then: it seemed uncivil to request the man to stand in the street like an errand boy, but I was uneasy at the prospect of inviting him inside to wait unattended while I went upstairs. I excused myself and shouted for Ned. A muffled reply gave me the confidence to invite Mr Spencer into the house. As he stepped into the hall, I was struck by an odd feeling of tension as I saw his dark, attenuated shape silhouetted against the bright light of the morning. It was the proper thing to do to bring the man into our home to wait, and yet I wished that I had not been drawn to do it. I had to shut my imagination to the thought that he represented some kind of harbinger, a foreshadow of events to come. I was relieved to see Ned breast the stairs. I asked him to conduct our visitor to the plate room, next to the kitchen, and to give him a mug of beer and bread and cheese, if it pleased him to accept it.

I hurried upstairs and tiptoed into the bedchamber. I was anxious to close the business with Spencer before Nash woke and changed his mind about the twenty pounds. I felt a strong urge to comply with Felix Spencer, so that we were done with him for good, otherwise I feared that he might haunt our household with his soliciting. Quietly, I lifted the pot that hides Nash's key. I opened the locking box and pulled out the velvet case where Nash keeps cheques and notes. I found the promissory made out to Spencer and stole with it on tiptoes through the bedchamber. Nash was lying on his stomach, breathing through his mouth. He looked beautifully vulnerable, a condition in which I rarely behold him in his waking life. On my way downstairs, I paused at my writing box and drew up a brief letter of bond to record Felix Spencer's receipt of the sum of twenty pounds from Oliver Nash.

Spencer was sitting at the small table in the plate room, hollow-cheeked, grasping the handle of a pewter mug. I showed him the promissory and offered him the bond to sign. He looked at the note and expelled a cough like a reproach.

He said, 'But I venture to say, madam, that Ollie owes a great deal more than this.'

'That is a revelation to me, Mr Spencer. How much more?'

'One hundred pounds.'

'Do not try to play me, sir. You are lucky to get even this note for twenty.'

Spencer leaned forward and fixed me with his gaze. 'Mrs Nash, I am not a casual acquaintance of your husband's, I will have you know. Our friendship commenced four-and-twenty years ago when we were at the Merchant Drapers' School in the City. Did Ollie tell you that?'

I saw no reason to advertise my ignorance of that fact to Spencer, so I made no reply.

'We were young and both of us had been in some trouble; then our fathers died at about the same time. Ollie's left him high and dry, but my father was more forgiving and I got a bequest. It was an opportunity to make a new start. Ollie was of the same mind and we determined to go out to India. It seemed natural to me to help my comrade. I bought myself a commission in the Bengal army and Ollie a passage and the means to set himself up in Calcutta, and we both quitted England. I asked no bond for the money, because I was convinced I did not run a risk. I took Oliver Nash for a man of honour. But I was decommissioned unexpectedly and I am weakened by the malaria that I contracted in Bengal. I am severely out of pocket, Mrs Nash, and it seems to me even by a cursory glance at your residence that Ollie is in an opulent situation and has the means now to acquit the debt.'

The haunted look in Spencer's eyes, added to the sincerity of his tone, inclined me to give credence to his story.

I lowered my voice so that the servants would not hear.

'In fact, Mr Spencer, the opulence you see here is a pretence. Everything is on loan.'

He nodded with a bleak smile. 'I can believe that, madam. Ollie was never a good economist.'

'The twenty pounds you hold in your hand is my personal saving and it is all I have. We pay it to you as a sign of good faith, sir.'

Spencer nodded heavily, then he folded the note and inserted it into his pocket. He got to his feet with an effort and wiped away the perspiration that had sprung up on his forehead. He said, 'I promise you, if you were of a mind to make inquiries yourself as to the veracity of my account, you will find that I am not a liar.' The broken expression on his face made me feel uncomfortable. 'If Mr Nash improves his situation, he might discharge the remainder of the debt, if not to me then to my wife.'

'Yes,' I said, knowing that such a thing was very unlikely to occur. 'Perhaps by means of an annuity.'

He said, 'Marsh Lane, near the sign of the Falcon at Humerton. That is where you may reach us.' He screwed his hat on to his head, and added, 'Thank you, madam, for doing justice to me. I will not forget it.'

As I walked in the direction of Fleet Street, my thoughts returned to Mr Spencer and the remarks that he had made concerning Nash. I could not recall Nash ever saying much about his school days except to mention that he had attended the Merchant Drapers' School and that he had won a scholarship to take up a place at the Middle Temple, which is one of the Inns of Court. There, he was set on a course to become a barrister, a prospect that had filled his father with joy. Nash the elder had looked forward to a repairing of the family's fortunes, through the efforts and elevation of his son, and a pampering of the Nashes' blood, but unfortunately, and typically, as Nash tells it, his father could not be relied on to play his part in this ascendancy. The clothier's business failed, due to his having the acumen of a gnat, Nash says, and he could not support his son's training for the Bar. Poor Nash was obliged to leave the Middle Temple and resign himself to an attorney's work in the common courts. After that, there was no love lost between Nash and his father.

We might not have lived so precariously at Hood Street had Nash been able to bring himself to return to the London courts. After all, even the shabbiest attorney can charge stiff fees for litigating. But Nash's experience of the law had been tainted from the beginning. It piqued him that the direction of his life had been formed by the requirement to compensate for his father's thwarted aspirations. In any case, I do not think that Nash's character is well adapted for the law. He tends to be speculative and fired by novelty. If he notices a hawker of news-sheets in the street, he obliges himself to go out at once to discover the latest scandal. I can imagine how it happened that his career in Calcutta miscarried. If Nash were assigned to a court case that lacked bustle and import, he is the kind of person who might become indifferent to its outcome and find it hard to stir himself to bring it to a satis-factory conclusion; but, at bottom, his chafing at the duties of an attorney stem from the law having been his father's choice for him.

Even if I had any idea how to go about confirming the truth of Spencer's story about fitting Nash out for India, I was not inclined to do it. Nash is entitled to keep his past to himself; in fact, I envy his ability to shun events that have gone before. I try to be as forward-looking as he, but some-how I am compelled to keep looking back. Drinking is the devil for that. One drinks in order to forget; but liquor has a nasty habit of turning on you and making you remember.

Presently, I arrived at Fleet Street and found my way to Ink Yard, where the printer, Arthur Wheeler, keeps his shop next to the sign of the Blue Anchor. It has a double frontage of tall bow windows on either side of a yellow door. The shopmaid, Wheeler's daughter, recognised me as soon as I entered and offered me a greeting. She was attending a cus-tomer, so I paused to browse the shelves with their many hundreds of volumes in elegant calf bindings. Wheeler spe-cialises in books concerning natural philosophy and history, biography and travel, and translations, of course, of these subjects. He also sells fine papers, ink powder, sealing wax and other stationery ware. He prints some of the titles him-self and the others he buys at trade sales and by private contract. A volume called *The Visionaries of Asia* caught my eye. I stowed my parcel at my feet and rifled through the book. I was engaged by the titles of the chapters and by the illustrations and maps. As I turned from one passage to another, I felt in my heart an unusual sensation of expansion; it was the thought of the magnitude of the world and of all the marvels that it must contain.

'The work is complete in five parts octavo,' Miss Wheeler said with a smile. She was dressed modestly in blue broadcloth and a white cap. Her demeanour was calm. 'We have an Irish edition as well, published in twelves, if you prefer. Both editions are rather scarce.'

With regret, I returned the volume to its place and said ruefully, 'Each time I come here to see your father, I have already spent my fee in the shop before he pays it to me in the parlour.'

She laughed. 'Books are a temptation, aren't they?'

If Wheeler had accepted credit, I should probably have bought *The Visionaries of Asia*, but he ran a strictly ready-money business. He was a singular tradesman in that regard, and a shrewd one. Although some customers were offended by this approach, it meant he had the cash to print and sell books at a cheaper rate than many of his rivals. He was able to increase his stock by commissioning translators and paying authors for their manuscripts and copyrights, whereas other printers could only afford to pay a pittance to hirelings who pumped out all kinds of trash on bad paper with loose bindings.

I retrieved my parcel and let Miss Wheeler conduct me to the back parlour, where her father sat in his shirtsleeves at a table, marking up a manuscript in red ink for the typesetters.

In the background, I could hear the creak and thump of the two presses in the printing room.

'Good morning, Mrs Nash.' Wheeler climbed to his feet and doffed his linen cap. He bowed, showing a bald pate ringed by fluffy greyish curls. The habit of bending over typecases had stooped him and his face was screwed up in a permanent frown from squinting at fonts. 'What have you got for me?'

'It's the end of Degoutte.' I placed the parcel on the table and undid the twine.

Wheeler began to thumb through the pages – and at once protested the inclusion of the footnotes. 'By Jove, madam, you have redoubled your interventions, it seems. Am I to be bankrupted by the cost of setting them?'

'I doubt it, Mr Wheeler.' I laughed. 'Your business booms, doesn't it? Your stock seems to have increased since I was last here.'

He replaced the cap on his head and harrumphed. 'I will say that reading is becoming more of a general amusement and there are signs that I may sell more often to the public at large and not just a coterie, which is very good for business. I can't sit around waiting for the gentry to send to me for a title now and then at their leisure.'

'What does the public like to read?'

'Voyages and travels. History. Biography. Anything with a personal touch. People have become very curious about the workings of things and the otherness of the world. I have a manuscript, there, by Mr Jamison –' he nodded at the tower of pages by his chair – 'describing his exploration of the Nile. I will put it out as a small octavo on good paper, I think, and I expect it to do well. Jamison is economical with his observations, Mrs Nash, unlike you.'

'I did consider deleting some of them.'

Wheeler rubbed his nose with an inky finger. 'Your footnotes do have their own peculiar character, I will say that much.' He stared before him intently, lost in a thought. Then he said, 'I suppose it might be possible to make a virtue of the annotations. I might compose an advertisement that mentions our translation offers additional remarks by an English lady. As an appeal to women. I would need to deduct the cost of the extra paper from your fee, of course. That would leave you with three guineas to come.'

I agreed to the proposal and Mr Wheeler straight away went to a cupboard and took out an iron box and unlocked it. He removed a ledger and marked the sum on a page that was devoted to my transactions with him and gave me my three guineas.

I made my way back to Covent Garden, thinking of the *Visionaries* in Mr Wheeler's shop and wishing that I had bought the book. Were I to write anything, perhaps it might be in a similar vein, proceeding out of a motive of curiosity about people and places which are as yet strangers to me. The thought of it quickened my mind for some minutes, but then, as I wended my way along Monmouth Street, with its plethora of apparel shops, my vision of travel and exploration was overwhelmed by a familiar fixation. Like a needle upon a lodestone, I was drawn to the display of trifles in the shop windows and almost spent the money I had got for the translation on a pair of velvet sleeves. They called to me like little sirens on their rock . . . *Buy us, buy us, take us home and love us, oh do, please do* . . . No matter that I would not wear velvet again until October, still I craved the compensation of the sleeves with a fervour that I was barely able to resist. However, since the flowers at Hillier's are also an infatuation of mine, I tore myself from Monmouth Street and struck out for the market square. On I rolled, like the wheel of wanting itself.

Hillier's Garden Warehouse is in Burleigh Street, a little south of the market. Whatever is fashionable in the garden may be found there, from bulbs and flowering shrubs to a small forest of trees in moveable containers. The shop is a great lifter of mood, especially in the dark months. Even as the river iced over this January past and a numbing fog crept into every cranny of the town, the heating pipes at Hillier's never once gave out. The luxuriants, with their suggestion of enigmatic fantasies, continued to thrive behind glass in a marvellous tangle of green. The pomegranate shrubs, the Persian jasmine, the gardenias, the butterfly bushes, the Indian thorn apples with dark, toothed leaves and trumpet flowers tinged a malignant violet – they cast their spell over me. The exuberance of them, the pushing of leaf and bud! The warehouse is divided into departments of floristry, perennials, ornamental shrubs and so on. There is a department of rarities, too, with so many new plant introductions one can hardly keep up with them, and another for catalogues and botanical prints and pamphlets of instruction.

The department of seeds I never pass by without thinking of my mother, Marie Ravine. Dearest Mama. If I close my eyes, I can see her still in the hazy light of the seed loft in the garden nursery that was our home. She is working on the catalogue that my grandfather put out each January and September for his customers. She writes with unflagging attention to detail, while I tip seeds on to the weighing machine and transfer them to packets. Jenny and Maryanne, my little sisters, are playing at our feet. Jenny is stuffing paper bags with the chaff that comes out of the threshing machine that we use for the seedheads. She ties the bags at the neck and waist with packthread and turns them into rudimentary dolls. Maryanne has arranged them around herself in a circle, as if for protection. Oh, poor, dear, lost Maryanne.

There is an area at the rear of Hillier's where plants are hired out and various administrations made. I repaired to the counter to pay the forfeit of two guineas for the pine-apple that we had violated after Gifford's supper party and suffered to endure a lecture from the shopman concerning my tardy return. At the far end of the counter, another shop-man was serving a customer. They were examining an object spread in paper wrappings that lay open before them. The customer was a hawk-nosed man who was above six feet high. He wore a light linen coat and a cocked hat. My gaze dropped to the short sword that he wore at his hip in a strangely worked leather scabbard. Its owner looked capable of using it. He was not from London, I guessed, where the flaunting of swords has fallen out of fashion. Nash would never be so boorish as to wear a weapon about the town. I was a little curious to know what the pair was discussing. As I strolled by them, my glance took in a few slim pieces of blackened root that were exposed in the wrappings on the counter.

'In no manner is this root edible,' the swordsman said firmly.

'It is Indian liquorice from Bengal,' the shopman retorted. 'The dealer told us so.'

The swordsman removed his hat, pushed back the blond-ish hair that waved up from his high forehead, and said, 'It is without a doubt *abrus precatorius*. A toxic vine. You must dispose of it if you do not wish to poison your customers.'

The shopman made a put-upon face and said, 'Is that so?' without the least sincerity.

'Will you call your superintendent?' the swordsman ordered. He looked around, apparently in search of an authority higher than a pimpled stripling with spectacles tied on with a string around his head. His searching eye caught mine as I was turning away. He had a plain countenance with rather raw features. His eyes, though, were uncommonly expressive and his gaze was direct. It seemed to pin me to him. I do not mean in any salacious way, for there was nothing of the philanderer about the man. But, oddly, he took a step in my direction and I had the distinct feeling that he sought to engage me. He was detained by the business at the counter, however, which had assumed an urgent nature. As soon as I had quitted the shop, I felt the absurdity of the notion that he should have wanted to apprehend me. It displeases me that, underneath my gaiety and my going about on the town, I cannot ever seem to shake off the habitual fear that a stranger is about to menace me or that a distressing proposition is imminent.

Chapter 6

The Paring Knife

My mother was born in Spitalfields, the year of 1730, to a gardener named John Durand and his wife Caroline, who is my namesake. Now, Spitalfields is in decline, the fine houses of the silk merchants subdivided into mean apartments, but at that time the area teemed with descendants of Protestant dissenters, Huguenots, who had fled France at the turn of the century. My grandfather used to say that you could still hear French spoken everywhere on those east London streets when he was a young man. It was a close-knit community and my mother never strayed from it until the day that she took passage for India. Her own mother having died in childbirth, she kept house for her father at Durand Gardens, a nursery he had established on four acres that he leased at Bethnal Green. At nineteen, she met Daniel Ravine, a twenty-four-year-old gardener who had come to work at the nursery. They married at a French church on Brick Lane, called L'Eglise de l'Hôpital.

My grandfather must have welcomed the match at first. The son of a French-descended gardener, Ravine was a personable young man and one who was accomplished in the operations of horticulture. He had studied vegetable physiology and chemistry in Holland and seemed an asset to the nursery. People found him attractive. He had quick features and dark good looks. My mother's temperament tended in general to be contained, but she was often girlish and blushing in my father's company. To everyone else, she was low-voiced and careful. I recollect her as a preserver and an organiser. She kept the nursery's books – the time book, the cash book and the plantation book. She gave me quiet tasks of a meditative quality, which appealed to me, even though I sometimes stole to the window during those placid hours and looked down on one or other of the apprentices in the garden and imagined the taste of his mouth and the secrets of his body. Then, on I would go, attaching dried specimens to cards in order of their flowering and filing packets of seeds according to the hierarchies. I can see my grandfather, John Durand, sitting close by in this scene, a big-shouldered, dignified man, cracking his knuckles, while motes of seed dust float in the dry yellow light.

Most of the days of my childhood, there was a settled, untroubled feeling at Durand Gardens. The fissure between Durand and Ravine took many years to widen, but even as quite a young child, I understood that Papa did not share my grandfather's traditional approach to his *métier*. He held no great veneration for greens and I often heard him despair of the nursery's stock of forest trees and hedges, which he found dreary and intolerably slow to raise. He urged Durand to improve the business by adapting to new fashions in the garden for exotics and luxuriants. My father was an interventionist by nature and possessed the hybridising skills to cultivate these barren beauties and produce lush blooms that were bigger and better than their progenitors. My grandfather thought these hybrids a risky proposition. They commanded high prices, but they were tricky to breed and demanded a great deal of maintenance. Nevertheless, he gave in on the question of pineapples and melons and allowed Ravine to construct a stove where they could be nursed. That was the thin edge of the wedge. While my grandfather was away visiting his customers in the country, my father had bark pits dug and a hothouse thrown up and purchased dozens of exotic parent plants in order to begin a new programme of cultivation.

I was a favourite of my grandfather's. He did not mind that I was a girl and he often took me out and about with him on the operations of his work. I enjoyed the life of a hoyden, with my petticoats tucked up and my own little knife and dirt under my fingernails. I hardly recognise myself in the recollection. I cannot explain how a tomboy managed to grow into a woman whose head has been turned by fashion and artifice. I suppose the transformation began when my parents enrolled me at the age of thirteen at Mrs Leonard's boarding school in Kensington. Grandfather had agreed to pay the fees. Most of the pupils at Mrs Leonard's were the daughters of ambitious tradesmen and artisans. We learned French, English, arithmetic, needlework and dancing for twenty guineas a year. It cost a shilling for the stage home, once a week. My parents were certain it was an education that would improve my marriage prospects. I estimate that it was not long after I began at Mrs Leonard's establishment that Durand Gardens began to founder.

Each Saturday, I came home from school to spend Sunday *en famille*, but in the spring of my fifteenth year I developed the feeling that some sort of storm might be gathering. I noticed at home an accumulation of vague tensions in the form of simmering silences, averted gazes and forced cheerfulness, and my mother seemed often in a distracted mood, ruminating in her closet. She seemed so unlike herself that eventually I was presumptuous enough to ask her if anything were amiss. It was a Sunday afternoon and we were walking on the boundary of the nursery, among the seedling trees. A sense of their redundancy weighed on me. I had heard often enough from Papa that no heir in these times of novelty would thicken up his plantations with dull English trees when he could ornament his estate with showy American species. I wished heartily that Grandfather would not be so stubborn and that he would vary his stock. As a child I had thought the steadfastness of his character to be admirable, that is, I felt instinctively that he could be relied upon like a mighty oak, but now that I was out in the world, I was learning that a person more often than not needed to sway with the wind. I had witnessed with my own eyes the wreckage left after a gale. If the onslaught were malevolent enough, even an oak tree could come crashing down.

Mrs Leonard liked to say that a truculent mind is the

doorway to disaster, at least for young ladies. To be affirmative and supple is the thing, since no man likes to keep a
sullen, disagreeable woman at his hearth. Mama herself had
given me similar counsel in anticipation of my future state
when I went away to school. One must be trifling and easy
and love one's husband, as Mama put it, 'above oneself'.

She had not responded to my question about her well-
being. I asked again if she were quite in order. Her small,
rather swarthy face was thinner than usual, perhaps. She had
dark, heavily lashed eyes that drooped at the corners. She
always looked faintly melancholy, but I remember particularly noticing it that day, for I have gone over those last
meetings between us innumerable times. Still she did not
reply directly, but said instead, 'I have a great fondness for
you, Carey. You do know that, my dear, don't you?'

I took her arm and kissed her cheek. She gave off a faint
scent of rosewater. As we walked on, Mama sighed and then
she said, 'I have been preoccupied by your grandfather's
affairs. I am afraid that the nursery business is not as robust
as it once was.'

It was difficult for me to be persuaded of such a thing,
especially in early summer, when all was in bud and new
leaf, swelling with promise, and the light was young and
green. I stopped on the path and withdrew my arm from
Mama's. I looked up at the house in the distance, with its
weatherboarded, half-timbered façade. How dear my home
was to me. I could hear the deep barking of one of the dogs
and a distant hammering that came from the packing shed:

they were the familiar sounds of my childhood. I said, 'Then let Grandfather give up the payment of my school fees. I should prefer to be at home. To be truthful, Mama, I do not absolutely like Mrs Leonard very much. She frightens me a little.'

'Ah, child,' Mama sighed. 'You must not leave the school. It gives your grandfather such pleasure to feel that he is doing something for you. If you were to come home, you would rob him of that satisfaction. I am of the same mind. I should like to see you settled in a good marriage.'

'But I do not need Mrs Leonard to find me a husband.'

'She gives dances, Carey, and makes introductions. She knows merchants and gentlemen. If you stay in Bethnal Green, you will never be perceived as anything other than a gardener's daughter.'

'That is what I am, Mama.'

'But in Kensington you may pass for someone else. Some-one better.'

I opened my mouth to protest, but my mother said, 'Do not argue with me, *chérie*. It is almost my only comfort to know that you are on a useful path.' At that moment, the dog, Bibi, shot along the path and startled Mama, who broke off and clapped her hand hard upon her bosom. Bibi skidded to a halt and looked abashed. Then he wheeled around and went loping off back towards the house. I looked at my mother. I could hardly believe that old Bibi had frightened her so. She kept her hand pressed above her heart, as if to quell some emotion.

'What is it, Mama?'

We were standing by one of the seedling beds. Mama bent down and righted a name-stick that had fallen over. She straightened up and said quickly, 'Oh, child, I find myself in a dilemma and I know not what course to steer.' Then she at once made a dismissive gesture and said, 'I hardly know myself at present. I have been stupidly out of sorts. Let us go to our dinner.'

She would not say more, but it was clear to me that some important matter had been left in suspense. One week later, I discovered what it was.

I was met in the usual way by a cart outside the Salmon and Ball, on the west side of Bethnal Green, where I had quitted the stage coach from town. It was a Saturday afternoon. The cart was driven by Harry, one of Grandfather's under-gardeners, and it brought me to the dwelling house at Durand Gardens. The house was placed near the road and as soon as Harry reached the gate I jumped out of the cart and ran to the side entrance. The parlourmaid, Lottie, welcomed me and went to take my bag from Harry. I was surprised not to be greeted by my mother and offered refreshments. She was usually hovering at the window, awaiting my arrival. There was no sign of Bibi, either, and his welcoming bark. I thumped up the stairs to the living room of the house and went to the window, which looked down on the packing court. It was about four o'clock in the afternoon and the sun was slanting through the trees. Strewn about the court were a number of the hooped boxes that we used for sending out plants in leaf. They were empty and I remember thinking that it was strange they were left in the court instead of being stowed in the packing shed.

On the open side of the court, a large parterre displayed a range of plants grown in the nursery, so that potential customers could inspect them. A covered seat had been put in by the parterre for the ease of visitors and my mother was sitting there with Maryanne on her lap and Jenny crouched at her feet. Mama was wearing a flat straw hat, a greenish dress and a striped apron. Papa reclined on the opposite side of the court, on a bench against a wall of the packing shed. He was sharpening his knife, but he was not dressed for work. His coat was pale blue and he was wearing stockings and buckled shoes.

Even now, I can never see a certain kind of small wooden-handled knife without thinking of my father, of that ever-present blade working at some tuber or leaf, the earth beneath his fingernails, the faintly suety smell of his oilskin apron. I am reminded of how he would lift his head from his work in the forcing house, aware of my watching him, and smile. Looking back on him, I see that he very much sought admiration in order to be gratified. In that respect, he had the ideal wife, because Mama, I understand more completely now, had a deep capacity for adoration. She was profoundly in love with her husband.

I recall that I was perturbed by the atmosphere of the house. It did not seem its usual self, although I could not put my finger on the source of the alteration except to say that the familiar rooms felt peculiarly unoccupied. I came downstairs to the office, where I expected to find my grandfather bent over a book or his papers, as was his custom on a Saturday afternoon. As I entered, he would look up and pretend to frown at the interruption – then his craggy face would crease in a smile. He seemed always pleased to see me. Everything was in its place in the office on this particular occasion – the writing desk, a bookcase, a map of the garden on the wall, a cabinet for specimens of plants and a drawing board – but Grandfather was not there.

I left the office and entered the court. I remember the scent of lilac and honeysuckle. The cats that were usually domiciled in the back sheds to keep mice at bay were sprawled in the pale sun. They seemed to be making a point of having nothing to do. At the sight of me, my father put his knife to one side and stood up. He opened his arms and flicked the dark hair out of his eyes with a toss of his head. It was a habit of his, which made him seem rather rakish, I think. There was always something about him of the buck, although I did not recognise it at the time. I had no perspective on him. He was simply my father and an absolute.

He cried, 'There's my girl! How is everything in the world, *petite*?'

I curtsied to him and said, 'It is awfully quiet here.'

As I made the remark, I realised how true it was. Where were the women who usually worked in the plots and bantered as they did their weeding? Where were the labourers who came to pulverise the soil and mulch and water? Where was Bibi?

Papa chuckled. 'Quiet we are indeed, Miss Kensington. You are already out of the ways of we simple country folk.'

'Where is Grandfather, may I ask?'

'Is he not here? Perhaps he went to take a box to the King's Head.' He looked across at my mother, who had climbed to her feet, with Maryanne resting on her hip, and yet she seemed rather immobilised. I had the impression that she was gazing at me as if across a vast distance. She even put up a hand to shade her eyes, the better to distinguish me. But in fact her gaze was directed at my father. Something passed between them at any rate, a shared *frisson*.

I was glad to hear that Grandfather had a customer who needed a box to be sent. I bounded across the court to my mother and the little girls with their bright eyes and plump cheeks. Jenny cried, 'Care-wee!' and hugged my legs. She was only three years old and Maryanne was less than two.

'What are you doing, poppet?' I asked. 'Are you grooming Tansy?'

Jenny nodded and stooped to her pet, a long-haired rabbit. She was trying to comb out the burrs in its pelt.

I kissed Mama and Maryanne and hunkered down on the ground beside Jenny. I gave her a squeeze and took up the wooden comb and showed her how to tease out a tangle in the rabbit's fur. The animal was very tractable. As I raked the tines of the comb through the fur, I had a satisfied feeling, as though a problem were being solved. Harry arrived in the court and began to haul away one of the storage boxes, but Mama called out and asked him if he would help Jenny to take the rabbit to its hutch. As Jenny tottered off with Harry, I noticed that my father was still standing where I had left him. My mother put her hand on my arm and she looked across at my father, who seemed to raise his shoulders in a sigh, before advancing towards us. There was a gravity about their actions that made the hairs stand up on the back of my neck.

Maryanne gurgled and I said, 'Shall I hold her?'

But the child protested as I tried to take her from my mother's arms and she twisted away from me. 'Oh!' I cried, 'I am only gone a week and she forgets who I am.'

'Ah, Carey,' Mama said in a low, choked voice.

'What is it?' The stricken expression on her face alarmed me.

Papa said, 'It is Durand. He and I have come to an open rupture. He will no longer permit me to work with him and we must quit the nursery.'

My mouth opened and closed at this shocking news and I lifted my gaze to the house. I could not think what to say. Instead, I had a wild impulse to burst into laughter. How ridiculous it was to think of our leaving the nursery. It was our home!

Papa said, 'The arrangements are already made.'

Mama's voice trembled. 'Your father must find a way to make a living. He knows someone . . .' Her words trailed off.

'It seems that someone of my skills may find a good contract in Bengal,' Papa said. 'So that is what we must do, child. We shall take a passage to India.'

'When?' I asked, stunned.

'In a fortnight.'

'Oh!' A smile came to my face then at the thought of leaving Mrs Leonard's establishment. That was some recompense for this violent change in circumstances.

Papa said quickly, 'But you shall stay here with your grandfather. You must continue at school.'

'No,' I cried in disbelief. 'You cannot leave me behind. Or must I look after Jenny and Maryanne?'

I turned to my mother and saw tears well in her eyes. She said, 'They are too little to leave in care. It is really not in our power to do anything else.'

'I do not understand,' I said.

Papa sighed. 'Carey, my dear, the Lord knows that we wish it had not come to this, but your grandfather has forced the situation, has he not, Marie?'

My mother nodded, the tears spilling on to her cheeks.

'What else can I do? He has ordered me to withdraw,' Papa said.

'But why?'

'Dear girl, I know how difficult it is for you to understand the turbulent relations between your grandfather and me – I can hardly make sense of them myself – but Durand has resented me for some time. Now he accuses me of encroachment on his territory and is jealous even of my very presence. I fear, with age, his faculties are beginning to disintegrate and—'

'Dan, please,' my mother broke in, sadly. She looked as

though someone had slapped her face. 'It is only that he is old and afraid of losing what he has spent his life building up. It is his confidence that fails, not his mind.'

Even my young self could see that this exchange showed a glimpse of a much larger argument that must have been going on for a long time.

'In any case,' my father sighed, 'the situation cannot be repaired and we have had to face its consequences. We are to go.'

'How can I bear the idea! Why mayn't I come with you?' Sensing the distress in my voice, Maryanne began to wail. My mother tried to hush her, and rocked from one foot to the other, but the child only cried harder.

I appealed to my father. 'If you are not here, will not Grandfather's business fall into danger? You have said that, if he continues so set in his ways, he will destroy our livelihood.'

My mother raised her voice to be heard over Maryanne's howls. 'Even though your grandfather's intransigence has brought us to this, his heart is broken over it.'

I wanted to say, *But isn't your heart broken, too, Mama?* She and her father had always had a strong bond.

But my mother had stepped towards my father and thrust the shrieking child at him. 'Daniel, please, I can't . . .' As soon as Maryanne came into Papa's arms, she ceased her racket.

Mama turned to me and said in a cracked voice, 'I believe that your remaining in your grandfather's care will preserve him from despair.'

'But if you do not go, he will not despair!' I cried.

'That is not a choice I have,' Mama said in a low, halting voice. 'I must follow my husband in this matter.'

'Carey,' my father said, 'there is no need to become desperate over this. We shall be reunited in two or three years. You will graduate from Mrs Leonard's school a mighty marriageable young woman, I am sure, and then you will come to us when we are in a state of prosperity and comfort. It will all be for the best, you shall see.'

My mother put her arms around me and hugged me close. Then she stepped back and looked into my eyes with an expression of such love that I found some comfort in it even in the midst of the maelstrom. 'I know that the Almighty will preserve us to one another,' she said. 'My constant prayers will be that we may be enabled to support this separation with fortitude.'

I passed an agonising fortnight then at Durand Gardens, while the final arrangements were made for my family's departure. My grandfather returned, but he was still and silent and awkward, as if he did not know how to behave. He seemed remote and hardly aware of my presence, although I fluttered around him, bringing his tobacco and pipe, making fair copies of his correspondence, most of which consisted of pleading with customers to honour his bills and begging suppliers to give him more time to pay. I tried to maintain a cheerful demeanour in order to spare my mother's feelings. It can hardly have been less harrowing for her to leave me than it was for me to be parted from her – and she must quit her own father as well. Over the course of those last days, I convinced myself to remain strong and to conduct myself with calm for the sake of my mother – for, to all intents, I was to be left behind to make up to Durand for the loss of his beloved daughter. Neither my parents nor my grandfather mentioned the causes that had led to the schism or the impending exit. The focus of the household was on the routines of the nursery and the packing up of my parents' possessions. I don't think I truly believed that the removal would actually take place until the morning arrived when the waggon was drawn up in the road outside the house and porters began to load the baggage.

The day was cruelly bright. The gardens were filled with birdsong, and sunlight streamed into the house. My composure began to desert me as I helped my mother to dress the girls and I had to pause to mash my wet eyes with the heels of my hands. Then I dressed Mama's hair, determined to fix in my mind every detail of her face. When, at last, I was finished, she looked at me through the glass and I knew the moment of separation had drawn near. She opened her mouth and I leaned forward to hear what she would say to me. It was, 'Do you know, Carey, I was very fortunate to win the heart of Daniel Ravine. My wish for you is to find a similar love.'

After that, she went to farewell her father in his office. I walked into the living room and looked down into the court, watching Grandfather's door. Presently, I saw him open it and lumber across the yard and make his way into the garden with the dog at his heels.

I came downstairs and my parents and I embraced in the narrow little garden at the front of the house. Papa said, 'You will see us again before you know it.' I hugged the little girls tightly and covered their fat cheeks with kisses. They did not understand the import of the occasion, which was a relief. My mother said, 'Pray for me, my beloved child. God bless you, dearest girl!'

I stood at the gate for a great while, watching the waggon become smaller and smaller as it made its way down the dusty road.

I returned to school and the routine of coming home on Saturday afternoons, but I felt severely the shock of deprivation. It was heartbreaking to find my grandfather seated in his office or, more often, in the seed loft with his hands resting on his knees, looking into space with a dark, blank eye. We went on in these miserable conditions for many months and I came to both long for and dread the visits home. In all this time, I remained in a harrassing state of suspense, awaiting news of my family. It could take as little as two months or as many as six for the ship to reach Bengal. But at last, one day, a letter from Calcutta arrived for me at school – and with it my gravest fears came to pass. My father wrote with heavy heart to announce that my mother, and my sisters, had succumbed to those malignant fevers that seethe in the heated parts of the world. My sisters had not survived the voyage. My mother had died only a week after arriving in

Calcutta, so swift and violent was the onset of delirium in that place.

My grief was boundless. It went on and on and, just when I thought that perhaps I might come to terms with it, the universe shovelled fresh new losses into my vast pit of despair.

In regard to Durand Gardens, my father's prophecy came to pass. My grandfather sank under the blow of his daughter's death and the nursery fell to bankruptcy. One evening, when I was at school, John Durand was seized with violent pains of the heart, Lottie told me later, when I came to collect a trunk of my possessions. He had died alone in his office. As for my father, I never heard from him again. I wrote to the address in Calcutta that he had given me, but there was no response – and even if there had been, how could I have received the letter, since I was by then incarcerated, in a way? (But I do *not* want to think about that.) I wrote to the East India Company at Leadenhall House in London, seeking to find if there was a record of Daniel Ravine, horticulturalist, having taken up a contract in the British establishment at Bengal. The Company was well known for the meticulousness of its records, but no one had heard of him.

Sometimes I fantasise, even all these years later, that our family is intact at Bethnal Green. Had Durand been able to trust Ravine, everything might have been different, but now my ghostly sisters and phantom mother are unreachably in the past. They recede while I move forward, the distance between us growing ever wider.

Chapter 7

A Stranger at the Eclipse

June the 30th, 1776

By some perfect accounting of the universe, the twenty pounds that went out of Hood Street one month ago to Felix Spencer bounced back last Tuesday in the form of an instalment from Fenton Gifford – and not before time. The first I knew of it was the vision of Nash in the hallway in a fantastic Chinese yellow silk coat that I had never seen before. My mood had been overcast in the hours before he made his vivid appearance. Since evidence of the maintenance that Gifford promised had been slow in coming, I had taken on the translation of a volume of libertinage, called *The Castle of Pain*. The assignment did not come to me from Mr Wheeler, it goes without saying, but from Stephen Norton, a printer in Pasternoster Row who makes a specialty of these kinds of texts. Translating *The Castle* was, to be frank, a dejecting experience. Although I am a freethinker and a sensualist, I prefer a merry frolic to a mordant one, the playfulness of the masque over the despair of the dungeon. There was not a great deal of pleasure in this particular memoir, with its cold, stony structures and complicated debauchery. The translation needed to be completed in a rush, since the printer had a nobleman waiting for its publication. I had been grinding away at it day and night, but my spirits were flagging. I thought of dispatching Jane to the pawnbroker's with my best sacque and jacket in order to produce a sufficient sum to allow me to abandon the seedy book and go out gambolling, but conscience drove me to work on, labouring over double entendres and searching out cognates for the equipment used by riding masters. In between, I nagged the servants to stir themselves at least a portion of the day to keep the house limping along. I resented Nash a little, for he was disporting himself with the *beaux esprits* of the town. I do not know why I found fault with him about it, because it was nothing out of the ordinary for him to be out and about. I felt restless and dissatisfied by my present line of existence. It seemed in want of something, only I did not know what it was.

Then Nash came home with that coat and some money from Gifford, and the world seemed a better place. We did not hesitate to partake of a pint of wine in celebration, sitting in Nash's office. He stretched himself out on the divan and I lounged on a chair with my stockinged feet tucked up under me. Nash had hung his coat over the back of a chair and it glowed with pale sumptuousness, a third presence in the room, one that was swell and bountiful. The decanter was hardly emptied before we decided that we must throw a *soirée* at the tavern on the corner of Hood Street, which is something we have done from time to time to signal to people of our acquaintance, as one must, that we are still alive and in circulation.

Nash stepped into the hall and shouted for Ned to bring another bottle of wine from the cellar. When he sat down again on the divan, I said, weakly, 'I have a deadline, alas.'

'We are nearly in the same boat. Gifford wants my piece by Thursday. If we reserve two rooms upstairs at the Eclipse for Thursday night, it will serve to celebrate my debut for *The Discoverer*.'

'Gifford has taken his time asking for your essay. I was beginning to wonder if he had gone back on his word.'

Nash turned a cool gaze on me. 'There is no danger of that, I assure you.' I had a feeling, just as I had when he snared Gifford in the first place, that there was something behind Nash's confidence that he had not yet disclosed to me. Then he looked away with a mischievous smile. 'Nemesis is about to be unleashed.'

'Nemesis?' I couldn't help but laugh.

Nash laughed, too. 'My pseudonym. It's got quite the ring of authority, don't you think? Nemesis! A brave man to write brave things about the politics and personalities of the times.'

'Have you a topic for your first column, Mr Nemesis?'

'I might circle around that business with the *Garland*.'

He was referring to a ship from Calcutta that had been robbed of diamonds and opium while she was moored in the Thames awaiting the unloading of her cargo. Twenty-four hours after the crime had been discovered, two customs officers were arrested for corruption and theft of goods from the ship. They were hastily brought to trial at the Old Bailey and found guilty, despite a complete lack of evidence to show that they had ever gone aboard the *Garland*. The officers are due to be hanged next week. There has been an outcry among the public about the impending executions.

I said, 'The more that good men weigh in on that sorry affair, the better. The moral there is very clear.'

'Is it? What moral is that, my stern evaluator? Ah, look, here is Ned with our claret.' Nash took the bottle, waved Ned away, and refilled our glasses.

I said, 'The moral of hypocrisy. The customs men have been stitched up for falling foul, in some manner that has not yet come to light, of the *Garland*'s mysterious proprietors.'

'So say some of the more hysterical broadsides.'

'How else to explain the hastiness of the arrest and trial?'

Nash took a swallow of his wine and put down his glass. 'Here is a fact that not everybody knows.' He paused for effect. 'Sir Rollo Hayle and Mr Gifford are the owners of the *Garland*.'

I stared, and at the same time my heart sank.

Nash raised his eyebrows meaningfully and tilted his head back. 'So you see,' he said, addressing the ceiling, 'my angle is likely to be somewhat against the grain of public opinion.'

'Oh, Nash,' I laughed in disbelief, 'you said yourself at the time that the customs men could not possibly be culpable.'

'That was before I had an investment in the outcome.'

My smile faltered. I wanted to believe that everything Nash did and said was amusing and fundamentally benign, but it was unsettling to think that he might have revised his opinion of the officers' innocence. I will admit that moral indignation is not his style, but he has always been tolerant on the subject of civil liberties. That a miscarriage of justice had been served on the customs officers in the affair of the *Garland* was something on which we had been very much agreed.

Nash must have seen the dismay on my face, because he said, 'I will simply offer an alternative angle on the matter.'

'No one will like you for it. You know the sentence of death on the men is widely opposed and for good reason, too.'

Nash shrugged and sipped his wine.

I said, 'How do you expect to win followers if you begin with such an unpopular stance? It is rather perverse, don't you think?'

'Carey, my love, you are missing the point. This is not about the whys and wherefores of the *Garland* case. It is about the advancement of my name. Nothing provokes notoriety more than an unreasonable position. I will kill two birds with one stone by satisfying my masters and bringing myself to prominence. The accuracy or not of my statements is hardly here nor there.'

'But if you pass over the truth of a thing in favour of your own considerations you are nothing but a pragmatist.'

'Where is the flaw in that?'

'Well, the want of a conscience, of course.'

Nash smiled indulgently, which irritated me. 'It is only a little opinion piece. It's not the judgement of Solomon. Have a drink.' He beckoned me to hand him my glass.

I shook my head. 'I must deliver Norton his pages in the morning.'

'How much remains to be done?'

'A chapter only.'

'What is its subject?'

'*Bijoux indiscrets.*' Lascivious toys. I felt that Nash was brushing my concerns to the side and I did not like it. 'I am upset about your essay. What is the significance of Gifford and Hayle's prosecution of this wretched case? And why have their names been kept in the dark? Is there something they are trying to hide?'

'They have nothing to conceal. The only reason their names have not come out is because the bleaters frothing about the trial have not bothered to search the records that would have revealed the *Garland*'s owners. There is nothing sinister in play. You know very well that the same mob that goes running after a so-called injustice with their pitchforks and pikes will have forgotten about it in a week.'

'I wish you would find another topic to write about, nevertheless.'

'Enough, Carey!' Nash said sharply. 'I am bored by the conversation now. Why don't you fetch down Mr Norton's manuscript and read to me from it? That, at least, is bound to amuse.'

I sent Ned out for a copy of *The Discoverer* as soon as it was published and sat down with it in the parlour. Nash had not shown his essay to me before he had taken it to Gifford's press at St Bride's Lane. Now, here it was: 'Nemesis Speaks'. I read the piece with mounting disquiet. Nash had not given up the topic of the *Garland*. Despite his having warned me that he would take a contrary view, I found it disturbing to read his endorsement of the death sentences levied on the customs officers, as he railed on the pressing matter of safe storage of our traders' commodities. The real issue here, Nemesis opined, is London's desperate need for secure warehousing. Theft from the ships is endemic; new docks need urgently to be built. The same public that is sentimental about the fate of the two officers protests loud and long when it must pay higher prices on the goods it buys and higher insurance premiums. The death penalty for the customs officers is the gravest of deterrents. Without it, we might as well throw open our warehouses and invite every man to help himself. And so on.

I threw the paper aside and sat, lost in thought. I ought to have been preparing myself for the evening at the Eclipse, but the condemned men were on my mind. One's humanity recoiled at the thought of the forthcoming executions. I could not understand Nash's taking up, instead, the cause of dockland developers and insurance agents.

I was roused from my preoccupation by the arrival at the house of a messenger with a parcel for me that was delivered with the compliments of Mr Gifford. His note regretted that he could not attend our *petit-dîner*, but that he sent me a token of his esteem. I unwrapped the parcel and flung off the top of a cardboard box. Dear God, but the gift was a horrid one. It was a short cape of soft black fuzz that appeared to have been peeled from the back of some juvenile creature, killed before its time. I almost shuddered to look at the garment. It was lined in black satin and there were two large pockets attached to the interior that suggested necrotic lungs. Nash came in as I was holding up the cape, appalled. He was very amused by my insisting that I would never wear it, and reminded me that Gifford had ships in whaling and seal hunting. The thought of the cape's being fashioned from battered seal pups made me loathe it even more. I hid the thing in the back of my closet and then I made myself sit down to write Gifford a note of thanks.

When I was finished, I found Nash and told him that I was disappointed by the essay he had written in *The Discoverer*. He was putting on his coat, the Chinese one, and we were about to leave for the tavern. He made a face to indicate that he was sorry about my opinion, but then he said, 'I am afraid, my love, it does not matter what you think. I am charged to defend with tenacity the interests of Mr Gifford.'

'What are his interests in this case? To have on his conscience the death of two men who may well be innocent?'

'Just drop the subject, will you? You are decked out in a new gown that was paid for by Gifford's money, so do not come preaching to me. You will not like the next piece either, since you may read it as an endorsement of the war in America.'

This was another surprise to me, since Nash had previously been of the opinion that we ought to give up the fight with the colonists and let them rule themselves.

Seeing my mouth open, Nash held up a remonstrative hand. 'Hayle and Gifford have their army contracts to protect.'

'I did not realise that you were to be quite so completely Gifford's creature.'

'It is only all a game, my love, you know that, and I will play it until we are secure and then I will enjoy the luxury of the rebel's opinion.'

We had plenty of everything at the Eclipse – a baked ham, roast chickens, wine, punch and ale, and two fiddlers. Our guests numbered around twenty people, mostly men-about-town and their companions. My misgivings about Nash's work were not forgotten, but I could be pragmatic, too, and the point of the evening was to enjoy ourselves and be seen to do so. I had buttoned up the skirts of my gown and Nash and I were dancing a reel as mad as hops, his new silvered-lace cuffs flashing among the lights, when all of a sudden the air seemed to go out of him a little. His hand fell from mine and he brought me to a halt on the edge of the floor. I looked at him inquiringly, but he dredged up a smile and said he would take a break. He handed me off to a new acquaintance of his, a bookseller named Doyle. My feet continued the pattern of the reel, but my gaze followed Nash as he shouldered his way through the crowd. The fiddles scraped away as I galloped up and down with Mr Doyle, their strings sounding flabby and rather out of tune in the heat. Then it was my turn to lose my place in the reel, as I caught sight of the person that Nash was approaching.

I begged Mr Doyle's pardon and stepped away, my eyes on Nash. He was heading towards a lanky, earnest-looking figure standing at the door. It was the man I had noticed at Hillier's Garden Warehouse in Covent Garden. Nash must have known the stranger, because he disappeared from the room with him. I supposed it might be another creditor sniffing around, since news of money, its loss and its gain, always travels like lightning. Nash was not gone for long. He slipped back into the room, glanced about and, catching my eye, he bowed and smiled.

He signalled one of the serving girls and waggled his hand in a tippling gesture. As soon as his brandy was delivered, he cried, 'Come now, friends, bung your eyes!' and downed the drink in one shot. Then he called me to his arms and we charged back and forth under the demands of a quadrille, and when that was done, I sat myself down at a seat next to the window and called for a tumbler of beer. The evening was thundering along with a hiss and a roar and I was sorry that Selina had not been free to attend. She was engaged with her noble dotard, flattering him into a belief in his vigour. I should have liked to ask her opinion of Stephen Norton's new offer to me to translate another grimy duodecimo, called *Mademoiselle Amourette*, but I could probably guess Selina's response. She was likely to advise that there was no harm in wearing out my pen on low work if I were well paid for it. I glanced down into the street – and saw, with a start, a figure looking back up at me. It was the man who had spoken with Nash half an hour before. What was he doing there? Waiting for Nash? I thought of the sword hanging at his belt.

'Here you are, missus.' The alewife handed me my drink and asked me if I had heard that Nelly had been seen walking the streets with false eyebrows pasted on and rouged cheeks and her bosom whitewashed. We gossiped about the scullery maid for a few minutes and, when the alewife moved away, I looked out of the window again. The man had gone.

I found Nash and pulled him into a corner and told him about the stranger I had seen lurking in the street.

'It is of no moment, lovely. He is only someone who wanted advice on the recovery of a debt. I let him know I am not in that business any more.'

The dancing went on until one in the morning before it was finally given up. By two, the company had broken apart and only Nash and I were left among the dregs. We stayed to drink a bottle of wine with the landlord. I cannot remember what we spoke about. I do remember Nash's saying that he must meet Doyle about some literary speculation with which he intends to startle the town. He saw me into the house and then almost immediately went out again, saying he would be back within an hour or two.

I sat up in bed trying to read a book, but I was too squiffy to take it in and the light was dim in any case. Shadows jumped around the room and everything seemed slightly at a tilt. I curled up on my side. I had forgotten to draw the curtains and a shaft of moonlight reached towards my plants. The white blooms had decayed and fallen away. I was reminded of another moonlit night, riding in a chaise with Nash. It was not long after he had returned to London from Calcutta. I had been introduced to him at a supper party of Selina's at Golden Square and was attracted at once to his appearance. He did me the honour of a great deal of notice and the next evening we made up a party to go to a performance at Sadler's Wells. The Wells was as louche then as it is now and I discovered, as we wandered among a rough crowd of beribboned servant girls and their labourer lovers, that Nash and I shared a taste for equivocal places. He spoke to me with the freedom of an old acquaintance and deluged me with compliments. 'I am making an effort to live life in a more regular manner,' I remember his saying, 'but it is difficult to know how that can be done without someone to take me in hand.' I thought him the most amiable man in the world.

Had something gone awry between us?

I felt as though it had. Then, as sometimes happens when I am maudlin after a long night, I fretted about our want of a baby. Nash and I cannot seem to conceive a child and I do not know why. We never discuss it. I have been saddened by the regular arrival of my flux and disappointed at the absence of new life; but on other days there is a miserable satisfaction at being free of children when I wish to indulge myself. In any case, I suppose I only want a child that would follow me faithfully and admire me. I want one in order to feel like a grown woman. I have reached the age of five-and-twenty already and yet there is something about me that is very juvenile. I do not exist with any degree of depth. I envy Nash, for he has seen the world, but then again, he has eleven years on me.

The bedchamber swirled in a nauseating way and I closed my eyes against it.

I woke after an hour or two, to judge by the burned-down taper in the candlestick next to the bed. I had a raging thirst. I raised myself on to my elbows and slowly swung my legs over the edge of the bed. I found that I was still fully dressed. My sides hurt where the stiffening of my stays had chafed the skin. I stumbled towards the chest of drawers and lifted the pitcher that sat on top. It was empty. There was a stone cistern of water in the scullery, but could I be bothered to go all the way down there? The lamp by the door had gone out and I could not think where the flint was to light it. I trudged out of the chamber and felt my way down the stairs to the first-floor landing. My eyes had adjusted to the dark and I saw by the flicker of light beneath the door of his office that Nash was home. Sometimes he sleeps there on the divan after he has made a night of it, so as not to disturb me.

I was nearly at the foot of the stairs when the office door opened slowly and quietly. Even in my muddled state of mind, the deliberately muted way in which that door swung wide told me that something was wrong. I froze, my heart beating fast.

A tall figure stepped noiselessly into the hall. I knew at once that it was not Nash. I opened my mouth to scream, but the sound stuck in my throat as the intruder stiffened and turned his gaze on me. I could not make out his features in the darkness, but I recognised him by his shape. It was the stranger who had trespassed on us at the Eclipse.

To my intense surprise he said, 'Forgive me, Mrs Nash. I did not mean to alarm you.'

'Who are you?' I cried.

'My name is Adam Martenson.'

'Get out,' I urged, my voice breaking. 'We have nothing left to steal.'

'I am not a thief. Your husband has something that belongs to me.' He took a step towards the stairs.

'Get out!' I shouted. 'Or I will call for your arrest.'

He did not move. He said, 'I knew your husband in Bengal.'

'Ned!' I cried, looking up in the direction of the landing.

The intruder turned on his heel then, pulled open the front door and left the house. For a minute or two I waited, trembling, for Ned to appear, but when I realised that he was not going to come, I stole to the door and stood out on the step. There were carousers staggering in the distance, but the intruder was nowhere in sight. I examined the latch on the door and found it was undamaged. I shut the door with a bang and returned to Nash's office.

I struck a flint and, when the lamp on the desk was lit, I scanned the room. Nothing seemed to be missing that I could tell. Nash's silver snuffbox was still sitting on the chimneypiece and there were other knick-knacks evidently untouched. I walked around the desk and saw that one of the drawers was open and that papers were spread out on the blotter. I drew the lamp closer and bent over them. They appeared to belong to a company contract. I moved the lamp closer, and read: *Allowing the Assignees to trade as the Neela Company. Sign'd by Rollo Hayle, Baronet, Fenton Gifford, Esq., The Right Hon. Frederick Viscount Casserly.* I could not see that there was anything immediately significant about the document. I went to the window and drew a crack in the curtain. The street was empty.

I checked the front door again – it was locked fast – and returned to the bedchamber. I propped myself against the pillows while I waited for Nash in the dark, feeling turned inside out, my nerves stretched taut and alert. All at once, a realisation struck me.

Martenson. I knew that name. He was the army surgeon who had written the reports on the poisonings in Bengal.

'Your husband has something that belongs to me,' he had said. Did he mean the dossier?

The darkness in the bedchamber began to alter and lighten until it resembled grey gauze. I figured the hour to be near four – dawn was approaching. I felt compelled to look at Martenson's reports again with a sense of urgency that would not wait. I removed the key to the locking box from beneath the pot where Nash always kept it. Once I was inside the closet, I groped around in the shadows until my fingers brushed the smooth material of his coats. As they shifted on their hangers, it gave me a feeling of unease, as if avatars of Nash were present. I dropped to my knees and reached out my hands until they encountered the locking box. I drew it out of the closet, fumbled with the key in the lock, opened it. The pocket inside the lid was empty. With some effort, I wheeled it out into the chamber. Painstakingly, I searched the contents of the box to ascertain that I had not overlooked the dossier. It was the size of a quarto and the pouch had the distinctive texture of oilskin. It was not there. I returned the box to the closet and the key to the pot, and climbed into bed. For a few minutes I entertained the disturbing thought that the intruder had entered the bedroom while I was asleep, but I could not believe that had happened. I did not see how anyone other than Nash could have removed the dossier, but what did that signify? It was his property and he was entitled to do what he liked with it.

Exhaustion overcame me then and I drifted towards sleep. The hoarse barking of a dog in the street and the clip-clop of horses' hooves became mixed up in a dream in which I tracked through dense vegetation. Threatening creatures heaved in the undergrowth. I could not see them, but I knew they were there. No matter how furtively they moved, they left an imprint of themselves in the atmosphere and my senses detected their presence. I climbed up a ladder and reached a loft that was used for storing fruit and vegetables. It smelled of apples. With an enormous sense of relief, I realised that I was at home at Durand Gardens. I opened the shutter under the eave, expecting to look out on the nursery with its neat paths and parterres. Instead, I gazed down on thick jungle that went on for miles, all the way to the horizon. I could not understand if the sight were one that I found horrifying or elating.

The clock had struck eleven before I got up. I dressed and made my way downstairs, my head in a fog. I knew the intruder ought to be reported to a constable, but I did not want to do it without speaking to Nash first, in case there was some mitigating factor of which I was not aware. He was in his office, sprawled on the divan. He had been asleep, but sat up unsteadily as I came in, newspapers crackling beneath him. He cast a somewhat sheepish gaze in my direction and said, 'Good morning, lovely.'

'I did not hear you come in.'

'Doyle and I dropped into the Crown and Cushion. One thing led to another and we went around the traps all night. We didn't close off the evening until four. And, even then, Doyle went on to a dog fight in Smith Field. I feel a faint glow of virtue at having drawn the line somewhere.'

Indeed, he looked relatively fresh for someone who had been up all night. I told him about the intruder. 'He half-killed me with fright, Nash. You must go to the justice about him. He actually gave me his name. It is Adam Martenson.'

Nash seemed to look at me askance.

'You said he had asked you to recover a debt.'

Nash scratched his head without saying anything.

'Martenson is the name of the surgeon who wrote the reports that were . . . that are in your locking box. Can that be a coincidence?' I did not wish to tell Nash that I had looked in the box again and found that the dossier was missing. I sensed that he would not like that. 'I saw this Martenson earlier, at the Eclipse, as well. What does he want with you, Nash? He said you had taken something from him. What did he mean?'

'Martenson,' Nash muttered to himself. Then he looked up. 'He's a blackguard.'

'We must lodge a complaint.'

'It is not worth the bother. If he wants the dossier, he is too late, I have disposed of it. After you mentioned it to me, I realised that I had no reason to keep it. I had forgotten that I had been given it to read quite some years ago when Martenson tried to engage my firm to bring an action against Sir Rollo Hayle. He is obsessed with the notion that Hayle ruined his livelihood.'

'Did Hayle do such a thing?'

'Of course not. Martenson is well known in Bengal as a failed planter and an addict who conceives strange obsessions about things. He is rather unhinged, I am sorry to say.'

'Then it is even more terrifying that he got into the house.'

'Did he come upstairs?' Nash asked, and got me to go over the encounter with Martenson again. It struck me that he seemed very little outraged at the danger that I might have faced. Something more pressing was occupying his thoughts.

'I don't believe he went further than this room.'

Nash glanced around the office.

I said, 'I do not think that he took anything. Your snuff-box is still here.'

Nash did not heed me. He looked across at his desk and something on it caught his attention. I knew what it was – the company contract I had noticed after Martenson had left.

I said, 'I had the impression that he had been looking at that contract. Had you left it out?'

'Yes, I believe I did,' Nash said, strolling over to the desk. He opened a drawer and put the contract away.

I said, 'What is the Neela Company?'

'One of Gifford's ventures.' Nash frowned. 'Do not concern yourself. Martenson won't be back.'

'How do you know?'

'I will see him off.'

'But do you know where to find him?'

'He lodges at Wild Street.'

That was not far away, near Lincoln's Inn Fields. 'Since we know his identity and his address, oughtn't we to send a constable to warn him not to menace us again?'

'For God's sake, Carey, will you stop your harrassment!'

I flinched at Nash's outburst. He reached out a hand vaguely towards me and said, 'Forgive me, it has been a long night.' He rubbed his chin. 'Would you rustle up Ned for me and ask him to bring hot water for my shave?'

I nodded and turned to the door.

'Carey –' Nash managed a weak smile – 'please be reassured. There will be no more Martenson. Now do find Ned for me, will you?'

While Nash was upstairs, I sat in the kitchen with Ruth

for our weekly reckoning of expenditures and drew up a list of provisions in order to victual the house in the coming week. Then I went to find Nash. He was standing in the door of his closet, tying his stock.

I said, 'I will feel at ease if I know why Martenson should have been interested in the contract that was on your desk.'

'Who is to say that he was interested in it?'

'Will you tell me what kind of company it is?'

'It makes commonplace items for the navy, I believe. Bengal lights, that sort of thing.'

'What are Bengal lights?'

I had the sense of Nash's having to restrain himself from snapping at me. 'Flares. Ships' signals. Have you seen my hat?'

'I think you left it downstairs. I suppose they are made from saltpetre. Gifford told me that he imports vast amounts.'

'Yes, he imports it from Patna as ballast in his ships. His manufactories use it to make the signals and glassware that he sells to the navy and he hawks some of it to gunpowder manufacturers. Does that satisfy your curiosity?'

'Are you writing something about it?'

Nash shot his cuffs, plainly irritated. 'Gifford gave the contract to me. He gives me all sorts of things to read to inform my work. Why do you fixate upon it?'

'Because I like to *know* things, Nash! Because you are my husband and I am interested in what you do.'

'You are vexed about what I do.'

'Well, I hope that you do not plan to write boosting praises of the Neela Company so that its stock will climb.

That would not be ethical. I worry about the expedience knitted into your work for Gifford and Hayle.'

'All I am trying to do is offer you the life you would like. I am heartily sorry that Martenson distressed you so. Now, will you let me deal with him?' There was a dismissive tone in his voice.

I said, 'Have some breakfast first, at least, before you go.'

But he strode away, shouting for Ned to discover his hat.

I stood at the window and watched Nash cross the street. I hated to quarrel with him and I did not wish to be suspicious of him, but I struggled to reconcile my instincts with what he had told me of Martenson. Perhaps those instincts are unreliable, but as I recollected my encounter with Martenson, I felt confirmed in my impression that he was not a blackguard, despite his breaking into the house. True, he had frightened me, that is to say the *situation* had been frightening, but, in retrospect, I could not quite take him to be felonious. I had witnessed him warning the clerk at Hillier's that the roots the shop had advertised as liquorice were likely to be poisonous. Moreover, in my life I have been exposed to my share of rogues and if there is one thing they have in common, it is their caginess – and their disinclination to identify themselves to the person they are robbing. I am used to debtors haunting our doors, but it seemed peculiar to me that two reprobates from India, Spencer and Martenson, should turn up in less than a month.

Chapter 8

The Playhouse

July the 9th, 1776

Nash and I forced our way through the crowd and managed to secure advantageous places on one of the benches at the back of the auditorium. They were almost at the same level as the circular line of boxes where the nobility and the gentry sit. I had never seen the playhouse at Drury Lane so packed. There must have been near two thousand people railed into the place. We had at least half an hour to wait before the performance began and, while Nash returned the salutes of his acquaintances, I looked up at the blazing chandeliers and reflected that I had not lost my taste for the glitter of our lives. It amused me to study the sparks in their finery, the fabulous ensembles worn in the boxes, the headdresses and the jewels sported by great ladies affecting boredom, and I was exhilarated, too, at the prospect of seeing Mrs Abington perform again in *The Suspicious Husband* with Mr Garrick.

'Who is that?' I asked from behind my fluttering fan. It was so hot I could feel the powder congealing on my face.

Nash was offering a respectful bend to a person in one of the boxes, who wore a crimson satin coat and a glinting cap on his head, in the style of a Mohammedan.

But I realised before Nash answered that it was Sir Rollo Hayle. The baronet bowed, his eyes fastened upon me. As I inclined my head to him, I whispered to Nash, 'Was it he who gave you the tokens for the play?'

'Yes, awfully decent of him, wasn't it.'

Sir Rollo made a beckoning gesture in our direction and Nash stood up at once and called for a couple of seat-men to occupy our places and guard them against other patrons. We climbed a narrow staircase to a lobby, where a footman showed us the way to Sir Rollo's box. The baronet was on his feet when we arrived, drinking champagne. He was accompanied by a liveried servant and a Negro woman in diamonds and satin and a blanched wig, whom he introduced as Madame Guadeloupe. There were a couple of gentlemen at his back engaged in conversation. They did not remark Nash and me at all, nor did Sir Rollo introduce them. The scene gave the impression of important business unfolding in the background even as Sir Rollo amused himself. Madame Guadeloupe turned away almost immediately and sank on to a chair. She took out a spyglass and aimed it at the audience in the pit.

Nash introduced me to Sir Rollo and I curtsied deeply, my hands at my waist. I maintain my jaundiced view of those white nabobs who have ransacked Bengal, but I had never met one before and it was difficult not to be fascinated. Moreover, this nabob had become our patron and required a respectful attitude.

'Mrs Nash,' the baronet murmured, 'how delightful to

have you among us.' His voice was attractive, smoky in timbre. His face was pitted with the scars of smallpox and yet they did not detract from his air of self-assurance. I judged him to be in his early forties, but there was something ageless about him, as if he had never been young. With his hooded gaze and oriental outfit, he might have passed for a figure from an occult sphere, an alchemist or a master of arcana, which I suppose in some ways he was, given his magical ability to conjure up one fortune after another.

'Are you as zealous about the theatre as your husband?' he asked.

'I believe I match his passions in that regard. I greatly esteem Mrs Abington.'

'Ah, Nosegay Fan,' Sir Rollo drawled. 'She generally meets with applause, particularly in her under parts. Women are very attracted to drama, don't you think, Nash? They crave their highs and lows.' He offered me an astringent smile. 'I mean no offence, of course. You must come to Underfall, Mrs Nash. We run a relaxed establishment there.'

What did he mean by that? I raised an eyebrow at Nash, but his attention was fixed on Sir Rollo. 'Who owned the house before you, sir?' he asked. 'Was it the Earl of Pomfret?'

'Pomfret had married as badly as he played cards and was ravaged sufficiently by debts that I got the estate for a song.' Sir Rollo made a circular motion of his finger at the footman, indicating that our glasses needed filling. He was a man the French would call *cynique*: one who entertains a contempt for people, which his manners barely conceal.

I wished that I could recall in more detail the part that he had played in the case of the poisoned subaltern. Weeks had passed since I had read Martenson's report and I could only remember the generality of the case. Sir Rollo had run a medical trial in which a volunteer had suffered a fatal allergic reaction. Martenson was not satisfied by the circumstances of the victim's death and suspected that the young man had been poisoned by a substance other than the *Ammannia* leaves being trialled. Perhaps Sir Rollo objected to Martenson's report and had ruined him out of spite – and now Martenson had come to England to avenge himself. The case continued to intrigue me and I would have liked to ask Martenson about it directly, but it was unlikely that I would see him again. Nash had spoken to him the day after the break-in, he told me, and had seen him off. I accepted that, one way or another, the business with Martenson had been solved or taken care of to Nash's satisfaction, because his mood was easy about it.

I felt less untroubled, though, about accepting Sir Rollo's largesse. I did not care for the faintly suggestive air with which he addressed me. He seemed to take for granted that he could deal with me with liberty.

Sir Rollo asked, 'Do you enjoy the mysteries and devotions of a masquerade, Mrs Nash?' There it was again - a certain heavy-lidded gaze and knowing smile, which made me wonder if it were possible that Nash had disclosed to him something of my past.

'As much as anyone, sir,' I said.

'Come now, Carey.' Nash laughed. 'You know you are an enthusiast.'

Madame Guadeloupe stood up and, with a distant nod at Nash and me, left the box without a word. Sir Rollo watched her go, his lip curled. He turned to us and said, 'You would think that lady would have the good manners to stand and converse, since I have fixed her with a salary of two hundred a year and board wages of ten guineas a week.'

Nash laughed, but I looked away from Sir Rollo's superciliousness. It was distasteful enough of him to make a point of remarking Madame Guadeloupe's kept status, but it also occurred to me that her payment almost exactly matched the amount that my husband was to receive. Did Sir Rollo mean to imply that there was something whoreish in Nash's situation too? One could not quite read the baronet's intent, but its effect was clear enough. One felt rather off-balanced and unsure.

Sir Rollo said, 'I fear I have displeased you, Mrs Nash.'

I offered him a reserved smile.

'Yes, I have, I can see it on your pretty face. As some trifling atonement for my boorishness, let me invite you both to a ball that I am to give. It will be a masquerade for members and guests of my Soma Club. Please do agree to come.'

'We should be honoured to attend.' Nash bowed.

Beneath the din in the auditorium, the orchestra began to tune its instruments and a ripple of anticipation ran through the crowd. With many reverences, we took our leave and returned to the pit. As we settled on to our bench, Nash said, 'That was a lucky invitation.'

'I hope so.'

'I know so. Were I ever to be admitted to the Soma Club, we should be very much established.'

I turned to gaze at Sir Rollo. He was holding his head at a peculiar tilt, as if listening to something beyond the hearing of ordinary mortals. Nash followed my gaze. He said, 'I wish I could become like that.'

'Like Sir Rollo?'

'Rich like Sir Rollo.'

'He is not a man who is limited by moral compunctions, I wager. No doubt it is the great spring of his power. But you have goodness in you, Nash, and that is priceless, I believe.'

'Is it? I am a little aggrieved at the unfairness of a world that lets Sir Rollo make three fortunes, while I have failed to make even one. But it may be possible that I can ride to victory on his coat-tails.'

The prompter rang his bell and we sat forward in our seats. The audience began to stamp its feet and whistle and cheer as the green curtain rose and the light flared from the lamps at the front of the stage.

Don't the times go up and down like the swell of the ocean? We had certainly found ourselves on a crest, because when we got home after the theatre, Jane greeted us with the news that a note had come to Hood Street. I followed Nash into his office and lit the candles for him while he broke the seal of the letter. It was from Spencer.

My Dear Nash,

I am sorry to disturb you once more, but I wish to settle my business with you. I have determined to strike the remaining debt that you owe me. This grievance has already proved a heavy burden for me and I wish to throw it off before I die.

The malarial fever has recently returned to me. I am told that attention and care, aided by the Peruvian bark, will alleviate my sickness, but I do not believe it. Sometimes our instincts will strongly tell us what our reason does not wish to hear, and I suppose I will not survive this new onset.

I am glad to have had the pleasure of making the acquaintance of your wife, who is an ornament to you. Mrs Spencer joins me in cordial compliments to you both. I will ask no more favours except to be remembered kindly.

Believe me, I am, my dear Nash, your well-wisher and most obedient servant,

F. Spencer

Throwing down the letter, Nash cried, 'I am off the hook!' and proposed to raise a toast to good fortune.

'Ah, Nash, it is bad luck to toast a friend's affliction.'

'I will have a splash of brandy then and call it a nightcap.'

He chucked off the contents of his glass and smiled at me. 'Won't it be arousing, my love, to go to Underfall House? It is a while since we have amused ourselves at a bacchanal.'

'So it is.'

'Spencer is quite right. You are an ornament, indeed, to

me – and you have charmed Sir Rollo, too. We must make the most of our invitation to the Soma Club.'

'How shall we do that?'

Nash grinned. 'Come here, pretty.' He stood over me and pulled me close. He brushed back a lock of hair and nuzzled my neck.

Suddenly, he dipped at the knees and took the hem of my petticoat and pulled it up in one swift motion, so that my legs were exposed. Still with the hem tight in his hand, he seized me by the waist and lifted me up and sat me on the edge of his desk. I was aware of papers falling to the floor and the brandy glass fell against the ashtray with a loud *clink*. He nudged my legs apart, stepping hard against me so that I could feel the swelling in his breeches in the softness of my groin. I wrapped my legs around him and opened my mouth to him with its rich, acrid taste of brandy. 'Be a good girl, Caroline,' he murmured. I felt a horrible, indecent pleasure at giving in to him.

Later, I lay awake against Nash's back, thinking that there was something wild and uncertain about the love I had for him that alarmed me, even as it aroused me. I sought to plunge into its depths, but something always pulled me back. I was afraid that I had misjudged its capacity and might break my neck diving into unexpected shallows.

Chapter 9

A Dark Morning

July the 13th, 1776

On Selina's birthday, she and I had hoped to take an airing in Green Park, but it happened that the customs officers sentenced for the theft of the *Garland*'s cargo were hanged that day at Tyburn and the west end of town was packed with thousands of gawkers for the occasion. I had thought that the officers would receive a stay of execution – at least, I could not credit that they really would be sent to their deaths on a dearth of evidence – but last night Ned came in with the news that they were for the drop the next day. I abhor executions and the atmosphere that surrounds them, for it is one that is hardened to human suffering. The carts bearing the wretches to the horror of the scaffold rumble through Holborn on their way from Newgate and I always feel sickened by the excitement of the crowd as it watches the prisoners pass by. Before we had taken breakfast, we heard the mourning bells of St Sepulchre's church begin to toll, and Nash straight away went out, saying that he was going to the public gallery at the House of Commons, as he often does, to soak up intelligence. But as Parliament does not sit until the afternoon, I believe he wished to avoid discussing the subject of the *Garland* with me.

By noon, I judged that the procession of the condemned had probably reached Tyburn, and swept the rabble along with it, which meant that the walk to Selina's lodging would be less fraught with *joie mauvaise*. As I made my way to Golden Square, a hot wind whipped up the rubbish in the streets and veneered my face with a coating of dust and I was glad to reach the sanctuary of Selina's house. As soon as her maid had shut the door upon the turbulent weather, I felt much calmer. Selina was waiting for me in the front parlour. We embraced fondly and settled ourselves on the sofa, and the maid was sent to bring us hot chocolate. I looked around and remarked the bunches of roses in crystal vases on the marble chimney-piece. The establishment was nicely fitted up with swagged silk drapes, gilt brackets and a sufficiency of garnish. It made the interior at Hood Street look effortful in comparison. In all respects, Selina's judgement is more confident than mine and more calculating. I thought, as I always did in her company, how very pleasurable it was to have the steady attachment of friendship with a woman one has known for a long time; a woman who understands when you begin to cry over a hurt, or laugh outrageously at a travesty that no one else finds amusing. Someone who will lend you her best gown in a social crisis and offer advice on the wearing of it; someone who will not turn away, whatever your need.

She unwrapped the present I had brought for her and with a cry of delight held up a pair of pretty gloves worked in creamy Spanish lace. She slipped her elegant hands into them and made a dance of her fingers so that I could admire the effect. She declared that she would wear the gloves in the evening to supper at Lord Newington's townhouse. 'And,' she added, 'Newington has given me a ticket to Sir Rollo's masquerade.'

'We have our invitation, too!' The packet had arrived only the day before from Underfall House. It contained two tickets to the Soma Club ball and an inscription of the rules of the event. They were the usual: at the masquerade, everyone would be permitted to amuse himself according to his own disposition. The guests were to be admitted in masks and would not unmask until the revels ended in order not to meet with an unwanted acquaintance; and no lady was to be surprised against her will, either by her husband or another gentleman.

'Perhaps I will go with you and Nash, if that is not an inconvenience,' Selina said. 'God forbid that Newington should assume I will accompany him.'

I was glad to hear that she would join us at the ball. I asked if Newington had spoken to her about the activities of the Soma Club.

'He has mentioned "eastern ceremonies", the burning of incense and invocations to heathen gods. Sir Rollo acts as the high priest. As for the soma itself, apparently it is some kind of Spanish fly that rouses the members to spill their sacred seed.' She directed the maid, who had arrived with our bowls of hot chocolate, to put them on the little gilt table in front of the sofa.

The day before, I had gone to Wheeler's bookshop,

hoping that the printer might have another commission for me. I was unsuccessful in my quest, but while I was there I bought the octavo concerning sages of Asia and, as soon as I was home, I began reading it with avidity. I said, 'Soma is a kind of mystic nectar, so I have learned. Its foremost imbiber is an Indian deity named Shiva. He has blue skin and wears a serpent for a necklace. The nectar is intoxicating. It causes one's mind and senses to expand in some way and is supposed to give one the powers of a god. Its great revelation is that the carnal life is also the divine life.'

'What a surprise.' Selina smiled. 'Debauchery dressed up in philosophy, as usual.'

'I met Sir Rollo, you know, at the theatre. He was there with a Negro mistress called Madame Guadeloupe. She was remote, though, and did not speak with us.'

'They famously come and go, Sir Rollo's women. What did you think of him?'

'He is compelling, of course, and also faintly unpleasant. I didn't care for him, but I paid homage to him, as I must. Nash says that Sir Rollo will soon be elected to Parliament on Lord Casserly's interest and his influence will be greater than ever.'

'All you need to know about him is that he is enormously wealthy. As a result, he does as he pleases and he has not suffered a disadvantage from it yet. Newington says that Hayle sometimes gives jewels away to women at his assemblies. If he treats you with partiality, you must make the most of it, my dear.'

'That is what Nash tells me.'

'No one will dare cut you, or Nash either, if you are one of Hayle's favourites.' Selina smiled at me with the air of a conspirator. We understand the impulses of wealthy men, she and I, and the tightening of the viscera that takes place when their interest is piqued by a woman or a precious object that they must bring into their possession.

Selina reached for the tongs and dropped another lump of sugar into her chocolate. I stood up and wandered to the window. Birds were hurling themselves about in the heavy, grey sky. It is the time of year when the pits at Durand Gardens were filled with tender annuals, and Papa's stove plants, the cannas and euphorbias, were in flower.

Selina asked, 'And how is our Nemesis?'

'Providence is delighted with him, it seems.'

Selina eyed me quizzically. 'But you are not so very delighted.'

I sighed and came and sat down again. 'Do you know, Sel, I am quite disturbed by the character of the opinions that Nash turns out for *The Discoverer*. They are written by a man I do not recognise very well. We argued about his stance in regard to those poor men who went to their deaths this morning.' Selina frowned slightly, and I added for clarification, 'The *Garland* case.'

'Oh, that.'

'No one believes the customs officers stole opium and diamonds from that ship. And now Nash intends to aim his dart at Crispin Ellis.'

'A member of Parliament, isn't he?'

'He opposes the American war and the trade in slaves.'

'Ah, Mr Gifford won't like that.'

'Exactly. Nash is hinting that Ellis is a hypocrite, because a nephew of his has links with the Africa trade, which is not true, by the way. Nash discredits the character of the nephew and says how appalling it is that he should have a contract from the army's victualling board.'

The gloves I had given Selina were lying on the sofa. She picked one of them up and slipped it onto her hand again and tilted her head to one side as she assessed its effect. I felt a little flutter of panic within my breast at the realisation that I was boring her with my earnestness. It caused me to raise my voice and over-plead my case, when really I ought to have changed the subject to one that was more entertaining.

'I protested to Nash that his so-called exposé was a dirty piece of work. I said, "You are thwarting a man of virtue and all because Gifford and Hayle are jealous of his victualling contracts." Nash is vexed that I do not understand his position. He says that if men like Ellis prevail and the fight in America is given up, then the troops will come home and lucrative military contracts will vanish, contracts that Hayle and Gifford depend on, as do we by extension. He said, "I cannot imagine why you admonish me, when I am only prosecuting my profession."'

'Upon my soul, Carey, why do you press the poor man so? Mr Ellis does not need you to defend his interests. He is a big boy and quite at liberty to commence an action against *The Discoverer* if he does not like its aspersions.'

It dispirited me that Selina did not support my stand. I said, 'But Ellis can't really bring a libel suit, can he, because everyone knows that is a double-edged sword. You can sue for damages, but you cannot refute the imputations and an airing in court only gives them greater currency.'

'Really, Carey, where has your sense of humour gone?'

'That is what Nash says, too. I have always thought that he and I are attuned—'

'So you are. Everyone knows the Nashes are a love match between two confiding hearts.'

I could not tell whether Selina was being just a little mocking. 'But every so often,' I went on, 'the differences in our point of view strike a very discordant note and I worry that he is reckless with what he writes. You must know that he was let go by his firm in Calcutta.'

'He was rather lax about his appearances in court, I think.'

'And he published satirical doggerel that lampooned the conduct of his colleagues at law. I still struggle to understand why he would provoke the very men he depended on for employment.'

'Perhaps they were humbugs and deserved a ragging.'

'Perhaps they were. But Crispin Ellis is not a coxcomb and his nephew does not deserve to have his business ruined in order to fill Gifford's pockets.' With her rosy skirts puffed out around her like a cloud, her ankles neatly crossed, Selina seemed queenly and rational. I, by contrast, was a bolus of confusion. I stood up again, somewhat restlessly. On the console behind the sofa was a figurine of a Harlequina I had not seen before, striking an exaggerated dancer's pose. I touched its tiny, cold hand.

Selina said, 'I am sorry to hear that you and Nash are at cross purposes.' Then her blue eye fixed on me. She said, 'May I make an observation? Nash is the same as he has always been, but you have altered. Haven't you always given him to believe that you are easy with the way you lead your lives? He has never claimed to be anything other than what he is. You ought to have more confidence in your husband. You have been with him long enough to see how he prevails. He has kept a good enough roof over your head these last two years and met your needs.'

I had never disclosed to Selina that it was I who had paid the day-to-day expenses of Hood Street ever since my marriage. I feared that she might think less of Nash if she had known that. I wished her to hold him in regard, although perhaps that was for my own sake as much as his.

She was saying, 'You know Nash: throw him naked into the river at low water and he will bob up at high water with a laced coat and a sword.'

I smiled at the image. Then I asked her, 'How have I altered?'

'You are less complaisant and more critical of the company that you keep.'

'I had not noticed that I was different.'

'That is because you are rather fond of the drama of

yourself, you know, my dear, and you cannot see past the clouds that you project. I wonder if, deep down, you are disappointed in Nash and seek to find some way of blaming him so that you can say, "There, see, he is irredeemably flawed and clearly not the man of my dreams." But it is not his fault, is it, if he does not match your heroic ideals?'

I found myself chastened by Selina's observations and, as I walked home from Golden Square, a feeling of oppressiveness grew inside me. What an aimless life I led. It seemed to me that I passed my time stupidly in the house and lived my days in a trivial way, without understanding anything. Gloves, hot chocolate, swagged curtains, porcelain figures. What was the meaning of such things? In this glooming state of mind, I arrived at St Giles and saw up ahead the Sun and Moon Inn, where a coaching stage eastwards begins. At that moment, the church bells struck three. My footsteps slowed as an idea presented itself. I would be easily in time to catch the coach that went to Humerton. I told myself that it would be only courteous to visit Mr Spencer and acknowledge in person his striking of Nash's debt, but that was not the true reason for my intention to see him. Spencer and his Bengal history were soon to pass from our lives. I could not imagine that I would ever see him again. Suddenly, I could not bear to lose the chance to put to him the question that haunted me: When you were in India, did you ever come across a man by the name of Daniel Ravine? I had promised Nash that I would quit tormenting myself with an inquiry that was as obsessive as it was fruitless, but I could not yet give it up. I craved an answer to it as much as I craved to shop when I was sad and to drink when I was anxious. In other words, the impulse was irresistible.

I took the coach without any inconvenience and disembarked less than an hour later at the King's Arms. I was glad to see fields and trees as I set off along the road. I passed a patchwork of market gardens and eventually, an alehouse came into view, bearing the sign of the Falcon. I had reached Marsh Lane. On the far side of the Falcon, I paused outside a small dwelling that had a stable attached. A woman was bent over in the strip of land at the front of the cottage, cutting herbs from a lumpy bed. A boy of perhaps ten stood listlessly at her side with a basket in his hand. She straightened at my approach and smoothed her bright, cross-paned apron. Her hair was frizzed under a flopping cap and her pendant gold earrings flashed in the sunlight. It was an appearance that conveyed a gaudy, forced glamour, kept up in difficult circumstances. There was something affirmative and energetic about her that I liked instinctively.

I introduced myself and learned that she was Mrs Spencer. She instructed the boy to continue the harvest of the herbs. He squinted at me curiously, a gangly child with ears that stuck out. Mrs Spencer wiped her hands on her apron and said she feared that her husband would not last. 'I am a soldier's wife,' she added in a matter-of-fact way. 'We learn early to steel ourselves.'

She invited me indoors. In the dingy interior, a second

child, a girl, was squatting in front of the hearth, shelling peas. 'Judy,' Mrs Spencer called, 'put the water to boil. This is Mrs Nash, who has come to visit Dad.' The ginger-looking girl stood up and bobbed me a curtsy. Mrs Spencer pushed aside a curtain in a doorway and said something to the occupant that I could not make out, then she turned and cocked her head at me.

A lamp flickered on a small table next to the bed where the invalid was propped up in a stew of blankets. I noticed at once that a copy of *The Discoverer* lay folded on the table. Despite the warm day, the window was shut. Spencer's eyes were sunken and his unshaven face wore a melancholy aspect. Recognising me, he lifted a thin hand in salute. I sat down on a rush chair beside the bed, and said, 'I am sorry to find you in this condition, Mr Spencer.'

He said, 'I did not expect to see you again, Mrs Nash.' His voice was weak.

'I was touched by the generosity you showed towards us and I wished to thank you in person.'

Mrs Spencer arrived with a pitcher and two tumblers, which she placed on the bedside table, and then left the chamber. As I poured Spencer a measure, the scent of mint rose from the infusion. He took the tumbler from me and sipped at it and put it aside.

I asked, with a glance at *The Discoverer*, 'You have been reading Nemesis?' I did not mention that it was Nash's pseudonym.

'Bengal breaking down,' Spencer said. I knew the essay he was referring to. Nemesis had fulminated against Bengal's resentful peons and their attempts to sabotage the East India Company's opium fields. Military support must be forthcoming, Nemesis had thundered, if restive natives were to be prevented from putting the Company's enterprises in India at risk. This was a theme to which Nemesis often returned, urging the government to increase its spending on the army. In the last resort, he said, the Company's trade was an armed trade and commercial opportunities could not be realised without the aid of force. If the government did nothing to find a solution to its empty magazines and under-manned regiments, it would find itself in danger of losing Bengal as well as the American colonies.

'Do you agree with Nemesis?' I asked.

Spencer was silent.

I said, 'Since you spent some time in India, your opinion must be an informed one and I am interested to know it.'

'I was a lieutenant in the Bengal army. Cantonment at Dinapore. That's when I last saw Ollie.'

'Is Dinapore very far from Calcutta?'

'Four hundred miles.'

'What was Nash doing at the cantonment, I wonder?' He had always given me to understand that he had remained in Calcutta for the duration of his tour.

A sheen of sweat had broken out on Spencer's face. He swiped at his forehead with his shirtsleeve.

'Work for his firm,' Spencer said.

A spasm of shivering overtook him and I leaned forward to pull the blanket up around his shoulders. I said, 'Is there anything more I can do for you, sir? If you do not mind my saying so, now that I see your circumstances, I am not sure if you can afford to write off Nash's debt. I would like to find a way of alleviating your distress.'

Spencer raised a limp hand and made a vague swatting motion. 'Nothing you can do,' he said. He sighed and his eyes seemed to look inward. He muttered, 'I had no choice, you know. They were bent on cashiering me if I did not go.'

'He does not know what he is saying.' It was Mrs Spencer, who had come silently into the chamber. 'Sometimes he does not make any sense at all.'

I looked down at Spencer's drawn face. He closed his eyes and the lids twitched.

Mrs Spencer said, 'He is easily tired, I am afraid. The tea is made, if you will take a cup.'

'Of course.' I wished to remain in conversation with Spencer, but I saw that his strength was exhausted. I said, reluctantly, 'I will leave you to rest, Lieutenant.'

Mrs Spencer pushed the door-curtain aside and stepped into the parlour. I watched her go and then I could not help but ask the lieutenant, 'When you were in India, did you ever encounter a man named Daniel Ravine? A small, dark man from Bethnal Green. He worked with plants.'

Spencer gave no sign that he had heard me.

I came to standing, saying, 'I do not wish to tax you, sir. I will go now.'

His eyes fluttered open. 'Blue falling lights,' he said in a low voice.

I did not know what he meant. 'Bengal lights?' I asked, although I had no idea what colour those signals were.

Spencer moved his head slightly and met my gaze. He said something that sounded like, 'No unicorn, you see?'

'Unicorn?'

His eyes closed again. I waited by his bedside for a minute longer, but he said nothing more. I glanced towards the parlour and saw the shape of Mrs Spencer with an air about her of impatience. I bade the lieutenant farewell and passed out of the chamber. With a curt gesture, Mrs Spencer indicated that I should sit down at the table and then she said, 'What do you want with Felix?'

'He wrote a note to my husband, which mentioned that he was indisposed. I came to wish him well in Mr Nash's stead. They were once acquainted, you know.'

'Judy,' she said, 'take those peas and finish them outside.'

The girl picked up her bowls and sidled out of the door with an interested backward glance. Mrs Spencer poured tea into two chipped cups and handed one of them to me. She stared thoughtfully into her cup for a few seconds and then she said, as if I had asked her a question, 'I will speak plainly, Mrs Nash. It was me who got Felix to write that letter. He is bound to die, I fear, and I do not wish to see him play out his last days chasing Oliver Nash for money, no matter how justified. I know that Ollie will never honour the debt and that you did not come here in his stead. Ollie cares nothing for Spencer now that he has no use for him.'

I was amazed, not only by the familiar way in which Mrs Spencer referred to Nash, but also by the bitterness of her sentiments. Evidently she read the wonder on my face, because she said then, 'I daresay I have known Oliver Nash a great deal longer than most people. Certainly longer than you have, since I grew up with him.'

That was startling to hear. 'In Clerkenwell?' I asked.

'Our people – Felix's, Ollie's, mine – were all in cloth. I lived across the street from the Nashes, and the Spencers dwelled close by. Ollie was always a terror, even as a lad. He was persuasive, though, you have to give him that. He led a rowdy gang of vandals at school and Felix followed in his wake.'

'You amaze me, Mrs Spencer. I cannot imagine that Mr Nash was so brutish.'

'Oh, his surface is smooth, I will give you that, but underneath he was always a roiling lad. He had a particular animosity for those escutcheons that the quality like to fasten to their coaches. He and his gang would set about levering the emblems from the coaches with a pair of tailor's shears. I used to think it was because he could not stand to see the quality flaunting their entitlements. It chafed him that his people were undistinguished. He always thought he was made for better things.'

A load of dunderheads and toadies was how Nash described his schoolmates, I recalled, who knew no better than how to price cloth or make linen last clean for a fortnight. In fact, I could imagine that those conceited coats of arms and smug Latin mottoes emblazoned on the panels of coaches might have inflamed Nash's spleen, but not to the point of malice.

'He was a bright boy, without resources,' I said. 'It must have been onerous for him to see his career at the Bar terminated before it could even begin.'

Mrs Spencer snorted. 'Whose fault was that? Ollie had his stipend from his father and he could have made do on it.'

'But he was obliged to leave the courts because his father could not afford to support him.'

'That is not true. His father had money enough, but Ollie was wild and his father punished him for it by withdrawing the allowance. It was the same thing all over again in India. A promising set-up, soon squandered. Felix lent him funds to establish himself in Calcutta. Ollie might have made a decent enough living had he stuck to law, but he could not help being drawn into ventures on the side, which interfered with his business at court. I was sorry when he arrived from Calcutta. He came to the cantonment to see Felix and got in thick with him. It was all bad news after that. I cannot say that Felix's being cashiered was Oliver Nash's fault, but what I do know is that, whenever he came into our lives, we were the worse off for it.'

'What an indictment that is! It does not seem like Nash at all.'

She laughed as if I had made a jest.

Lowering my voice, I said, 'May I ask why your husband was cashiered?'

'You may ask, but you won't get an answer. We do not know ourselves.' She stood up and said, 'Thank you for coming, Mrs Nash,' in a tone very much loaded with dismissal.

She showed me out of the front door and I stood blinking in the glare of the sun. I said with sincerity that she must apply to me if she found herself in difficulties and that I would help if I could. She gave me a look that I can only describe as enigmatic.

As I struck off for the west, I looked back and saw that she remained standing in front of the house, watching me go.

Nash said that he did not know, either, on what grounds Spencer had been cashiered. When I asked him why he had not told me that he had known Felix Spencer from childhood, he said, 'You have scenes from your past that you like to draw a curtain over, don't you? For no other reason than they have become irrelevant to your life? I feel the same way about the Spencers. We happened to be neighbours when we were young, but then I came to move in very different circles and I am sure they resented me for it, but I owe no apology to anyone for the divergence of our destinies. I am sorry that Felix is dying, but you know what my attitude is, Carey: among the survivors, life must continue.'

Recollecting Selina's observation about the impossibly high standard I held Nash to, I began to wonder if I had been too judgemental and I did not press my questions. After all, Nash had not exactly lied. Rather he had omitted to mention certain things and, even then, I could not really say what the omissions signified. I did know that I did not wish to enter into a dispute. No doubt it is the lawyer in him, but Nash is devilish hard to argue with. Altercating with him is like wrestling with a muslin curtain on a breezy morning: the thing is too light to pin down and one ends up batting at air.

There was certainly nothing bothering Nash's conscience, because he fell asleep almost instantly that night. I stretched out next to him, feeling the warmth of his body. He turned over with his back to me, pulling the bedclothes with him, and I pushed myself up against him and I draped my arm over his hip. The air was cool on my bare shoulders. We were comfortable together. An intimate fug surrounded us, of warm, stale breath and the spicy scent of our bodies.

Chapter 10

The Soma Club

August the 20th, 1776

I had been before the glass in my bedchamber for two long hours, surrounded by a legion of cosmetics, and still *monsieur le friseur* had not finished setting my head. His name was Jacques d'Oray. He had a leathery countenance, which was at odds with the femininity of his *coiffure*, a fall of golden curls that tumbled with brazen artificiality from his crown to his waist. Like all practitioners of his art, he was a most voluble talker and my cheeks hurt from maintaining a false smile as he offered damning indictments of his patrons. 'You will not believe it, madam,' he was saying, 'but I now count among my clients an accountant who has become a Methodist and will not have his hair dressed on a Sunday. Now it must be done on a Saturday night and, to prevent it from being discomposed, he must sleep in a chair.' I was undergoing the last operations of my toilette before setting off for Underfall House and the Soma Club ball. Jacques was deploying a spatula to mould my hair with gum and silver powder into something that was supposed to look like a cloud, which it did, in a way. The creation was a veritable thunderhead. 'Did you hear,' he went on, 'that Lady Celia Malet is being divorced by her husband?'

'Poor Lady Celia,' I said. 'Her husband has treated her with indifference.'

'They say that Sir John is very well pleased to be rid of his wife as he might get a handsome sum from Lord Dexter by a prosecution for criminal conversation.'

'I did not know that Malet was so in need of money.'

'He has thrown his guineas away on the nymphs at Dove's Bagnio, they say. But do you know that Lord Dexter says now that he never bedded Lady Celia, save for a joke. Haven't you seen the lampoons of her? She is stuck up in caricatura in print shops all over town.'

I had seen the lampoons and I had felt a pang of sympathy for Lady Celia. She had been giddy and foolish, but she did not deserve to be so thoroughly humiliated.

'Sir John is at the pinnacle of happiness,' d'Oray rattled on. 'He has rid himself of an old wife and got a good price for her, and seen her reduced to a scanty pittance. There, madam, you are done!' With a flourish of the silver dust that was loaded on a big, fat badger brush, d'Oray stepped back to admire his handiwork. I complimented him upon the artifice, for certainly my head was set into a shape of shimmering durability that was bound to last throughout the masquerade and, possibly, for all eternity.

There was a thump at the door and Jane appeared to announce that Mrs Colden had arrived.

'Give her a glass of something and tell her I will be down

in an instant,' I called. A few minutes later, as d'Oray was packing up his implements, I heard a chariot draw up outside the house. Voices and the nickering of a horse floated up from the street. D'Oray gave himself permission to go to the window and look down on the activity in front of the house.

'I did not know you kept a carriage,' he said, managing to sound both impressed and scornful.

'It has come courtesy of Sir Rollo Hayle.' He had undertaken to supply transport to those of his guests who had not their own equipage. It was generous of him to offer us the ride, but I wondered if we were to pay in some other manner.

I bustled d'Oray out of the bedchamber and called for Jane, who took my articles of toilette away to be stowed in the chariot, while I tied a protective calash over my *coiffure*. I came downstairs to find Nash at the looking glass in the hall, setting his hat at an angle. Selina was watching him from the doorway of his office. She looked up at my approach and blew me a kiss of greeting. Nash complimented my appearance; I smiled, and putting my fingers to my head, felt the gritty powder covering my hair. I felt a flush of excitement at the prospect of the masquerade. It was like the thought of entering a room that is out of bounds.

The chariot was very comfortable. It boasted walls of padded leather and a network hanging from the ceiling, where Selina and I lodged our shawls and Nash his hat.

'The traffic is awful,' Selina said. 'Shall we play a hand of gleek to pass the time?'

Nash took out a pack of cards and let down the table from its leather strap. We commenced playing for pennies, while we crawled along High Holborn. We could hear the driver expostulating at the frequent obstacles in our path. My hand was a poor one and I soon folded it. Selina passed on hers, too. I looked away, out of the window, and saw that our vehicle had come level with the frontage of Dove's, the bagnio that the *friseur* had mentioned. There was a figure in black outside Dove's that looked familiar. It was a jeweller called Jacob Dezevedo. Nash had once recovered a debt for him. Dezevedo's customers were courtesans in the main with expensive tastes. They often liked to buy for themselves some glittering jewel while they were in between keepers and Dezevedo would give them credit to almost any amount.

'Declare your gleeks, ladies,' Nash said.

I turned over my cards to show I had none that was a three of a kind, nor did Selina. Nash won without a showdown and raked in his winnings.

Dove's is a house of intrigue, but one of high repute. When I first met Selina, she had operated there. It is where she assembled the connections that have allowed her to set up an independent life, even if it must be lived on the backs of debilitated peers whose amorous abilities are not in their first flush.

'Why don't you deal us another, better hand, Nash?' she said.

I rested my chin on my fist and gazed out of the window

as the stone of the town gradually gave way to trees and sky. It was very warm in the chariot and I fell into a doze until the driver's horn woke me. We had arrived at the Green Man, a large tavern that stood at a fork in the road, with the forest pressing at its back. We had reserved a room there for the afternoon in order to refresh ourselves and change into our masquerade costumes.

We ordered brandies to sip at while we dressed. Nash was going as a heathen god, in a loincloth and taffeta toga. Selina was the picture of an Arcadian shepherd boy, in a short white tunic with a silver belt and silver sandals and I was rigged up as an Arabian sultana, with a piece of tulle pinned to my cloudy hair as a veil. We were ready to make an exhibition of ourselves.

The honeyed light of the sinking sun streamed through the trees in a haze as we joined a stream of vehicles heading north along a narrow road that ran through groves of oaks and hornbeams. By the time we reached the eminence where Underfall House stood, the sun had set. The high walls around the estate threw long shadows over the queue of carriages and coaches waiting at the gates, where men armed with firelocks inspected our tickets before giving us leave to pass into the grounds. In creeping darkness, we made our way along a driveway illuminated by flambeaux. Sir Rollo's mansion did not look especially beautiful – it was made of red brick with a front of seven bays behind a line of stolid

Doric columns – but it had scale and weight. We disembarked before the grand portal amid a great knot of carriages and masquers - and jugglers and fire-eaters, who were making a show to amuse us. The more illustrious guests had brought their own servants with them, but we were content to place ourselves in the hands of Sir Rollo's dark-bearded stewards, who were got up in white skirts and cockaded turbans. They ushered us into an entrance hall with a chequerboard tile floor and painted ceiling panels. Everything was oversized – the tall, bare-chested footmen, their upper arms clasped with metal bracelets, the massive chandelier and hanging lanterns of coloured glass, the cavernous chimneypiece surmounted by a gigantic marble head wearing a garland of vine leaves and grapes. We were conducted to a small apartment on the third floor, where our luggage was lodged, and where we could rest if our energies should fail us. Refreshments, we were informed, would be served throughout the course of the night; breakfast was at ten, but those in want of their own equipage, who had pressing business in town, might take advantage of a coach that would depart at five in the morning.

We descended once more to the tumult of the hall, where the din of conversation nearly drowned a small orchestra playing instruments that were unfamiliar to me. The masquers were a medley of goddesses and nawabs, Persians and Turks, and idols with the heads of animals. An elephant deity had taken a seat on a dais above the throng. His grey head and trunk were painted with occult symbols and wreathed in marigolds. His tusks were ringed with bangles. He owned a muscular, stocky body and lolled, legs wide open, lazily handling his penis like a butcher offering a fillet at market.

Young women, costumed in a superb manner as dancing girls, offered us glasses of champagne and conducted us, in groups, on a tour of the masquerade's precincts. The girls welcomed us into a long gallery, furnished with couches and low tables. It was lined with side-rooms for *tête-à-têtes* or games of cards and there was an apartment that had been fitted out for supper. Then we followed our willowy guides down a winding stone staircase to the lower part of the house. At the foot of the stairs, a stone sculpture sat on a plinth on a tigerskin. It was a likeness of the deity that the Hindus call Shiva, the great lord of time, who destroys our illusions and erases our old memories, so that the universe may keep in order. The so-called temple of soma was situated at the rear of a low-ceilinged cellar complex, hollowed into a series of intricate vaults lit by braziers. A pleasant scent of rosewater and of Persian tobacco wafted through the air. There were already numbers of men smoking hookahs that were set out on embroidered rugs. They were making a great ceremony of it, fussing with the chillum and the coil of piping.

In a play of light and shadow between the braziers, Indian goddesses, painted in a frieze on the walls, seemed to dance and to beckon us. As I looked at them more closely, I saw that the lush figures were actually rather martial and ferocious. Their multiple arms wielded weapons of spears and curved knives and batons of bones and the bowls that they held in their hands were upturned skulls.

When the tour was concluded, we dispersed to do as we pleased. Nash and I returned to the gallery, arm in arm. Glasses of Madeira, sherry and burgundy made frequent circuits as we fell into the kinds of initial conversations – the teasing chit-chat, the *do-I-know-you?* and *do-you-know-me?* and every species of compliment – that take place at such events. I was laughing and drinking, drinking and laughing, when Nash touched my arm and steered me towards a couple who had begun to disport themselves upon a couch. He, in the costume of a rajah, pushed aside the petticoats of a nun to open her thighs. As he played her, a crowd congealed around them, watching with an air of affected ennui until the woman gave herself up to a rapture. Nash, who was standing behind me, pressed me close against him so that I could feel the hardness of his cock. I felt a gaze upon me and turned to see Sir Rollo Hayle. He had not bothered very much with the mystification of disguise. A skimpy half-mask covered the upper part of his face. It was bright blue, with eyebrows like huge caterpillars, and he wore a painted golden coronet. His long ringlets were oiled and bound up in a knot on top of his head in the centre of the coronet. He wore lengths of gemstones around his neck and a belt studded with brilliants over thin silk breeches, and diamonds in his ear lobes.

As I curtsied, Nash said, 'Here is an Arabian beauty released for a few hours from the harem.' There was something eager in his tone that reduced him in my eyes, although I do not know why I should particularly remark that now, since I have always been aware that it excited him to see men who were socially superior look on me with desire.

Sir Rollo bowed, and said, 'I am overwhelmed by the satisfaction of seeing you. I am Ravana, arch demon of the Hindu epic *Ramayana* and emperor of three worlds.'

From behind his mask, I could feel the boldness of his gaze. 'Ravana,' he said, 'is possessed of the nectar of immortality. Do you know where he keeps it?' He took my hand and I thought he meant to kiss it, but in a swift movement, he pulled it into the recesses of his robe and pressed it against a penis that was half-erect. He said in his husky voice, 'Do you admire my contrivance, madam?'

I snatched back my hand, utterly affronted by his liberty, but Nash widened his eyes at me in warning. I was not to offend the mighty Sir Rollo.

'I admire it, of course,' I said, my voice thick.

Sir Rollo took my arm firmly and was very much in my way. Nash gave me a gesture of relinquishment, since it was a favour to himself that his patron should fix on his wife.

Sir Rollo put his lips close to my cheek and breathed, 'Pretty dove, you will do me the honour to come to the temple. It is our sanctum, where the soma works its wiles.'

I accompanied him for a few steps, while looking for an opportunity to escape. Sir Rollo, however, held fast to my arm. Then a mature nymph, resplendent in ropes of jewels and little else, rushed towards us, crying in mock terror, 'Save me, sir, from this uncourtly miscreant!'

A gentleman came stalking up to her with a beseeching remark. He looked ludicrous in a new curled wig with a feathered headdress, a half-mask and a pair of violently yellow pyjamas.

Sir Rollo laughed and said, 'I have no difficulty recognising this coxcomb.'

The befeathered creature flashed a smile that was full of false teeth. The veneers must have cost him a fortune, for they were mother of pearl. He patted his mask with one hand and wiped the other on the skirts of his pyjamas.

'Mercy on me, who is it?' the nymph cried.

'That is a great lord,' Sir Rollo replied, amused. 'You will not want to run away from such a man of influence.'

Sir Rollo had let go of my arm during this interruption and I managed to slide away, hiding myself in the nearest room, which was packed full of company gathered around tables that were covered in comestibles. All too quickly, Sir Rollo appeared at the door, but fortunately a distraction occurred at that instant. A young woman, clad only in a silk petticoat, climbed up on to the table, destroying several dishes of delicacies in the process, and began to perform a sinuous dance. She was the worse for wine, however, and could not accomplish her purpose. She entangled her feet in one of the dishes and, as she toppled, candles and plates and glasses fell with her amid screams and unsuccessful attempts to catch her. I escaped under cover of the crowd, dodging behind Sir Rollo's back, and rushed into the gallery. In the distance, I saw a familiar halo of blonde curls and I ran to catch up with the figure in its shepherd costume.

'How goes it, my dear?' Selina smiled.

'Avoiding our host. Have you found Newington?'

'If you see a stag with ambitious antlers and bandy legs, it is he.' She laughed. 'But I am after other game tonight.'

I looked over my shoulder, hoping not to spy Sir Rollo's blue demon mask. Selina invited me to take refuge with her in an alcove, and we sank on to the semi-circular seat at its rear. Selina pulled out her pocket looking-glass and her little pot of rouge and remade her carmine mouth. I asked her if she had seen Nash.

'I have lost him,' I said.

'But you cannot expect to dally with your husband tonight, my dear.'

'Why not? The masquerade has always been an amorous recreation for us. I have no desire to impale myself on these dry old monsters.'

Selina looked away at that and my face flamed. Surely she did not think that I made a criticism of her; and yet I felt a chill pass between us. Then she said, 'Is that why you are so sullen with your host?'

'How do you know that?'

'Nash told me. You have embarrassed him.'

'He does not expect me to prostitute myself with his patron.' I very much wanted to find Nash, but at that moment two romping ladies took their chance at the entrance to the alcove and my way out was blocked. One of them was perhaps the ancient Carthaginian queen, Dido, and the other something from a harem. They were joined by a bull, who was missing his breeches.

'This is not about your pleasure. It is work,' Selina said, 'don't you know that?'

I felt a flush of anger. 'Who are you to instruct my evening, Mrs Colden? I will do as I please. Is not that how you conduct yourself?'

Selina turned her head towards me. 'Your depression is perfectly visible, you know, and it is an insult to the occasion.'

One of the queens, Dido, had slid to the floor with her back against the wall and her knees drawn up, while the bull fumbled beneath her bunched-up silks. I don't think I have ever been irked by Selina before, or even been at odds with her. Dido threw back her head and moaned, while Selina and I watched in silence. The bull stood up and left with the lady of the harem, leaving Dido crumpled on the floor. Selina rose suddenly, bowed stiffly to me, and moved swiftly away, leaving behind a trace of displeasure in the air. I felt a reflexive regret at having contradicted her, but at the same time I noticed, after Selina had left, that my mind had filled with an unaccustomed feeling of spaciousness.

I walked the length of the gallery again. In the rooms that led off it, I glimpsed pashas and Circassians pounding away at shepherdesses and gipsies to the gratification of the lascivious spectators. 'Oh, you creature!' cried a pretty young lady, seizing my waist. One side of her face was painted white and the other black. She breathed into my ear, 'I am a Chinese symbol,' and tried to kiss me. All of a sudden, the sound of a gong reverberated through the house and one could feel an accompanying ripple of anticipation emanate from the guests. 'Come downstairs and drink soma with me!' the Chinese symbol implored.

But I had spied Nash, at last. I seized his arm and he laughed in his wolfish way and said he was tight enough to burst. A creature hung on his other arm, a woman in a black habit with a feathered mask like a fantastic bird. She leaned towards me and whispered, 'You must ask him to tease you.' Did she mean Nash? 'He teased me.' She laughed.

Nash pulled me away from her and said we must descend to the cellar, where the ceremonial was to take place. Nuzzling my neck, he said, 'Drink soma with me, my beauty, the sacred elixir.' He had got a head start on me and was already somewhat slurred. I was eager to join him. I was in need of something to boost my mood, which was not as effervescent as it ought to be in the midst of such revels. I linked my arm in Nash's and we made our way down to the cellar. Dancing girls with bejewelled breasts and hair bound up in garlands swayed among the buzzing crowd. Bells tinkled at their ankles. From the painted walls, demon slayers and enforcers armed with swords and sickles looked down on the pleasure seekers lounging upon the divans.

The dancers began to circle around a structure in a corner of the cellar that resembled a large sarcophagus, although it was unadorned.

A voice, attractive, murmured, 'It is a tomb, a *samadhi*, where we practise the rite of death and rebirth.' The mouth was close enough to my cheek that I could feel its heat. I found myself face to face with Sir Rollo Hayle again. I was sorely incommoded by his determination to distinguish me among the company. I looked around for Nash, but he had melted away. Fortunately, Sir Rollo's eye was drawn by the arrival of an elaborately bedecked palanquin, carried in by bearers in turbans and loincloths. A perky girl dressed as a pony, with a tail buckled upon her bare rump, pulled open the fringed curtains of the palanquin to reveal a little *fille de joie* operating upon the lord in yellow pyjamas. Their cavorting was brought to a halt by the sudden beating of drums and wailing of pipes. A cheer went up as the dancing girls arrived with trays of burnished bowls. They were led by an odalisque wearing a headdress two feet high. It was composed of greenery that appeared to be a sheaf of hemp. She climbed upon the sarcophagus and began to perform, with a wanton smile, a lewd posture dance. Hollow brass rings about her ankles increased the commotion with which she extolled her body and she played with two pieces of bell metal, which she worked between her fingers.

The attendants ladled draughts of the libation into small

tumblers of coloured glass and passed them among the guests.

I thought I glimpsed Nash sitting on pillows on the floor, a woman – naked save for her stockings, her mask thrown to one side – buried in his lap, but it was only another man passing for a god. I could not see any sign of Selina, either, and I wished that I had not offended her. I stared at the statue of Shiva again. I have read that when he loses his temper, his third eye opens and anything in its gaze is reduced to ashes. I turned away from the statue. Something had caused my spirits to dissipate as if I had been abruptly released from the spell of the masquerade. I looked around for one of the attendants. I was in urgent need of one of those libations in order to counteract the inexplicable feeling of estrangement that had overcome me.

At last, one of the trays came near me. I seized a tumbler and retreated with it to a pillar beside the stairs. I had always thought it wonderful that convention decreed one could not attend a masquerade disguised as oneself, but now I chafed in my costume. At the same time, I found these thoughts distressing, since I longed for pleasure and the satisfaction of my desires. I sniffed at the libation. It had a herbaceous, grassy smell. As I raised the glass to bring it to my lips, a restraining hand touched my arm and a voice said, 'Don't drink it. It is a narcotic.'

I turned to find that a tall domino of no character was standing at my side in a colourless silk habit.

He spoke again, close to my ear. 'In Bengal, they call it bhang. It has many useful qualities, but not in this setting.' I wondered if I knew him. There was something familiar about his voice.

'Who are you, sir?'

'My name is Adam Martenson.'

Martenson! What was he doing here?

I did not acknowledge him, but I put the glass aside. In our line of sight, the yellow-trousered lord was lying in his palanquin and another masquer, with the head and horns of a goat, was speaking into his ear.

Martenson stooped to me a little, as if he wished to curtail his height and present himself as a less looming figure. He said, 'That is Lord Casserly in the yellow, and the creature speaking to him is his banking partner, Benjamin Packham.'

So that was the mighty Lord Casserly, Sir Rollo's political backer. He did not look so very estimable with his snout buried in his bowl of soma.

Martenson indicated a fat pasha, sunk into a huge floor-cushion. 'Over there is Thomas Strong, a nephew of Fenton Gifford's. He is a director of Hayle and Gifford's company, Bengal Glass. Strong owns warehouses and often accommodates the overflow of Hayle and Gifford's trading goods.'

But my attention was on another figure. Sir Rollo had spotted me and was making his way towards my lurking place by the stairs. This was the moment when I could do the most good for Nash, and for myself, of course, by extension. All it required was to allow Sir Rollo to do as he liked with me – but I could not bear to be secluded with him. I glanced to the side and saw that Martenson had disappeared. Obviously, he had entered the gathering without an invitation.

I turned on my heel and quickly ascended the stairs before Sir Rollo could pounce. A footman held open the portal that led into the ground-floor gallery and I passed through it in haste. I experienced a momentary thrill of elation, as if I had escaped a danger. As I strode away – I was nearly running – I saw, at the far end of the gallery, the retreating figure of a tall man in the cloak of a domino.

Chapter 11

The Hothouse

August the 20th, 1776

As I walked on, following Martenson at a distance, a group of shrieking merrymakers ran by me and I stepped aside to let them pass. It was clear to me that only a matter of great urgency could have provoked him to steal into Underfall House and risk his freedom by it. There was no doubt that he would be thrown into prison if he were unmasked in this particular lion's den. Either that or he was unhinged, as Nash had described him. Instinct, however, continued to suggest to me that Martenson was a sound man. He had advised me not to drink the soma and I was glad that I had not. I did not know what effects the libation might have unleashed, but I felt relieved that my senses and thoughts were not under the influence of a drug. I watched as Martenson took a turning to the right and disappeared from sight. Hurrying to catch up to him, I took the same turning myself, into a narrower hallway that was dimly lit by lamps placed at intervals along its length. I saw that he had come to a halt and I too slowed my footsteps. I did not feel a sense of danger. Martenson had stooped and was reaching out, perhaps to try a door handle. I became aware, before he did, of two figures approaching from the far end of the hall. They wore turbans and the candlelight glimmered on the metal bands around their muscular arms. Sir Rollo's footmen.

Impulsively, I ran forward on light feet and called to Martenson with a somewhat forced peal of laughter, saluting him in an apparently tipsy manner. He looked up, surprised, but then he too noticed the footmen and he understood at once that I was creating a diversion. He returned my laughter, although it did not sound very natural, and suddenly opened his arms. I rushed forward, with a great deal of false giggling, into his embrace. As he wrapped me close to him, the novelty of the moment caused my heart to thud.

'Pray forgive the intrusion, sir − ' it was one of the footmen − 'but you cannot remain in this part of the house.'

I continued to laugh like a maniac, while at the same time eyeing with curiosity the tall glazed door that we stood before. It was ornamented with metal plant forms.

'My companion is a little worse for wear, as you can see,' Martenson said.

'We will show you to the gallery,' the second footman said, 'where you may place the lady in a more comfortable situation.'

The zealous servants loomed at us with cold smiles and escorted us back the way we had come. Martenson did not protest and went along with the footmen, while I hung upon his arm, as if it made no difference to him where he was. As soon as he spied a couch in the gallery, he pulled me down upon it with him and put his mouth close to my ear. I suppose, to the footmen, it looked as though we were continuing an amorous dalliance. Out of the corner of my eye, I saw them leave our proximity and take up positions standing guard at the entrance of the hallway. Martenson said, 'I appreciate your quick thinking, Mrs Nash. Thank you.'

His breath was warm upon a spot just below the lobe of my ear. The cloth of his domino had a faintly musty smell. Music and drums sounded from very far away and I had a feeling of invigoration, as if a window had been opened, letting sunlight and fresh air into a stuffy apartment. It was absurd to attribute my elevation in mood to the presence of Martenson, but I did feel quite suddenly improved and glad that he had drawn me away from those morbid excitements taking place in the cellars.

'They have gone,' Martenson said, drawing back. 'I will try again.'

In a determined manner, which I was beginning to interpret as a foundation of his character, Martenson replaced his visor and stood up. I scrambled to my feet, too. As he turned away with a brief nod of his head, I asked, 'What is your scheme?'

'Please be at leave to return to the revels, madam.'

I found his abruptness and lack of charm oddly refreshing. I stepped along beside him, saying, 'I should like to know how it is that you are acquainted with my husband.' Martenson paused and looked down at me, and said in a kinder tone, 'Really, Mrs Nash, do not risk your host's ire by accompanying me.'

I glanced over my shoulder at the masquers who had drifted up from the cellar, then I turned to Martenson and said, 'Whatever your clandestine mission is, I would prefer the novelty of being your lookout than the familiarity of this bacchanal. And, to be candid, it is my host that I very much wish to avoid.'

Martenson did not reply. He pressed on; but I dogged his footsteps, turning into the hall with him. I said, 'Do you continue your search for the dossier? You were looking for it the night you broke into our house.'

'Yes. Hayle has it. Your husband sold it to him.'

'How do you know such a thing?'

'Please go, Mrs Nash.'

'I will ask my husband, then.'

'He will not tell you the truth. You should ask at Packham's Bank. They will tell you that his account has swelled.'

Martenson removed a needle-like tool from beneath his habit and bent to the door. He began working the mechanism of the lock with the pick.

I whispered, 'Nash does not have an account with Packham's. Why do you slander him so?'

Martenson said hurriedly, 'I cannot speak more now.' A groan rose up from the hinges and he pushed the door. I felt a blast of humid air and an earthy, fecund scent. As the door creaked open, I caught sight of shadowy, tall vegetation. It was a hothouse at least two storeys high.

I hung at Martenson's shoulder. 'Doesn't it occur to you that I could go to one of the stewards now and expose you?'

'But you will not do such a thing.' Martenson's voice softened. 'You are not that kind of person. I bid you good night, Mrs Nash.' Just before he pulled the door shut, he said, 'Do not drink anything that Hayle offers you. It will likely be infused with an opiate.'

As I set off towards the gallery, the initial shock of Martenson's statements gave way to indignation. He had defamed my husband. But even as I fumed, a particle of my mind feared that there might be some truth to Martenson's revelations. Events had occurred before I met Nash, and their consequences were beginning now to leach into our lives.

There ought to be another entrance to the hothouse, I speculated, somewhere on the first floor of Underfall House. I was curious about the structure and its vegetation. I was curious, too, about Martenson's actions. I passed through the great hall and reached a wide passage that ran on the same axis as the gallery downstairs – which meant it must be adjacent to the hothouse. The passage was painted blue and white, with panels of Chinese wallpaper. It was illuminated by lamps in elaborate sconces. I could not find a door, though, that would lead into the upper level of the hothouse. I returned the way I had come, passing the panels of flowers and birds on the walls – camellia, egret, peony, palm . . . I paused and looked at the panel that depicted a palm in a boiserie frame ornamented with carvings of coconuts. I ran my fingers over the bas-relief of the frame, pressing randomly. And then the door, for that is what the panel was, swung open.

I stepped on to a gridded walkway and pulled the door to. A wave of heat washed over me and pinpricks of sweat broke out on my skin. I untied my mask, wiped the perspiration from my face and looked up into the rafters – they were entwined with vines, and shafts of moonlight beamed through skylights that studded the angled roof. A suspended walkway ran around the four sides of the hothouse. About twenty feet away from where I was standing, I could see the head of an iron ladder and, beyond that, there was an extraordinary structure that was built out over the walkway. It was a compact replica of an Indian bungalow, complete with thatched roof and a porch. It had been made, I imagined, so that Sir Rollo could sit out in a high-backed basket chair in the heat, as he had been habituated to do in Bengal. I felt a stab of fear for Martenson. If he were to be discovered here, in Sir Rollo's sanctum, he would surely hang for it.

Suddenly, Martenson appeared in the doorway of the bungalow and stepped on to the porch. He froze as he saw me, and then came forward on the walkway. At that moment, I heard a movement at the hidden door a few yards from where Martenson and I were standing. I dared not make any sound – all I could do was widen my eyes in warning. Martenson understood my meaning. He grasped the railings of the ladder and disappeared from sight, just as the door opened and a wedge of light spilled on to the walkway. I felt the grid beneath my feet tremble slightly as the ladder responded to Martenson's weight.

'Unmasked already, Mrs Nash?' It was Sir Rollo. He had

given up his mask, too, and I felt the heat of his stare. There were two gentlemen with him. One of them was the banker that Martenson had pointed out, Benjamin Packham. The other was done up as a domino with a black habit. From the outline of him, it might have been Gifford. The banker looked gingerly over the railing. Despite the urbanity of Sir Rollo's greeting, my presence in the hothouse was, of course, utterly questionable.

'Forgive me.' I laughed. 'I know I am out of bounds.'

As I took a step towards him, the structure gave an awful creak. I let out a girlish squeal.

'How did you get in here?' Sir Rollo asked with a cold smile.

'I came into the hall, looking for our apartment, when I saw a footman leave by this door. I was intrigued by the concealed entrance and could not resist trying to breach it. It is a wonderful hothouse. What an extraordinary place! Is that a Bengal bungalow, I wonder?'

'Do you like it?' Sir Rollo put an arm around my shoulder and pressed me tight against him as we gazed towards the structure. 'Perhaps you would like a tour of the interior?'

I twisted away from him, and said, 'How kind, but I must find my husband.'

He seized my arm with a steely grip, and said, 'Do not run off so soon, Mrs Nash. You know, I take no notice of any other lady here but you.'

'But I must disappoint you, sir. I am not the wanton you are hoping for.'

'You are rather hard upon me. Perhaps this will soften your mood.' He unhooked one of the diamonds from his ear.

I shook my head. 'I cannot take something so privately offered.'

'Of course you can.' He dropped the diamond between my breasts. 'You are at liberty to have its mate, if you can earn it.'

He thrust me hard against the wall; I gave a cry and pushed at him.

'Hayle.' It was Gifford. I recognised his voice. 'Leave the little strumpet.'

I tore myself free and made for the door. I thought I heard the sound of a *plink* as the diamond fell through the metal grid and was lost among the palms. Selina would call me a fool, but I did not care about it. I managed to retrieve my composure enough so that I turned and curtsied in farewell. Sir Rollo bowed gravely, while fixing me with his glittering eye. He had a smile upon his face, which suggested that, in his view, his conquest of me was only a matter of time.

I intended to shut myself in the apartment, but as I reached a landing I heard the crunch of wheels on gravel and a jingling of harnesses. Glancing through a window, I saw that a coach had drawn up in the forecourt below and passengers were gathering for their ride back to town. I continued downstairs, meaning to search for Nash, but as I entered the great hall, where a few weary guests were still in the last throes of fondling, I was met by two of Sir Rollo's bare-chested footmen. One of them bowed and said that his master would be honoured if I would adjourn to his parlour and take a bite of supper and a glass of champagne. I recalled Martenson's admonition, and shivered. The merchant I had been sent to live with after the death of my grandfather had employed a similar modus operandi at first: a cordial corrupted with an opiate, which I was given to drink in the evenings. Once it had operated on me and I was unconscious, the merchant entered my chamber and gave loose to his wishes. My saviour was the dereliction of his body, which refused to perform to his liking; but I was ruined in other ways. The thought of it still turned me to water. He had claimed to have a passion for me and pretended that I had *carte blanche* to live with him as I liked, but I was, in effect, his prisoner.

Fearing to provoke the footmen to use force against me if I refused Sir Rollo's invitation directly, I pleaded a few minutes' grace to take in a breath of fresh air.

The driver had slammed the door of the coach and was climbing upon his seat as I came out of the house. I pulled open the door and climbed into the coach. I was fortunate. There were six gentlemen inside, but they made room for me, and I shrank into my place with my veil pulled up around my face.

As we drove away from Underfall House, I hardly dared to breathe, fearing that the footmen might halt the coach and bring me back to the house, but we passed through the gates and began to bowl along the forest road. As soon as we reached the highway, I felt a burst of elation at having left the Soma Club behind.

An hour passed by as we rolled on. From time to time I caught a glimpse of trees through the window. I had loved walking through woodland as a child, beneath an overwood of oak and hornbeam. I thought of afternoons spent with my grandfather cutting scions for his rootstocks. He died quite suddenly and, by the time I was informed of it at school, the internment had already taken place. The fees for the school were paid until the end of the term and I went on with my lessons with the expectation that, when my father was in receipt of the melancholy news, he would send for me.

I do not remember weeping at all at that time. I rose in the morning, I went to my lessons. I wrote to my father care of the East India Company. I remember feeling insubstantial as if I had dematerialised in sympathy with the disappeared.

Then there came a day when Mrs Leonard told me that Durand's money had run out and that I had no choice but to go into service. She put me into a hackney coach and sent me to Chelsea. I knew that other girls at the school had suffered the kinds of critical alterations in their circumstances that required them to be sent away to unknown households. They would have been anxious, too, on the drive out of the school's gates. Would they have felt, as I did, an urge to leap from the coach and run for their lives? Calm yourself, Carey, I repeated in the close confines of that interior. Calm yourself, calm yourself. Since that journey to Chelsea, I have done nothing *but* calm myself with champagne and shopping and with a husband whose talent for amusement has kept me from brooding on the past.

I waited in the library of the tall house for my new master. The butler had taken away my bag and my writing box. The only other possession that meant anything to me was the one letter that I had had from my father in Bengal with its dreadful news. I kept it for many years until the paper became worn through and unreadable. All I knew of the master was that he was a former spice merchant named Tate, who had left the City to set up in salubrious retirement. I was to be a secretary, apparently. It was an absurd proposition, but I had not questioned it. I had been schooled to do as I was told. As I took in the disquieting objects in the library, the hairs on the back of my neck stood up. Cases of stuffed birds lined one of the walls and there were two hinged brass lamps at the foot of a table covered with green baize. I did not like that table or the lamps. It still astonishes me that I sat there so meekly, like a kid at its stake, but when Ambrose Tate entered the library, I jumped to my feet and ran past him to the door. The butler waiting outside – Porterhouse, his name was – simply manhandled me back into the library. He was a creature as dry and unpleasant as his master. The merchant was very ordinary in appearance, with a thinning pate and a withered face, and I remember he was sweating into a tightly tied stock and a heavy coat that night. I divined that he was a depraved man without knowing at that point how wide and deep is the possibility of moral corruption.

He ordered me to be stripped naked and to be placed on the green baize table. He said that Porterhouse would fetch me a blow about the ears if I did not do as I was commanded by my master. He lowered one of the lamps to examine me. I can still hear the slither of his slippers on the rush matting of the floor as he made his approach. He growled, 'Blast your eyes, girl, if you do not do as I ask, I will strike you a sharp one.' But it was not the prospect of a blow that caused my perfect terror.

Some years later, when I had learned to make my way in the demi-monde, I discovered that I was not the only pupil of Mrs Leonard's who had been bilked of her virtue. It was a habit among the school's trustees, wealthy merchants for the most part, to look for a sweetener from the headmistress in return for donations to the school's coffers. Those douceurs commonly came in the form of girls in unfortunate circumstances, who were sent to service. The lessons of loss and aloneness are hard ones and they will exact a toll. The only free will you have in a brutish situation is to decide how much of a toll you are prepared to pay. I tried not to pay with the entirety of my soul. I managed to withhold just enough for my own sustenance. This is not easy to do when you must make a payment every day.

The merchant proposed to me the terms of employment. He said, 'I am certain you will understand the difference between the comfort of a roof over your head, a supply of victuals and the possibility of monetary rewards much greater than a servant has any right to expect, and the alternative, which is to throw yourself upon the street. I might add that, if you do not please me, to the gutter you shall go. The choice is yours.'

Ambrose Tate could not pay his devotions to women in any regular way. His sexual pleasure depended on a detailed conception of himself as the guardian of a virginal niece on whom he expected to perform various indecencies without complaint. He sought a slender, clean-limbed girl, who could be modest in her manner, yet lewd in her conversation and postures when required. He expected her to be lively, airy and eager to do his bidding. In return, she could expect that he would not impregnate her, since the act of coition did not interest him. The ability to sustain his fantasies was the thing. He was willing to pay her prizes and bonuses if she used her imagination well and of course he would clothe her and fit her out according to her fabricated rank. However, should he see the least sign of sullenness or despondency in her demeanour, or should he grow bored with her, she must forfeit her post and he would turn her out without a thought. Or she could be thrust out of the door at that moment. No one would stop her from making her way towards whatever fate the streets had in store for her; and no one would care where she went.

I was compelled to submit to the merchant's measures as necessity dictated. I saw no other choice. Where else was there to go? To the workhouse or some other place of wretched confinement? I had heard that young people who could not find protection were sent abroad in merchant ships along with convicts to be indentured for life. Perhaps I might eventually find a position as a governess or a companion, but that could take time, which was a luxury I did not possess, and, even then, the wages would be pitiful. I was alone without a guide. Therefore, I accepted Ambrose Tate's demands. I remained in the merchant's house for five years and I learned, by force of will, how to survive. In all of that time, I kept looking for a sign that would direct me to the place where I was meant to go in my life and live in peace and happiness. I was convinced such a place must exist, but how one reached it was a mystery.

Chapter 12

Alive and Enmeshed

August the 21st, 1776

As we neared Ludgate Hill, the coach ran on over the cobbles with a jolting that began to sicken us all, and I was glad when it halted and I was released from its confines. I was without money and attired in a ridiculous costume, but one of my fellow passengers kindly hailed a cab and paid for it to take me home to Hood Street. Jane let me into the house. I asked her to bring hot water to my bedchamber and then I trudged upstairs. My cosmetic utensils were as I had left them and my wrapping gown lay in a heap on the floor, where I had dropped it alongside my slippers. I felt as though I had been away for weeks. One of the woundworts had come into early flower, I saw. I regarded the bedchamber with a sense of detachment. What was the point of all its knick-knacks and bric-a-brac? I went to my closet, stripped off my costume and put on a clean shift. I plumped a pillow on the bed – and then I punched it in frustration. I had made the mistake of letting Ambrose Tate into my head again and now he would not leave. The thought of him was exhausting; just as life with him had been, at least in a mental sense. One had constantly to dissemble to oneself. I used to pretend that the life I was sunk in belonged to somebody else. In that regard, I never succumbed to despair and I found the resolve to make provision for a future. I was always hopeful, in spite of everything. Tate had liked to boast of his trading days in the City. He still followed avidly the rise and fall of stocks. At first, only for the sake of gaining some release from my velveted prison, I persuaded him to show me the site of the warehouse at Blackwall, where he had formerly lodged the spices that he traded, and the Royal Exchange on Cornhill, but then I refined my role so that I, the 'niece', became interested in being instructed by my 'uncle' in the mysteries of the stockmarket. If only there were someone cleverer and older and wiser than I, someone of superior mental capacity, I mused, who could introduce my poor little woolly brain to the ways and means of investment. Presently, I began to accompany the merchant whenever he visited his stockbroker and I listened intently to their conversations. I soon began to improve my earnings. On my eighteenth birthday, I persuaded Tate to purchase stock for me in the Batavia Company with the money that I had got from him and, when the stock performed well, to act as a guarantor for me at Harrington's Bank at Cheapside. Although he jealously hoarded his gold, he delighted to see me win on the Exchange; as his pupil, my achievements affirmed his skills. In attaining the age of twenty-one, I was entitled to become a private customer of the bank. By the time I was twenty-two, I had accumulated five hundred pounds, which I intended to draw on to take a passage to India.

I had continued to write letters to my father, care of the horticulture committee of the East India Company in Calcutta, in the hope that he was alive. The waywardness of communication with faraway places offered a faint possibility that he was not dead, but only at the wrong address. *Please Forward*, I always wrote in an emphatic hand on the cover. In these fruitless letters, I claimed to have continued at Mrs Leonard's school in the capacity of a tutor, thanks to the benevolence of the headmistress. I was too ashamed to reveal the truth.

With my finances secure, I quitted the merchant's house for good one morning, without a word to him. I put up a few common things in a handkerchief and took asylum in two rooms in Silver Street, which I rented while I accustomed myself to my liberty. During the years of pretence in the house of Ambrose Tate, I had kept my emotions on a very tight rein. As a result, I felt alienated from myself and benumbed. But I began to thaw as soon as I became acquainted with Selina Colden. Her friendship consoled me and I appreciated her as a woman of spirit, who knew how to make her way without falling into folly or imprudence. She was adept at playing the coquette and sometimes getting, from this lord and that, a twenty-pound banknote. She showed me how it was done and how to live while giving up as little as possible to one's protectors. My years at Chelsea had altered me. I certainly could not hold any hard belief in virtue as an indicator of character. I loathe the hypocrisy of the conventional world, which trades money and sexual favours no less blatantly than the bagnios and seraglios, but dresses them up in religion and legislation. I came out of Chelsea being against the world, to be frank, and I wished to do as I liked.

I rushed towards anything that was bright and diverting. At first, that was Selina, who threw glittering little parties and made me feel that we were sisters in adversity, who had overcome it all and cocked a snook at the prigs and the pietists. Then I rushed towards Nash. When I met him, I had been in search of a man to fall in love with. I had been casting about for a man I could revere, a man who would repair my hurts and melt my heart. The instant that Selina introduced us, Nash's gaze met mine and mingled with it and I felt exhilarated as if something marvellous had happened. We must have recognised instinctively our similarities. We both liked to indulge ourselves in living after our own manner. Nash had an enticing style and I saw in him possibilities and pleasures. He was prepared to marry me, when most men of any acceptable station would have found me beyond the pale.

It was late in the afternoon when I woke up. Nash's office was in its usual state of disarray. I looked in the drawer where I had seen him stow the contract belonging to the Neela Company, but I could not find it. I had wondered if the Neela Company were associated with the dossier of poisonings. There were boxes on the shelves, containing files fastened with ribbons. Surely, I did not mean to search through them all – and to what purpose? I should like to be able to say airily to myself, *Oh, what does any of this matter?* But it mattered to Martenson enough to risk his life, and whether his assertions about Nash were true or not, there were connections that I wished to understand. I was still sitting on Nash's divan when he arrived home, dead on his feet. His face was blue shadowed and there were damp strands of hair stuck to his forehead. He called for Ned to help unload the luggage from the carriage and greeted me in a voice that was slurred. He climbed unsteadily up the stairs. I followed him and found him sitting on the edge of the bed, his shoes kicked off. 'Lord, my head,' he groaned. 'What made you run off? I was greatly inconvenienced looking for you and I fear that your rudeness offended Sir Rollo.'

'I was pressed by him, Nash, and I did not care to gratify his passions. When I saw the morning coach was to leave, I seized my chance to escape him.'

It was beyond Nash to make a response. He fell on to his back with the finality of a man who had been mortally shot.

Late that evening, I found him sitting at his desk with his legs stretched out, one crossed over the other, working at his pipe. The lamp on the desk lit up the pen and blank paper that lay at his elbow. He watched me somewhat warily as I closed the door and sat down on the divan. There were shadows under his eyes and his face was puffy. He forced a smile and laid down his pipe.

'What am I to think,' I said, 'when I learn that you keep a private account at Packham's Bank?'

He banged the pipe noisily on the rim of the ashtray to

dislodge its burned tobacco. 'Who told you such a scurrilous thing?'

'Someone at the masquerade.'

'What is his name?'

'It is true, isn't it?'

'Am I to seek your approval for every action of business that I undertake?'

'No, but why do you worry me about our debts, when you have the resources to pay them?'

'How tiresome you are, Carey, with your poking about. Can't you take up collage or something, like a reasonable woman?'

'Why can't you tell me where the money came from?'

'God in heaven, the account is provisional. It is only a loan from Gifford to be used for investment. I thought to take advantage of information that Lord Casserly is privy to as a member of the government and, being a party to these particulars, purchase stock from certain companies.'

'Under a false name.'

'That goes without saying.'

'Ah, Nash, I wish you would not.'

'Your objection is noted.'

'Is the Neela Company one of these investments? Don't you retain some sort of scruple about the things that Hayle and Gifford get up to?'

'Get up to? Do you know what Neela makes? Nothing but harmless glass. Bottles and tumblers and covers for lanterns.'

'If it is harmless, why is the company so secretive?'

'Because it also makes prototypes of glazing from new recipes.' Nash turned a sorrowful gaze on me. 'It pains me that you are not the lively girl you once were. You seem no longer ripe for any frolic and it is a shame.'

I thought Nash was about to remonstrate with me, as he approached me, but instead he took me by the arms and brought me gently to my feet.

'My poor, Carey,' he said softly. 'You are not yourself, are you? You are quite sapped, I can see that. It is the difficult recent times that have worn you down. What a beast I am not to have taken better care of you.'

His tender tone struck a chord in me that vibrated deeply in my heart. He sounded, I realised, like a fond parent re-assuring a child.

'You know, Parliament is nearly at an end,' he said, 'and will not strike up again for several weeks. Why don't we make a little trip to Paris? I think that is what you need – a respite from your cares.' Nash took my chin in his hand and tilted my face towards his. 'I should very much like to rise above my limitations, which are many, as you have not failed to notice. I very much wish to convince you that I am doing my best to bring us forward, you and me. Do you see that, my love?'

'Yes,' I said. 'I do know it.'

Nash smiled and said, 'Now let me write my piece while you go to bed. You look in need of rest.'

I went upstairs and undressed and stretched out beneath

the bedclothes. But still I could not sleep. It was very warm in the chamber and I got up to open the casement. As I stood at the window, I heard the distant thump of a door closing and then Nash appeared below in the street in the pool of light thrown by the lamp at the door. He clapped his hat to his head and walked away. I ought to have asked him if he had sold the dossier to Sir Rollo, but I was too afraid of what the answer might be and what it might mean: that Nash was involved in a bad business. Or was it Martenson who was playing a deep game, sowing seeds of mistrust? He had succeeded at putting me into a state of confusion, and I did not like it.

A faint breath of air wafted through the window. I let my thoughts drift to the cool of the mornings at Durand Gardens and the sensation of the soft grass under my bare feet as I ran down the avenues of trees. It was so luxuriant it needed to be mown every few days. Blackbirds sang in the trees and I would feel on my face a gentle breeze. Later, the breeze would drop and the day would sink under the heaviness of summer heat and sometimes a slow grey storm would break.

The sun was beating down as I arrived at Wild Street. The street runs on a north–south aspect, west of Lincoln's Inn Fields, and its apartments are mainly rented by clerks and pupils at the nearby Inns of Court. On a corner, an Italian *pâtissier* had set up a cart piled with ice and was selling ice creams in cone-shaped casings to parched passers-by. There are a couple of dozen identical houses in the street, but it did

not take me long to discover where Martenson lodged —
because I saw a tall, lanky figure leave one of the houses and
head north on the western side of the street. I recognised his
coat and hat. I was shielded by my paper parasol and he did
not so much as glance my way. I followed him at once and
presently the dome and mansard roof of the British Museum
came into view. I hung back as I watched Martenson pause
to show a ticket to the porter at the gatehouse. As soon as he
entered the gardens of the museum, I approached the porter
and obtained a ticket for myself. I passed through the gates
and stood at the head of a grand central promenade embraced
by tight parterres. The great blocky mansion that houses the
museum was situated at the far end. Numbers of visitors
strolled in the sunlight, admiring the sculptures. I have often
been to the gardens at the rear of the house. Martenson was
headed there, I thought, as I caught sight of his tall figure
striding among the people on the circumferential walk.

I set off in his wake, keeping my distance. Martenson had
a sense of purpose about him. He crossed the lawn and followed a path through the arboretum nearly to its edge, where
it gives way to fields that stretch north towards the wooded
hills of Hampstead and Highgate. I too followed on a path
that wound among the trees and sat down upon a bench. I
saw Martenson greet another gentleman, rather shorter in
stature, who came forward to meet him. I was able to keep
Martenson and his companion in view while remaining
concealed among the trees. They remained deep in conversation for ten or fifteen minutes and then Martenson's

companion took his leave. He passed by me in a hurry. With one hand on his hip and the other dangling his hat, Martenson watched him go. He gave the impression of a man who was greatly preoccupied. At once, I sprang up from my seat. When I called his name, he turned slowly to face me in a guarded way.

'Good afternoon, sir,' I said.

Blondish stubble glinted on Martenson's face. He looked at me with remote, greenish eyes and made no move to utter a greeting. He stared at me as if absorbed in some overwhelming thought. Then he said, 'Are you the daughter of Daniel Ravine?'

I stared at him, jolted by the question and confounded by Martenson's manner, which seemed almost hostile. 'Yes,' I stammered. 'Why do you ask me that? Did you know my father?'

'Of course I know him.' His tone was withering. 'He was the superintendent of Hayle's research station.'

'But he is dead!' I cried.

Martenson's expression tightened. 'What kind of fool do you take me for?'

He turned on his heel and strode away.

I stood for a minute in stunned silence, trying to take in the import of the words: I *know* him.

I ran after Martenson and seized his arm. He shook himself free of me as though I were something noxious. Passers-by turned to stare, but I did not heed them.

'Is he alive?' I cried.

Martenson frowned.

'Please, tell me! I had thought that he was dead.'

He gave me a look of great scepticism. 'Forgive me if I do not believe you. You, your father, Oliver Nash, Rollo Hayle – you are all very much enmeshed.'

'But where is he?'

He looked at me with a cold eye and walked off without a word.

My knees suddenly felt weak and I groped my way on to one of the stone benches that lined the path. There was such a racket in my head.

My father was alive.

Chapter 13

Called to an Accident

August the 22nd, 1776

I jumped at the sound of a bell. It was a signal that the gardens were about to close for the evening. I shook myself out of my daze and hurried after Martenson, desperate to speak to him. My emotions were in a maelstrom. The joy that had gushed up at hearing the news that my father was alive was tempered by confusion. Why had Papa failed to contact me in all these years? Had every one of the letters miscarried — or did he not want me? I could not see Martenson among the visitors leaving the grounds of the museum, but my mind spun with questions. Martenson said that my father had worked for Sir Rollo Hayle — as had Nash. I had learned from Lieutenant Spencer that Nash had been in Patna on Sir Rollo Hayle's business. My heart broke at the thought that he might have known that my father was alive — but, no, he would never have kept something so momentous from me. Such a thing was impossible. Nash can be cavalier, but he is not cruel. I went to Wild Street straight away. At Martenson's house, my knock was answered by a small maid with a pallid face and a limp cap. I said I wished to present my compliments to Dr Martenson and to wait upon him as a matter of importance. The maid seemed to struggle with the request, then she said, 'I am not his servant, ma'am. Besides, he is not at home.' And she shut the door in my face. I knocked again and when, after a long wait, the maid opened the door, I said that I should like to leave a note for Dr Martenson.

I feared that he might ignore my entreaty, but to my relief a messenger arrived at Hood Street at about eight that evening and delivered a reply from him:

> *My dear Mrs Nash,*
> *I can very easily imagine the very great emotion that my news must have given you. It took me by surprise, too. I had only just then learned of it. You may call upon me at your convenience and I will tell you what I can. Believe me to be at all times,*
> *Yours very faithfully,*
> *A.M.*

The sun was beginning to sink as I walked to Wild Street, but I cared nothing for the impropriety of visiting Martenson in his rooms after dark, so anxious was I to discover news of my father.

The same maid answered my knock, but before she could enter into a negotiation with me, Martenson appeared at her back and said, 'Thank you, Annie. Ask the lady to come in.'

Annie allowed herself a smirk. She dropped an ironic curtsy before Martenson as she retreated, before disappearing through a door at the end of the hall. Martenson remained standing at a little distance, as if already about to see me out. He wore shirtsleeves, a green waistcoat, pale breeches and riding boots. He repaid my greeting with a nod and showed me into a room that would once have been the back parlour. I glimpsed through the open window the rear of the house behind. Martenson would have had to tilt his head to be able to see the sky and I wondered at the contrast between the cramped chamber and the vast landscapes he must be used to. A table spread with papers was set before the window to capture the scant light. A lamp burned as well. He squared off a stack of pages and picked up a quill and replaced it in its holder. The room was systematic in its layout and I guessed that Martenson must use it for a sleeping chamber as well as a parlour – there was a tall, narrow bureau next to the fireplace and a divan that was probably his bed. A single armchair was placed beside the divan and Martenson invited me to sit down in it. He was polite enough to don his coat and tie his stock, although the temperature was very warm.

'I will attempt to fetch you tea,' he said, 'although Annie is hard to persuade to almost any task.'

I waved his offer away. 'I do not require refreshment.'

'I am afraid that I gave you a shock this afternoon.'

'It is your forte. Each occasion I encounter you is more jarring than the last. I really did not know that my father was alive, you know. I still find it hard to accept. My letters to him were never answered and I could draw no other conclusion than to believe him dead.'

Martenson nodded. He said, 'It amazed me to discover that you are Daniel Ravine's daughter. Bellamy had just informed me of the fact, when you detained me.'

'Who is Bellamy?'

'The man you observed with me at the museum's gardens. He is a high constable at a rotation house in Whitechapel and an investigator on behalf of the government. You were not at the museum by chance, I take it, although I can't imagine how you knew about my meeting with Bellamy.'

'I did not know of it. I happened to see you make your way to the museum and I wished to speak to you. But what does this Bellamy want with me? Why is he searching out my history?' My voice trembled. I felt sickened at the thought of an investigator poring over the intimate details of my life.

'Because you are the wife of Oliver Nash, who sold a dossier to Hayle that Bellamy and his superiors would have preferred to have brought out into the open.'

'Why is the dossier so important?'

'That is a long story.'

'But you think I am a party to the transaction that my husband is supposed to have made.'

'I do not know what to think of you.' Martenson's voice was low.

I could feel a damp band of sweat around my forehead. 'May I remove my hat? It's awfully hot. And please do not swelter in your coat on my account.'

I unpinned my hat and set it on the divan, while Martenson put off his coat and hung it on a peg behind the door.

There were no ornaments in the room, nothing personal to give away anything about his life. I said, 'There is so very little that I understand and so very much that I should like to ask you, Dr Martenson. I do not know why you should be suspicious of me, but please believe my sincerity when I say that I have not heard from my father since he wrote to tell me of my mother's death in Calcutta ten years ago. I sent countless letters to the horticultural committee of the East India Company in Calcutta, which yielded nothing, and eventually I was forced to accept that I would never know what happened to him. I beg you to tell me everything you can.'

Martenson sat down on the wooden chair by the table and regarded me thoughtfully. After a pause, he said, 'I met Daniel Ravine only two or three times and that was six, no, seven years ago.' He frowned in the direction of the empty fireplace. He said, 'Perhaps you know that the poppy is a plant that is easily injured by all kinds of diseases and insects. One can try to protect it by means of acrid waters and caustic powders, but when you are cultivating hundreds of acres of poppies as a singular crop, as the Company had begun to do at Patna, stronger countermeasures are called for.'

'Opium poppies, you mean.'

'Yes. About eight years ago, the members of the horticulture committee at the Company Bagh decided that it was a matter of urgency to discover a poison lethal to the animacules that burrow into the poppy.'

'What is the Company Bagh?'

'It is the East India Company's centre of administration at Bankipore in Patna. Hayle owned a big research station near Patna at that time. It was one of his many enterprises. The station is called Lalatola and Daniel Ravine ran it. Ravine was said to have a talent for curious and difficult horticultural operations.'

'That sounds very much like my father, but I did not know that Sir Rollo was a botanical man.'

'His fingers are sunk in many pies, Mrs Nash. He was originally a chemist and a talented one. He studied with Richard Mayer in Berlin.'

'You do not like him, I gather.'

'I always thought him a man driven by a dangerous animus of envy and despair, but in Patna no one else shared my opinion of him. Bengal society tended to revel in his inexhaustible supply of champagne. If he collected his revenues by force or inspired his tenants with fear, that was no concern of theirs. Anyway, Hayle and Ravine began to experiment with fumigants that might protect the poppies. One afternoon, a messenger came to the cantonment asking me to attend an accident at Lalatola. Ravine had suffered burns from a spilled lamp, I was told. I remember thinking it odd that a messenger had come all the way to Dinapore when other doctors were closer to hand, at Bankipore and Kumrahar.'

'Why, what did it signify to you?'

'That Ravine's injury was considered a matter for the military establishment.'

'Perhaps he did not trust the reputation of doctors who were closer.'

'It is true that there are some medical men who are not fit for the duties they undertake.' There was a hollow tone to Martenson's voice as he said this and it made me think that there was a story behind it.

'Was my father very badly injured?'

'When I reached Lalatola, I found Ravine lying on a chaise in a parlour. I noticed at once that his eyes were weeping, one of them copiously. He was not pleased to see me and blamed his steward for making more of the accident than it warranted. He said that he had only brushed against a lighted lamp, which had capsized and burned him; but when I examined his arm, I saw a pattern of blisters that suggested he had flung up a hand to defend himself from a splash of burning droplets. I questioned him about the sight in his left eye, whether he could distinguish any object before it. He said that a mote of dust had inflamed it and that he could bear the irritation without complaint.'

I stared at Martenson as he spoke. It was incredible that he carried in his head images of my father, the only images I had had of him in years. My picture of Papa, though, was of the vital man of my childhood, his bright eyes, his ready smile. I could not imagine him in any way debilitated.

'One could see, however,' Martenson continued, 'that Ravine's injuries were more extensive than contact with burning lamp oil would suggest. He was unable to rise from the chaise and he had difficulty speaking. He also had severe photophobia. I remember I asked a servant to lift one of the Venetian blinds in order to examine the burns and Ravine could hardly bear the sudden admission of light. I am sorry, Mrs Nash, it must be distressing for you to hear this.'

'No, tell me everything.'

'Ravine refused to respond to any questions, so after I had dressed the burns, I went to speak to the servants. I managed to piece together what had occurred from the gardeners and water carriers who were near the laboratory where Ravine had been at work. A combustion must have taken place, obviously of some mordacious compound, which had exploded and showered Ravine with burning liquid. I thought it likely to have released an acrid miasma, too, that had injured his eyes. Against Ravine's wishes, I stayed overnight at Lalatola so that I could bathe the eye every few hours. However, the left eye continued to worsen. I cleaned it as best I could, but then Hayle returned and ordered me from the station.

'Naturally, it puzzled me that Ravine would risk losing an eye rather than seek treatment. At Dinapore, I discussed the case with my superior, Surgeon-Major Douglas, and he assured me that he would dispatch another physician to Lalatola. I do not believe now that he did so. A few days after my conversation with Major Douglas, I received marching orders and was sent on detachment to Allahabad. I was away from Patna for six months. On my return, I found that Ravine had indeed lost sight in his left eye and that he walked with a limp.'

I recalled how nimble he had once been, how he would shimmy in a trice to the top of ladders, where he trained creepers on high poles and bound them into shapes with rods and pegs. I said, 'My father has shown extraordinary loyalty to Sir Rollo, then.'

'He has been well compensated for it. These days, since Hayle left Bengal, Ravine lives on his own estate. That is a story in itself. Neither Hayle's estate nor Ravine's has been come by legitimately, but the chain of ownership is a tangle that none of the government's auditors has been able to pick apart.'

'Is my father's estate in Patna?'

'No, he has retreated downriver, near a town called Murshidabad. The name of the estate is Kaligar,' Martenson said.

As the fact of my father's existence sank in, I was devastated by the realisation that he had chosen to estrange himself from me. Perhaps Martenson understood what had caused my stricken expression, because he said, 'May I venture to say, Mrs Nash, that you would not find many opportunities at Kaligar.'

'Have you been there?'

'No, but I am told that Ravine lives in a very reclusive manner. His servants come and go. I don't think there is anything happy about the place.'

'Is he married?'

'No, not married.'

'But he has a woman.'

Martenson nodded.

'I can hardly believe it. He has been alive all this time.'

'I am sorry, Mrs Nash,' Martenson said simply.

'Why are you speaking to an investigator? Has my father done something wrong?'

'He has a principal connection to the cases of poisoning that I reported on.'

'Because he worked for Sir Rollo?'

'Yes. The first poisoning occurred at the army hospital in Dinapore during a trial of a hybrid plant that had been raised at Hayle's station. I was the attending physician. In the course of the trial, one of the volunteers died, a gunner named James Kinch. I can still see him slouching into the ward room in a blue coat, and a forage cap turned around on his head.'

Martenson described to me Kinch's collapse and Hayle's intransigence when Martenson tried to take remedial action; and he stated his belief that Kinch's death was suspicious. I still hesitated to tell him that I had read the reports. Despite my desire to understand everything about their genesis, I wished to keep my distance, personally, from them, especially now that I knew they were under the scrutiny of investigators. I said, 'I don't understand how my husband came to be in possesion of these reports and why Hayle would want them. Didn't he have copies of his own?'

'No. My original reports were notarised by the magistrate at the Company Bagh and stored in the archive, as was usual. But no copies were made and sent out, which was not usual. I made my own personal copy of each report, but they were stolen from my house. Then the dossier with the original reports disappeared from the archive at the courthouse. Oliver Nash was in and out of the archive at the time, engaged on legal work for Hayle. I think he suspected that the dossier might be useful to him as a source of income. He would have known there was something odd about these cases.'

I put my fingers to my temples. 'It is so extraordinary to hear you speak of my husband so casually as a thief and a blackmailer. You must know that it is painful and insulting to hear such allegations.'

'I understand,' Martenson said gravely, 'but you asked me to tell you what I know.'

I nodded with a sigh. 'Please go on. Tell me what was odd about the cases.'

'Well, after I had submitted the first report, I expected there to be an inquest or an inquiry into Kinch's death. Usually, the Company is punctilious about these things. I went away on an expedition and, when I returned to Patna many months later, I discovered that no inquest had taken place and that my report had been filed and dismissed by the magistrate. Naturally, I began to ask questions. Medical trials, such as the one in which Kinch died, are almost always conducted under the auspices of the East India Company's horticultural or medical committees in Bengal. Instead, that particular trial was administered by a defence research committee. I thought such a thing was telling and raised the matter with my former commanding officer, Major Douglas. My attending Hayle's *Ammannia* trial had been my last duty for the army, you see. I had already decided to resign my commission in order to cultivate medicinal plants. However, Major Douglas urged me to leave the matter of the trial alone. I confess I was disposed to heed his advice, because by that time I had a won a contract to raise an experimental crop of hybrids at a small research station near the Company Bagh, and I did not want to jeopardise it. Making hybrids is a slow business, though, and the Company expected me to undertake other botanical tasks in the meantime. I was assigned to find specimens of grass that might be useful as a source of paper, and that is how I came to find myself in the Rajmahal Hills early in seventy-three.'

It had grown dark in the room. Martenson stood up and lit the tapers on the table and the lamp on the chimneypiece. He said, 'Are you sure that I cannot offer you something? Will you take a refreshment?'

He poured each of us a small measure of Madeira and added a splash of cordial water. I asked him to tell me what Rajmahal was like.

'It is an area beyond the rule of law,' he replied. 'Tribal people have always lived in its jungle, and bandits, but in the last ten years, numbers of people with grievances have moved there, too – militant holy men and dispossessed overlords, driven out from other places by the army. They greet demands for rent and taxes with eye gougings and beheadings. The Company's troops are stretched to deal with them. And there was a bandit queen named Rani Savriti, who was a thorn in the Company's side. Her clan had once ruled the region and exacted revenues from the inhabitants, but when the Company took over Bengal, the rani was ordered to give up her land and to remit much of her income to the Company. She was violent and resentful as a result. She had burned down a hill station and her men had seen off tax collectors and warrant servers and the troops accompanying them. No one could touch her, it seemed.'

'How could the Company send you to such a dangerous place to look for grass?' I asked. 'That seems unconscionable to me.'

'The *raison d'être* for the research stations in India is to find economic plants and that can hardly be done without facing danger. In any case, I had been to Rajmahal before and knew how to conduct myself. I had a little of the local languages. I expect that is why the horticulture committee chose me to go. Had Hayle, and the army, known about my assignment, though, I do not doubt that they would have done everything in their power to prevent it.

'The last leg of my journey in Rajmahal was to pass across a place called Shukra Hill. I stopped at a village of my acquaintance to hire bearers, but the headman refused my request outright. Shukra Hill, he said, was under the spell of a powerful evil eye. These are people, you understand, Mrs Nash, who worship spirits and believe in magic. It seemed that, several nights before, a woodcutter who had been gathering fuel on Shukra Hill, had seen lights in the sky, which he interpreted as spirits or souls departing the bodies of their hosts. The next morning, he arrived at a clearing and found fifty corpses. He identified them as Rani Savriti's men.

'Eventually, after a great deal of persuasion, I saw the scene for myself. The men were lying by their bivouacs, as if cut down unawares. Wild beasts had torn apart many of the carcases, but the weapons and the remains of their dress suggested that they were indeed bandits and probably followers of Rani Savriti.'

'Why did the villagers attribute the attack to an evil eye and not human marauders?'

'They could not believe that such men could have been caught off guard by mere humans, especially en masse. These were hardened fighters and yet they had not even drawn their weapons. I would have made a report on the incident as a matter of course, but I was even more inclined to do so because of similarities in appearance between the bandits' corpses and that of the gunner at Dinapore who had been poisoned during the medical trial. The bandits had died in attitudes of contortion and their skin showed evidence of cyanosis. They had suffocated, in other words, just like Kinch.'

'But there must be many poisons that produce a similar result.'

'A point that was also made by the magistrate at Bankipore when he read my Rajmahal report. He interpreted the scene as a case of collective palsy, which is not uncommon in Bengal. There are always unscrupulous grain dealers around, selling adulterated pulses to boost their profits. They tend to operate in areas, like Rajmahal, that lack settled agriculture. They have been known to bulk out quality *dal* with a cattle feed that is lethal if ingested in large quantities. According to the magistrate, this was a likely explanation for the deaths on Shukra Hill – the victims were mass casualties of accidental food poisoning. That was his verdict. My report was notarised and filed in the dossier in the archives of the courthouse at Bankipore, along with the earlier report.'

'Could the magistrate have been correct? After all, you can only speculate that there was a connection between the cases.'

Martenson smiled. I was surprised to see how much the smile transformed his face, making him seem pleasing in appearance. He said, 'You are right, of course. It's all speculation.'

'What about the bandit queen? Did she avenge the loss of her men?'

'That is strange, too, because she is of a character to fight to the bitter end for what she considers to be her territory. And yet she simply disappeared, never to be heard from again.'

'The Company must have been glad to be rid of her.'

'You would think so, wouldn't you? But nothing was broadcast in Bengal about the disappearance of the rani, perhaps presumed dead, nor about the discovery of slain bandits. That puzzled me, because there had been many attempts in the past to bring her under arrest. The deaths of her mercenaries, by whatever means, ought to have been a victory.

The news that fifty armed men in Rani Savriti's stronghold had poisoned themselves with bad *dal* should have been toasted high and long in the British establishment, but not a word of it was mentioned. Not long afterwards, the investigators arrived, men sent from Westminster, and everyone was preoccupied by that.'

I knew that the East India Company had been clinging on to solvency by the skin of its teeth. Parliament had agreed to pay off its debts, but in return the Company had been obliged to submit every aspect of its governance in India to auditors. 'When Lord North's party came to government, it decided to take exception to the Company's commercial aberrations.'

'Exactly, Mrs Nash. The prospect of auditors caused a commotion in the Bengal establishment. There was a rush to assemble teams of attorneys; there were sudden departures into exile. At that moment, the dossier vanished.'

Chapter 14

Spirits in the Sky

August the 22nd, 1776

The paving stones still smelled of the day's heat and there was a faint over-ripe tang of orange peels discarded in the gutter as Martenson and I walked in the direction of Hood Street. A large waxy moon hung above us and the balmy temperature had brought more people than usual outdoors. It was the supper hour. There were pie sellers out and about and servants hurrying by with pots from the cook shops. Martenson had offered to see me home, but we stopped at a teahouse in order to conclude our conversation. I was blunt with Martenson about my intention to relay to Nash the substance of my evening. How could I not, when there were questions that I needed to ask my husband? Martenson was unperturbed by this and said it was a matter of importance that everything connected with Sir Rollo Hayle should come out into the open. He even suggested that he should enter the house at Hood Street to speak to Nash, with the aim of recruiting him to give a statement to the investigator, Bellamy. I dissuaded him from the notion – at this juncture, at least – for I feared that Nash might call the watch on Martenson and I did not think the doctor deserved such a fate.

As we waited for the serving girl to bring our tea, Martenson was silent, as if gathering his thoughts. At length he said, 'I believe that the poisonings at Dinapore and Rajmahal are linked to a dark enterprise that had been put in train at Patna and concealed behind the activities of Hayle's and Gifford's provisioning companies, chiefly the Bengal Glass Company. Bengal Glass has a subsidiary, which manufactures something rather more sinister than plates and glasses.'

I could guess the name of the subsidiary, but I asked Martenson to tell it to me.

'Neela,' he said. 'They call it the Neela Company.'

'That is a strange word.'

'It means "blue" in Hindi. *Śiba mata nīla*. The skin of the dead men was blue, like the god Shiva. And the souls of the dead men were blue.'

'The spirits in the sky?'

Martenson nodded.

Blue. What was it about the colour blue that I knew, but could not quite retrieve from my mind?

'What does the Neela Company produce?' I asked. Something told me that it was not new recipes for glazing, as Nash had suggested.

Martenson said, 'It manufactures a poison.'

'The poison that killed the gunner and the bandits.'

'I believe so, yes. I do not know what it is exactly, but it dispatches people horribly and efficiently. I call it the blue agent. I think that this agent was developed at Hayle's research station at Lalatola. It probably originated as an antagonist against pests and then Hayle came to discover that it was lethal to human beings as well, and saw its potential.'

'My father was its first casualty.'

'In its early stages. I believe that Kinch's poisoning proved the toxin's efficacy and that the deaths of Rani Savriti's men at Rajmahal proved that it could be deployed in the field to inflict multiple lethal casualties. I do not know how that was done, though, and there are no witnesses to it.' He looked at me in a steady way. He could tell that I was trying to assess him. He had a cerebral presence that made it difficult to dismiss his theories about the dossier as overwrought.

'I investigated the record at the Grand Magazine at Patna,' he went on, 'which is the entity that signs out every army detachment sent on a sortie. The clerks of the Magazine issue weapons and ammunition. I could not find evidence of any detachment having been deployed to Rajmahal around the time of the deaths of the bandits. It does not mean that such a thing could not have occurred, but there is no history of it. I believe that, after the success of that mission, a secret committee of the Board of Ordnance commissioned a limited amount of the blue agent to be manufactured, presumably for military use.'

'What is the Board of Ordnance?'

'It convenes in London and has overall responsibility for the supply of armaments and ammunition to British troops, but it operates independently of the War Office.'

'So, the reports are important because they point to the existence of this sinister agent.'

'Yes. Since they are notarised with the Company stamp, it is at least an acknowledgement that these unexplained deaths took place and that the Company knew about them.'

'What about the members of the committee that commissioned Sir Rollo's trial? Could you have asked any of them what they knew?'

'I found that the members of the defence research committee, save for Hayle, very quickly dispersed after the trial and within months were either dead or redeployed to distant places that put them beyond reach. I suppose it could be a coincidence, but I do not think so.'

I remembered, then, the footnote that had caught my eye in Martenson's first report. Even as a disinterested reader, I had thought it odd that all of the committee members had been retired or removed or were deceased.

Martenson sighed. 'Of course, I wondered often if I had conceived a conspiracy where none existed. But recently I learned that I was not the only person who suspected Hayle and Gifford of wrongdoing. Gabriel Bellamy, the gentleman you saw me with at the museum, was one of the auditors sent to Patna from Westminster. Since he returned from there, he has investigated the Neela Company, but his determination to raise a case against it has been thwarted at every turn by Casserly and his connections. Some of those men I pointed out to you at Hayle's house. I assume that they, like Casserly, are investors in the blue agent. Fortunately for Bellamy, the political winds are beginning to shift and Casserly's enemies have increased. An exposure of the Neela Company

and its principals would serve their ends very well.' Martenson leaned forward and fixed me with a gaze that was so
intense, I nearly flinched. 'Would you agree to meet with
Bellamy, Mrs Nash?'

'But, how can I be of assistance to him?'

'It would help his case if Mr Nash would testify to the
existence of the dossier.'

'And he wants me to persuade Nash to do so.'

'He expressed that hope to me, yes.'

'It is very unlikely that my husband would agree to such a
thing. Even if he were willing to sign an affidavit, surely
people like Casserly and Hayle have too much influence for
a case ever to come to trial.'

'They have their enemies in government who think a trial
might serve very well as a reminder to Company servants
that no one may operate beyond the jurisdiction of English
law. They are ripe for making an example of. You see, Mrs
Nash, I keep nothing from you.' Martenson had an uncommon plausibility, I must admit.

I said, 'You are asking me, and Nash, to kill the golden
goose that keeps us alive. Hayle and Gifford are his patrons.
If a scandal blows up and Nash's involvement is exposed,
don't you see that he would be alienated from society and his
sources of income?'

'But you do not value money over morals, do you, Mrs
Nash?'

He said this with such certainty that it made me smile.

I said, 'I do not know if I care to toil in some moral

universe where I must choose the correct course of action at the expense of my comfort. Perhaps I prefer to be selfish. Perhaps I prefer to dance and drink and dress in pretty clothes and not care about anything.'

I could feel his steady gaze on me. He said, 'Or perhaps you have not yet become reconciled to your true nature.'

'You are very presumptuous.'

'I remark what I see.' He signalled to the serving girl and left coins on the table for our tea.

'Where does the advantage lie for you,' I asked, 'in exposing the existence of this agent?'

'The advantage is that I will be able to answer to my conscience. Hayle is expecting to take a seat in Parliament, furnished for him by Casserly's rotten borough, but if he is impeached for corruption, that will not happen. I believe that, if he gains political influence, the country will suffer for it. He is a man who will always press for war and conquest, and he will not care how it is achieved. He is not someone who takes a long view of consequences. And, in addition, I will admit that I want my contract reinstated at Bankipore.'

We came out into the street. It was one of those beautiful August nights when one feels the thrill of summer and its lifting of cares. As we walked towards Holborn, I asked Martenson what had happened to his experimental crop.

'After I wrote the second report on the poisonings at Rajmahal, Hayle was determined to oust me from the district, just as he had seen off everyone on the committee that had commissioned the trial. He did all he could to hinder my work and eventually he succeeded. It was destroyed by order of the Company magistrate at Bankipore. The operation of my own conceit played a part in it. A lawyer came to serve a writ on me of a charge trumped up by Hayle. Like a fool, I took a swing at the server and I was arrested and put in jail. I pleaded to be released to my fields while I was waiting to go before the magistrate. The timing of my harvest was critical. But the court would not soften the matter. My contract was rescinded and, by the time I was set at liberty, the crop had been ploughed under on the Magistrate's orders.'

We had reached Hood Street. We stopped outside the Eclipse tavern and Martenson said he would watch me into the house. He asked me to inform him as soon as I could concerning the result of my discussion with Nash.

I said, 'You ought to prepare yourself for disappointment, Dr Martenson.'

'If Nash needs further convincing that his masters are about to fall, I invite you both to meet with Mr Bellamy in short order. I will send you a note tomorrow to arrange a time.'

Just before I turned away, I said, 'What is the name, again, of the place where my father lives?'

'Murshidabad, a week's journey upriver from Calcutta.'

'Murshidabad,' I repeated.

'It is the city where the Nawab of Bengal usually resides. Will you go there, do you think?'

'I do not know.'

He smiled at me and said, 'Good night.'

As he spoke these brief words, I felt an odd lurch inside me, as if something indefinable had altered. It was with a sort of wariness that I offered him my thanks, and went away to my house, because I certainly did not wish to encourage in myself any feeling that Martenson could be meaningful to me.

As I entered the hall, I encountered Jane with a broom, sweeping on to a sheet of newspaper pieces of china. The casualty was one of my porcelain teacups. 'I don't know why they make 'em so brittle ma'am.' She eyed the shattered cup accusingly. 'They're always breaking, not like proper English ware.'

'It's just that you don't know how to handle them,' I said. 'You need to adjust yourself to the situation, not the other way round. It's not the porcelain's job to figure how to be held by clumsy hands.'

'I am sure I do not know what you mean,' she said. 'The master is at the Eclipse, by the way.'

I walked up to my parlour and unpinned my hat. I sat down and let a consideration of my father wash through my thoughts. I was in search of a degree of understanding about the severance that had occurred between us. I speculated that sorrow had infected his mind and that, without my mother by his side, he had been overcome by indifference and let himself slide into work and associations that were corrupt. I imagined that he could not bear to have the daughter who had been so devoted to him witness his decline; it was preferable to nurture an estrangement.

I stood up again and repinned my hat. I made my way

downstairs preoccupied still by thoughts of Papa. I was all that he had left of his family and, as long as we did not meet, he could believe that he was still admired as the god I had taken him for when I was a child. Such were the projections with which I comforted myself as I crossed the cobbles towards the Eclipse.

The alewife greeted me as I entered the tavern and, with an upward jerk of her chin, indicated that Nash was above. I climbed the stairs and scanned the noisy room with its fug of smoke and found him at a table near the chimney, playing dominoes. As he looked up to wave his cane at the serving girl, he caught sight of me. He stood up with a bow, kissed my hand and offered me a seat.

He pushed his game to one side as I sat down, and said with a grin, 'You will be delighted to hear that arrangements for our tour proceed. I have ordered two enormously smart trunks, nicely brass-bound, and have already written to rent an apartment near the Sorbonne.'

'Nash,' I said without preamble, 'I have learned that my father is alive.'

'How can that be?!' Nash cried in surprise. 'Where is he?'

'In Bengal. He lives on an estate near a place called Murshidabad.' I reached out and took hold of Nash's hand. 'My father has been alive all these years. And, hardly less extraordinary, he was contracted to Sir Rollo Hayle.'

'Blast my blood,' Nash said thickly, 'how did you discover such a thing?'

'Dr Martenson told me.'

'Martenson.' Nash's face darkened. 'There will be little truth in anything that he has to say. Damn that blackguard. I told him I would put an end to him if he did not leave us alone.'

'He did not seek me out, Nash. I encountered him by chance. Do you know how he discovered that I am Daniel Ravine's daughter? An investigator called Bellamy told him. Apparently, Bellamy was one of the auditors that Parliament sent to Bengal to investigate the affairs of the East India Company. Now he is working with the government to raise a case against the Neela Company and Sir Rollo and his associates. Bellamy believes that the Neela Company is connected with the poisonings at Dinapore and at Rajmahal. What ever did you do with those reports of Martenson's, Nash?'

Nash stiffened, then glowered at me. 'So, now you have become Martenson's proxy.'

I found myself mightily exasperated by Nash's evasiveness. 'Did you give them to Sir Rollo? If you did, no doubt Bellamy already knows it. He investigated my background because he is also investigating you.'

'So says Martenson, a delusional man who thinks himself the centre of a dozen conspiracies.'

'You don't have to take my word for it. I intend to meet Bellamy tomorrow—' For I had made up my mind in that instant that I wished to glean anything I could from the investigator that would throw light on the life my father had been living in India.

Nash raised a hand. 'Oh no you don't, lovely.'

'Nash, I implore you to come with me. If Bellamy confirms Martenson's contentions, then we are forewarned. You must extricate yourself from the affairs of Sir Rollo and Gifford. It may be that we could not have chosen a better time to absent ourselves from London.'

'I will not involve myself with such nonsense.'

'You may not have a choice. They will involve you, whether you like it or not, since you have made yourself Sir Rollo's cat's paw. Please listen to me. I am very afraid that, if you try to evade Bellamy, he will arrest you. You do not have the wherewithal of people like Lord Casserly and Sir Rollo to escape prison.'

Nash threw back his head and laughed. 'What a drama you have created. Nobody is going to prison, least of all me – and I certainly will not submit to be interrogated over nothing. Don't you realise the influence that Casserly has in government? Nothing that is investigated will ever come to consequences.'

'You must take this seriously.'

'Doesn't it occur to you that I spend my days with my ear to the ground in Westminster? Were there any hint of a move being made by a faction that might perturb me, I should have learned of it long before now. You must trust my experience, Carey.'

'Must I? My trust in you has wavered, since I have found so many of your assertions in recent times to be faulty. You never mentioned to me, for instance, that you had been in

Dinapore, working for Sir Rollo. Each time you dismiss my inquiries, I am confronted by another revelation more astonishing than the last. My father was the superintendent of Sir Rollo's research station in Patna. Now I wonder how it could be that you never heard of Daniel Ravine while you were there. It really does beggar belief, Nash.'

Nash seized my hands. 'Of all the rancorous, divisive things that Adam Martenson has done, this is the most reprehensible. He uses you to undercut me and raises your hopes about a subject that is painful to you. It is contemptible. He *has* undercut me, hasn't he? Whatever it is that he has told you, now you doubt me. I have my wastrel moments, I will admit. I am not the best man in the world. But it is extraordinary to me that you could think I would keep from you the fact of your father's being alive, when I have always known how you long to know his fate. God almighty, how heartless do you think I am?' Nash's expression was one of outrage. Then he shook his head, as if he could not believe the extent of my unreasonableness, and let go of my hands. He tipped a long draw of wine into his mouth and looked off towards the side. He said, 'How cruel of you to malign me so.'

'I do not say that you kept it from me, only that you might have encountered him without knowing his connection to me.'

Nash turned away from me and hung one arm over the back of his chair. His sigh gave the impression that dealing with me was a debilitating business. 'My God, Carey, you do see, don't you, how Martenson has preyed on your desperation?'

'But this is not about Martenson. It is about the Neela Company and Sir Rollo's clandestine breeding of a horrible poison that will kill people, without regard to the articles of war, and the determination of greedy men to profit from this wickedness.'

'While you were quizzing Spencer, you might have asked him about Martenson's obsession with narcotics. I do not suppose you know that Martenson travelled all the way to the mountains beyond the Bengal plain on an absolutely perilous quest and it was all in search of plants that cause visions and a derangement of the senses. The truth is, there is nothing rational about Martenson's actions. People say he was never in his right mind after the death of his wife. He was involved in an incident, I seem to remember, in which he tried to attack the doctor who attended Mrs Martenson. He presents himself as a rational man of science, but he is as combustible as a volcano.'

It startled me to hear that Martenson had been married and I could not help but reflect that I knew very little about the man.

'He is consumed by his hurts,' Nash went on. 'I believe that Martenson has come to fix the entirety of his bitterness on Sir Rollo, and by extension, it seems, on me. I do not think he can stand to see that I have a winsome paragon of a wife. Therefore, he begins to worm his way into your trust in a way that poisons the tender feelings that have always existed between you and me.'

My thoughts reeled between the polarised plausibilities of Nash and Martenson. I knew what it meant to be in a state of grief, and I could believe that it would throw a person out of his senses. And I knew that I must choose to believe that my husband had never met or even heard of Daniel Ravine during the time he had spent in Patna, because the alternative was too heartbreaking to contemplate.

Nash finished his wine in one draught and said, 'Tomorrow, I will begin to gather the letters of introduction and of credit we shall need to smooth our way in France. You ought to order a new riding coat, my love, and luggage, and look forward to our sojourn. We will unbend our minds and make ourselves a little easy. And I implore you to stay away from Martenson and his investigator. Please, Carey, will you do so, for the sake of our bond?'

He took my hand again and, when I nodded my assent, he pressed his lips to my fingers.

As we lay in bed that night, Nash pulled me close to him and rested my head on his chest. I leaned into him, longing to feel safe and nested, but, it was true that Martenson's revelations had infected my thoughts. They lurched along on waves of uncertainty and I did not feel fixed at all. Dear God, such somersaulting feelings! Among the last of the letters that I had written to my father, I had boasted of having five hundred pounds to my name. By then, I doubted that he was alive, but I evidently felt a need to reassure even his shade that he did not have to concern himself over me; and I think I wanted to impress him, as well, in the matter of my resource-fulness. But now, as I lay in Nash's arms, a sickening suspicion began to bloom in my mind. Surely Patna was a small place. How could Nash have avoided meeting his employer's right-hand man? And if my letters to my father had been forwarded to him from Calcutta, he might have mentioned to Nash that he had a daughter, nicely situated in London with guineas jingling in her pocket? Could Nash have known of the money I had accumulated? Such knowledge might have motivated him to contrive an introduction to me on his return to London. Certainly, he had been in sore need of funds. According to Mrs Spencer, he had arrived in Patna under the burden of a large gambling debt. It was horrifying to imagine that he could have engineered our marriage for the purpose of invei-gling my savings to his interest – but I forced myself to recall that, as soon as we were wed, scores of pounds evaporated almost immediately to pay mysterious debts. At the time I did not protest the swift disappearance of one promissory note after another, for I was in love and disposed to be boun-tiful. I felt that careless generosity showed me as a gay spirit, untrammelled by the banal concerns of the middling class. Such was the image of myself that I presented to Nash – and in that respect I was just as false as he.

But no, I could not believe that Nash had been so devious! It was shameful of me to harbour such suspicions of my hus-band. No, no, Nash had never known my father, of course he had not. He was my lover and my helpmeet. He could not be culpable of the deception that I feared.

As I lay awake, under the torment of these speculations, I seemed to see, in the dimness of the chamber, the wavering figure of my father vanish, as wraithlike as ever, down a long narrow road that returned him to the past. In that darkness, Lieutenant Spencer's strange words came to me once more. Blue falling lights. Unicorn.

Chapter 15

Green Medicine

August the 23rd, 1776

Before Nash left the house to go to the House of Commons, he urged me to visit the mantua maker and order travel apparel. Instead, I caught a post-chaise to Humerton. I had missed the morning stage, but there were always unlicensed conveyances to be had. I soon found myself squashed into a shabby chaise with four young maidservants. Their hair was tied up in ribbons and they were on their way to a fair at London Fields. I was obliged to disembark with them in Hackney, since the chaise would go no further, and so I looped up my petticoats, the easier to stride, and walked on. As I reached Marsh Lane, I saw a pair of harriers swooping low over the flat open fields in search of prey, and I envied them their lazy gliding on the updraughts. How pleasant it would be to float on breezy currents and look down on everything with detachment, instead of feeling, as Martenson had put it, enmeshed, without any idea what purpose this embroiling in events would achieve. Presently, the Spencers' cottage hived into view. A waggon stood in the lane and two brawny men in shirtsleeves were manhandling a trunk into its tray. They looked up with blank expressions as I approached, yet there was something about them that made me feel wary. The door of the cottage stood open and I glimpsed the figure of Mrs Spencer hanging back in that all-purpose front room. She preferred not to notice me, that much was obvious. I raised a hand against the sharp sun as I walked up the path and lingered at the low step before the door, until Mrs Spencer came reluctantly to the entrance. She did not respond to my greeting at first. Then she said, in a flat tone, 'My husband has gone to his rest.'

Ah, poor Felix Spencer. 'I am truly sorry to hear it,' I cried. 'My deepest consolations.' Spencer had been a good man and my sorrow was heartfelt.

'Well,' his wife replied, looking up at the sky, 'he has thrown off his burdens.' There was no sign of mourning crape on her. In fact, she was rather more handsomely attired than before, in a silk gown and a lace cap. As if reading my thoughts, she remarked, 'I should wear mourning if I was in town, but in the country it is not minded.'

She looked over my head and seemed to address the watchful porters, who were now standing in the path, hands on hips. 'I will be a few minutes,' she called. 'I must pay this chapwoman.' Mrs Spencer's gaze drifted from the porters to me and I understood her import – she was under the scrutiny of the men. It struck me that they might have been keepers rather than porters and I wondered who had sent them to pack up the Spencers' home.

'Thankee, ma'am.' I made the kind of bobbed curtsy one might expect from a peddler woman. I suppose I looked the part, with my free and easy dress and trailing hair and my hat in my hand.

'Come into the scullery, if you must,' Mrs Spencer muttered, and then, raising her voice in the direction of the porters, 'you may carry on with your hefting, sirs.' *Sirs*, she had called them. So, servants they were not.

As soon as I entered the cottage, I got a sense that the material situation of the lieutenant's family had improved. The boy and girl were sitting solemnly at the table, in new clothes, playing cards with a stiff, shiny pack. There was a bottle of French brandy on the shelf next to the hearth and a bonnet with glossy feathers sitting somewhat pridefully on a footstool. Mrs Spencer jerked her head at the youngsters and they turned over their hands of cards with grumbling sighs and stalked outside.

I said, 'It looks as though I have caught you just in time. You are going away.'

'I am surprised to see you return.' Her voice was kept low, as if we might be overheard.

'I wished to see Lieutenant Spencer again.'

'I am sorry you have had a journey into these wilds for nothing.'

'I esteemed your husband, Mrs Spencer. I knew he was dying, but I am still shocked to hear that he has gone. I offer you my sincere sympathy.' She acknowledged my statement with a tight nod. 'May I speak to you? It will take only a few minutes of your time.'

'I am sure there is nothing I can tell you.'

'It is a personal matter of importance to me.'

She turned without a word and I followed her down a narrow hall into a scullery. There was nothing in the scullery but a lump of sandstone soap sitting on the windowsill. Through a small, smudged pane I could make out the market gardens at the back of the house. The Spencers' boy was running across the rows at a tilt, like something thrown off course.

'Mrs Spencer, did you ever come across a man in Patna by the name of Daniel Ravine? He worked for Sir Rollo Hayle at a station called Lola . . . Lola-something.'

'Lalatola. I knew of the station, everyone did. It was a big house and there was an artificial lake in the grounds, I heard. Lowly garrison wives like me did not receive an invitation there. I never knew a man named Ravine.' She looked restlessly in the direction of the parlour. 'Pardon me, but some . . . some – relations – have paid to remove us to our new lodgings and we must not keep them waiting.' Her tone grew sharp. 'There have been merciless bills. I cannot manage on my own, you know.'

'Of course you can't. Is there some way that I could help?'

'No,' she said tersely. 'I do not need help from you. I . . . I have been given a pension.'

I said, 'But not from the army, I suppose.' Since her husband had been cashiered, neither he nor his dependents qualified for assistance.

Mrs Spencer stiffened and her reserve increased my curiosity about the source of the pension, but evidently, she did not intend to enlighten me. 'I am glad to hear that you have some support,' I said. 'Where are you going, may I ask?'

'No,' Mrs Spencer said, 'you may not ask. It would suit me if you would leave me now, Mrs Nash.'

'I beg a few more minutes of your time, please. You are the only person who can assist my inquiry. It is about a gentleman named Dr Adam Martenson.'

She looked surprised. 'Dr Martenson from Bengal?'

'He was an army surgeon at one time.'

'So he was. I remember him when he was at the cantonment in Dinapore. There was a terrible business with his wife and he went off to run a station at Bankipore.'

'Did people think well of him? Was he immoderate or ill-conditioned, perhaps?'

'He was a good surgeon, I recall. Reliable. He was anguished about his wife, I do remember.'

'She died suddenly, I understand.'

'She was poisoned by accident. While Dr Martenson was away from the cantonment, another of the doctors had pulverised pills for Mrs Martenson in a mortar. It turned out that arsenic had been beaten in the mortar previously and the doctor had not taken care to clean it. Carstairs, his name was. A great man for the bottle. Martenson came to the cantonment and searched Carstairs' house himself and discovered the contaminated mortar. But the colonel had already bundled Carstairs away up to Cawnpore as soon as he heard of Mrs Martenson's death, and a charge was never brought. And then Martenson ended up being the senior surgeon at Dinapore, undertaking Carstairs' work as well as his own.' Mrs Spencer shook her head. 'People will tell you that in matters of health women break down sooner than men. When it comes to grief, though, I find that men are the weaker vessels.'

'Lieutenant Spencer was awfully cut up about something, too, I think. Am I wrong about that?'

'Felix was prone to goodness, in spite of everything,' Mrs Spencer said, her eyes bright with unshed tears.

'That was apparent,' I said. 'I felt, when I saw him last, that something was weighing on his mind.'

Mrs Spencer glanced around at the small, cold room with a trapped look. 'Felix never wanted to come back to England, you know, but we had no choice. They made him forfeit his commission. Oh, Lord.' She cupped her forehead in her hands.

'Will you tell me why? I cannot imagine that he was not a sound soldier.'

She looked up. 'Believe me when I say that I do not know what went so very wrong. His last mission was early in seventy-three. He was sent out on a detachment, him and half a dozen grenadiers. It was in spring, before the rains came. They were asked to prove rockets. That is all he told me.'

'Did he go to Rajmahal?'

'I do not know. Soldiers are not accustomed to discuss their orders with their wives. He was away for about six weeks. After the grenadiers returned, they were all posted away from Dinapore for one reason or another and Felix was stripped of his commission without reimbursement.'

'And you could find no reason for it.'

Mrs Spencer opened her mouth and closed it again. Then she sighed, and said, 'He was drinking a great deal at the time. He had an altercation with his commanding officer. When they tossed him out they said it was because of "gross misbehaviour".'

'Your husband uttered a curious phrase to me just before we parted. He said, "Blue falling lights." Have you any idea what he meant?'

She shook her head.

'I wonder who it is that has given you the pension,' I said, making another attempt to coax the information from her.

'I must not say.' She pulled open the back door. 'Please go, Mrs Nash. I cannot speak more to you.' Her voice had dropped to a whisper. 'I have my children to think of. Leave by way of the stable. You can cut through to Broad Lane at the bottom of the field.'

I stepped across the threshold, and then turned back and said, low and quick, 'Only, will you tell me, Lieutenant Spencer's detachment went out in mufti, didn't it? The men were not in uniform.'

'I dare not say.' Mrs Spencer shut the door in my face.

Unicorn, Spencer had said to me, which had seemed to be nonsense at the time. But it was clear to me now that the word he had been groping for was *uniform*.

I made my way through the fields behind the Spencers' cottage, climbed a stile and followed a bridle path. It crossed an old ford, the water flowing at a trickle, like a dark damp ribbon. I did not mind to be out of the hurry of the town. I paused and tipped my head to the sky, where clouds were piled up like whipped cream. I stood still for some time and I gave thanks in my heart for being alive and I commended Lieutenant Spencer's soul to its rest. A breeze had set the hazel leaves fluttering and there was a lovely, tired, golden light splintering among the alders. I felt that events in my life were conspiring to turn me towards a calling, the nature of which was yet unknown to me. I knew that it existed, though, and I ought to move towards it.

At length, I reached a wide thoroughfare and made for the turnpike that I could see in the distance. I walked along to the accompaniment of axe blows. Arborists, up on ladders on either side of the lane, were cutting the overhanging branches of chestnut trees. As I walked on, Adam Martenson's name alighted in my mind like a dragonfly on a branch. I thought of the death of his wife and the suffering that must be bundled up inside him. Beneath my feet I felt a strange sensation, as if the earth had minutely shuddered. Perhaps it was the vibrations produced by the impact of the axes on the trees. I could imagine them travelling in waves down the trunks and along the roots in the ground.

At the turnpike, I paid for a seat on a cart heading towards the town. I was let off half a mile from Holborn and it was early in the evening before I reached Hood Street. I found that a note had arrived for me from Martenson, which Jane had left for me on my writing box. It was an invitation to accompany him the following day to meet Mr Gabriel Bellamy. It was with some agitation of mind that I left the house again. I did not lightly break my promise to Nash not to see Martenson or Bellamy, but necessity compelled me to go to Wild Street.

As Martenson showed me into his room, a puff of wind at the open window shivered the lamplight and stirred the papers on his table. Martenson leaned over and closed the window a little. There was a pronounced dustiness in the air and it felt like rain was on the way. I picked up a sheet of paper that had fallen to the floor and placed it on top of a pile. There was a single sentence written on it: *The bark is astringent, used in fevers to allay thirst, correct foul taste and—*

I said, 'I am sorry to have interrupted your work.'

'Not at all. It is a pleasure to see you, Mrs Nash.'

My fingertips brushed the page that I had replaced on the table. I said, 'Are you writing about Indian plants?'

'Yes. About medicinal plants and the method of their preparations.'

'I know a printer who is interested in this kind of work. I sometimes make botanical translations for him. Is this a catalogue of indigenous remedies?'

'I intend it to form the basis for a Bengal dispensatory. I believe it will be of great use. I am trying to convince the Company to have the remedies prepared under the sanction of the medical board and then sent to our hospitals in India for trial. Persuading the boards and committees is never easy, though.'

'If you left the business of the Neela Company alone, you might smooth the way for your own enterprise.'

'That is not a course that appeals to me.'

Martenson invited me to sit down. I sat on the divan and he turned around the chair that was at the table and took a seat facing me.

I said, 'Do you plan to return to India?'

'Yes, of course. It is my home. I was born there. As soon as I know that Bellamy has enough information about the Neela Company to bring his investigation forward into public scrutiny. The crop I raised in Bankipore was destroyed, but I will try again. I still have a contract to work for the horticultural committee and I want to keep it.'

'What was the crop that you cultivated?'

A few raindrops blew against the glazing and Martenson got up and closed the window completely. He sat down again with one leg crooked over the other.

'It was a hybrid of cannabis.'

'A narcotic hemp.'

Martenson nodded. 'Hayle passes off a poor variety of cannabis *indica* as his soma.'

'You warned me against it at the masquerade.'

'I warned you against the setting.'

'Indian hemp does not have a very wholesome reputation, I think. Why did you choose to grow it?' Everything about Martenson's character seemed to contradict Nash's assertion that he was susceptible to intoxication, but then, I would have claimed the same normalcy for myself, when the truth is that I barely pass a day or confront an attack of emotions without reaching for a drink to quell the inner panic that assails me.

'I would say that I was drawn to the plant. I was irresistibly attracted to it before I ever knew of its therapeutic potential. I first came across bundles of dried ganja leaves for sale at the stalls of the medicine dealers among the lanes of the chowk at Patna. I had just come out to Bengal as an assistant surgeon and I was already fascinated by native herbs and minerals. I asked what the leaves were used for and the vendor replied, "White man shaking." I did not understand what he meant and I was in want of the languages, at that time, to question him. When I inquired of my colleagues in the cantonment what they knew of ganja, I was told that it is a herb used for grossly sensual purposes by fakirs and other unsavoury characters and that it caused catalepsy and mental derangement.'

'You must have ingested the leaves yourself out of curiosity.'

'Of course. I drank it as a tincture, when it is known as bhang, and smoked it in a pipe. I was impressed by its ability to show everyday objects in a different and often much improved light. As my Bengali improved, and I was able to speak directly to native apothecaries, I learned that this green medicine, as they call it, has many medicating properties. It is much less addictive than opium and it has a way of cooling the body. I thought that the army of the Bengal establishment ought to find it very useful.'

'Do you use the leaves as a poultice to heal injuries?'

'You would think that most of an army surgeon's work would consist of treating wounds sustained on the battlefield, but the majority of my patients suffered from alcohol poisoning. It was not long before I understood why the vendor had called ganja leaves a remedy for "white man shaking". In the cantonment at Dinapore, I was confronted with many cases of *delirium tremens* and there seemed to be little that could be done for these men. I asked apothecaries to show me how to prepare the herb to benefit the symptoms of my trembling patients and found that tinctures of hemp helped them to sleep and to revive their appetites. My compatriots did not share my enthusiasm for the use of the herb, though. They regarded it as little more than a soporific, used by the lowest classes to alleviate the depression of their existence.'

'How can one hold that against them? I too am attracted to anything that alleviates pain.'

'But it is living through the pangs of life that makes us fully human, don't you think? Anyway, once I had discovered the analgesic qualities of cannabis, I began to prescribe it quite often, but it could be troublesome to calibrate a correct dose. Some leaves were ineffective and others had overwhelming psychical effects. It was difficult to bring the medicinal actions and intoxicating agents into balance.'

At the sound of something like ground glass being flung at the window, we looked up and saw rain dashing against the glaze. The light softened and a curious calm overtook the chamber – it seemed to become imbued with a confidential atmosphere that shut out the world. Martenson said, 'I was told by native apothecaries that the hemp that flourishes in the Himalaya mountains differs from the Bengal variety. It is a plant that grows tall and aromatic and its narcotic principles are more predominant than those in cannabis *indica* and more amiable in their effect. After I had submitted the report on Kinch's death, I travelled to Bhutan to gather specimens.' As Martenson spoke, I felt tension disperse from my body – indeed, I had not been aware how very tightly wound I had been. His voice was low and musical and the images conjured by his words transported me from one life into another – one that thrilled me with its depth and reach.

'Eventually,' he said, 'I found my way to a high plateau, where I discovered field after field of wild hemp, the plants eight and ten feet in height, with a distinctive odour as of mint and a yield of resin so prolific it was easily rubbed from the dark buds by hand. I took it to be a species quite distinct from the lowland plant. It struck me, then, that a hybrid of the Bhutanese *sativa* and the Bengal *indica* might answer the deficiencies that have prevented cannabis from being accepted as a useful drug in our pharmacopoeia. If I could cultivate a stable hybrid, I foresaw its use in British hospitals. It could be prescribed for cramping disorders in cases of tetanus and rabies and cholera. On my return to Patna, I applied for a contract to raise the hybrids. Hayle spoke against me in the district, saying the land around my station ought to be put into the poppy.' Martenson exhaled with a grumpy expression. 'That is a crop whose addictiveness and profitability are guaranteed.'

'You disapprove of opium.'

'I don't disapprove of any plant, but it troubles me that the Bengal's peasants must pull up food crops in order to plant poppies.'

'Do not poppies make a useful physic?'

'Physic has nothing to do with it. Opium is the only commodity that can rescue the East India Company from bankruptcy and pay its creditors in London. Its manufacture has become a political stratagem, a way of contending with China's trading superiority. We have a boundless appetite for China's silks and teas, its spices and porcelain, but Britain must exhaust its reserves of silver in order to pay for them. China, meanwhile, finds that there are few of our commodities that pique its interest. Save for the poppy. The more we smuggle opium into Canton, the more China craves it, so much so that we may use it as our coin of exchange – a ton of opium in exchange for a ton of tea – and, in that way, prevent the draining of our treasury.'

'How long did it take you to cross the two species of cannabis?'

'About three years to arrive at a strain that impressed me. But the plants were burned and ploughed under by order of the same magistrate who suppressed my reports.'

I took a deep breath and said, 'I confess, Dr Martenson, that I have read those reports. I read them when Mr Nash had the dossier in his possession, several months ago. I truly do not know where it is now.'

Martenson gazed at me from under his brows. 'You took your time with that admission, Mrs Nash.'

'I am sorry. I was not sure of you and I am dubious of being drawn into anything that concerns Sir Rollo Hayle. But I am willing to tell Mr Bellamy that I remarked the stamp of the East India Company on the dossier and can testify to the existence of the reports if that will help him to expose the Neela Company.'

Martenson gave me a searching look. 'Thank you,' he said simply.

'There is something else I think you would like to hear. You asked me if my husband had connections at Dinapore. I have learned that he was acquainted with an army officer named Spencer whom he had known in London. He lent Nash the money to be fitted up for India when they first went out there together years ago. This Spencer turned up at our house at the beginning of the summer and implored my husband to honour the debt. He was in poor health with a wife and children to provide for. But then he changed his mind and forgave the debt, which seemed extraordinarily magnanimous for someone in such difficult circumstances. Lieutenant Spencer has very recently passed away, God rest his soul, but last month I spoke to him at his home. The poor man was in a weak state and it was clear that he was near the end of his life. He told me that he had been a lieutenant in the Bengal army, but he had been cashiered. Then, as we parted, he said something odd. He uttered the words "No uniform" and "Blue falling lights". I could not get any more sense out of him, but I went away with the impression that his conscience was burdened.'

'Why so?' Martenson asked.

'Please bear with me, while I explain. Spencer was a grenadier,' I said, 'and grenadiers are elite soldiers, are they not?'

'Yes, they are usually commissioned for hazardous duties.'

'And I am sure that a grenadier's uniform is distinctive.'

'A red coat and a distinguished mitre cap.'

'I remembered your telling me that you could find no record in Patna of an army detachment being sent to Rajmahal around the time of the bandits' deaths. When I visited Mrs Spencer earlier today, she disclosed that her husband had been sent several years ago from Dinapore on a sortie of great secrecy. You can imagine how attentive I was to that intelligence. It seems that the lieutenant led a detachment of men charged with the proving of rockets. That is as much as Mrs Spencer knew. I felt convinced that these must have been the men who went to Rajmahal to test the blue agent in the field.'

'The blue falling lights.' Martenson's eyes narrowed with interest.

'The detachment would have been much noticed on their skirmish, I think, had they been attired in their red coats and mitres.'

'No uniform,' Martenson said.

'Exactly. They must have gone out in the camouflage of ordinary dress.'

Martenson stood up in a decisive manner and said, 'I must speak to Mrs Spencer at once and bring her to Bellamy. Where does she live?'

'I can tell you, but you will find her gone. Two men were packing up her belongings, when I arrived. Mrs Spencer said that she and the children were moving away, although she very particularly did not wish to tell me where. She is frightened and her only concern now is to protect her son and daughter. I had the impression that she had been paid money to remain silent.'

'Did you witness her departure?'

'No, but it seemed imminent.'

'It is worth the effort,' Martenson said, 'of trying to apprehend her.'

I jumped to my feet, too. 'Let me come with you. I am sure I must know London better than you do. I can show you the fastest way to Humerton.'

Rain was falling lightly as Martenson and I left the house and walked to the mews in the rear. At a stables under the sign of the Golden Ball, Martenson hired a light chaise and a chestnut mare. There was something other-worldly about that journey to Marsh Lane. The rain soon lifted and the clouds sailed away. It was a wonderful feeling, flitting through the summer night with a sense of purpose. Martenson and I hardly spoke, except for the directions I gave him from time to time. As the buildings rushed by and we gradually left the city behind, I felt that my life was more significant than I had realised and much bigger than I had been used to.

After leaving the Hackney Road, we turned at the junction at the Nag's Head and travelled further north on Mutton Lane. Martenson was a skilled driver and the chaise ate up the miles. By the time we reached Humerton, the colour of the sky had deepened to a velvety blue scattered with stars. Presently, I recognised the Falcon, its windows flickering with light, and we drew up at the gate of the Spencers' cottage. It was dark and silent. Martenson left me with the chaise while he walked around the cottage and hammered at the door. When he returned, he said, 'It is disappointing that we arrived too late.'

'I should not have delayed coming to see you.'

'Do not concern yourself, Mrs Nash. Bellamy will find Mrs Spencer.'

We stopped at the Falcon so that the horse could be uncoupled and rested before we made our way back into town and Martenson asked after Mrs Spencer, but no one could say where she had gone. It was an uncouth crowd at the tavern, but we sat in a snug in the rear and no one bothered us. As we ate supper, I asked Martenson about his origins and he told me he had been born at a Danish colony near Madras to a father, who had come out to India as an orientalist with the Danish East India Company, and an English mother. When Martenson was twelve, the family had gone to England and his father had obtained temporary employment at Oxford, giving classes in Sanskrit.

'My mother died when I was fourteen,' Martenson said. 'It was an event that made me think deeply about my beliefs.

I decided that Eastern ideas concerning the transmigration of souls were more to my liking than the Christian notion of heaven and hell.'

He had attended a grammar school in Oxford and then read medicine and botany at Edinburgh.

'I did not wish to become an intellectual like my father, though. I sought to lead an active life, not one that theorises and speculates. My father died while I was in Edinburgh and I used the money he left me to buy a commission in the Bengal army.'

He tried to ask me about my background, then, and I offered a sketch of Durand Gardens, but I preferred to change the subject. 'Do you think,' I asked, 'that a rocket really was the method of shooting the poison into the clearing where the bandits were camped?'

'It is a plausible theory. Patna is a centre for the manufacture of fireworks and there are many artisans skilled in rocketry in the region.'

'Is the blue agent in the form of a liquid?'

'I do not know. Hayle has always been extraordinarily successful at breaking through limitations. Perhaps he devised a way of dissolving his compound in water. It could have been enclosed in a container and attached to a staff, in the manner of a skyrocket. How else could Lieutenant Spencer and his grenadiers have come close enough to a bandit encampment to effect a successful strike? In this scenario, they were not grenadiers, but rocketeers. Whatever form the blue agent took, it would have needed to be carried in a canister or a vial that was attached to the staff of the missile.'

'Glass vials!' I cried. 'Who better to supply them than the Bengal Glass Company, I warrant.'

'I believe you are right, Mrs Nash. The vials are fired from a staff. They shatter and drift through the night sky and anyone catching sight of them sees nothing more sinister than falling blue lights.'

'Of the kind one might mistake for an ordinary signal, like a Bengal light.'

'Or a spirit of the dead,' Martenson said.

'Ah, yes, as the woodcutter in Rajmahal believed.'

'You have excellent powers of recall, Mrs Nash. That is a useful capability for a traveller.'

'How so?'

'One travels in order to talk to people and hear of their lives and customs and be informed by their stories; but it is bad form to sit poised with a notebook and a pencil at the host's hearth, should you have had the honour to be invited in to a local settlement. It helps to be able to rely on a good memory to record the occasion.'

'Well, your story was a vivid one. Certainly, I remember that the night before the woodcutter came across the corpses of the bandits, he saw the souls of dead people in the sky.'

'That is how I interpreted the phrase he used, because I knew it to be a common belief of Rajmahal people, who see spirits everywhere. They speak of *nīla ātmā*, the souls of the dead, which are blue. But, now, in view of what we have learned, I wonder if the woodcutter might not have used the phrase *nīla ālō*, which means blue haloes or blue lights? At the time I did not see the importance of the distinction. Lights, spirits, I took them to be the same thing – an entity of a metaphysical nature. In other parts of Bengal, in the marshlands near Calcutta, for instance, the wandering spirits of the dead are seen as lights. But now I understand that the woodcutter was describing something real. The blue falling lights in the sky were not spirits or souls. They showed the vaporous trace of a chemical phenomenon.'

'When the grenadiers, or rocketeers, ejected the glass vials, if that was how it was done, don't you think they must have run the risk of inhaling the noxious fumes? How would they have protected themselves?'

'The magazine at Patna keeps a supply of charcoal masks, which soldiers wear during dust storms, but as Lieutenant Spencer's detachment to Rajmahal was not recorded at the magazine, there can be no inventory of equipment issued. In any case, I do not see how the masks could have been protection enough.'

'Why would the army seek to deploy such a terrifying substance at all? It represents an egregious violation of the rules of military engagement.'

'The army in Bengal is undermanned and the Company overstretched. There is much talk of the tractable Hindu around the supper tables of Westminster, but those of us on the ground in India know that stubborn pockets of resistance remain against the establishment. Not only do those malcontents and rebels continue to threaten, but also, there are inevitably conflicts to come on the borders of our influence in Asia. It is cumbersome and costly to prosecute a war; but conceive of an alternative, where small units of assailants make daring strikes with weapons of stealth and then slip away. It is not an honourable way to proceed, but our over-lords will tell themselves that the end justifies the means.'

As we left the Falcon, I saw that the moon had climbed in the sky. I stood under its brightness, while I waited for Martenson to bring the chaise to the road, and wished that it could beam quite completely in to my interior and discover the possibilities that dwelled within and make them visible, for they were yet unknown to me. Then a cloud passed across the moon and I was plunged into obscurity once more. Well, is that not the rhythm of existence? The darkness *in actu* is light; the light *in potentia* darkness.

Chapter 16

The Rockingham Faction

August the 24th, 1776

Martenson deposited me at my door at midnight and I entered a silent house. I had hoped to find Nash at home, for I wished to inform him of my intention to see Mr Bellamy in the morning, but he was absent. As the clock struck one, I gave up my vigil and retired to bed. Rain had begun to fall once more. Nash would find that as compelling a reason as any to stay at whatever nighthouse he was in for another couple of pints of beer. He crept in around dawn, but I could not rouse him to speak to me and, when I rose an hour or so later, he was soundly asleep. We were in danger of becoming one of those couples who only meet in passing upon the stairs.

The sun came out and a faint mist rose from the cobbles as I walked through the damp streets to meet Dr Martenson outside a coffee house on High Holborn. He hailed a hackney coach and said in a tone of reassurance, as we set out for Whitechapel, 'Gabriel Bellamy is a man of character, Mrs Nash. Please know that he will not let you down.'

'Why is it that he has fixed so on pursuing Sir Rollo's gang?' I asked.

'He takes pride in his work. When the auditors arrived in Patna to investigate irregularities in the Company's business, Hayle was particularly arrogant. Bellamy suspected the Neela Company of dark dealings, but Hayle overwhelmed the auditors with bureaucracy. What could Bellamy prove, other than the fact that a supply agency in a territory abroad is a complex entity? He could report his frustrations to the Treasury at Westminster and his suspicions that accounts seemed to have been framed to thwart inquiries, but there would not be much of a response, since the Treasury's own secret committee was responsible for the enterprise that involved Sir Rollo Hayle, the Ordnance Board and the commanding officer at Dinapore, Sir John Lambert. But Bellamy has a dogged nature and does not like to be underestimated.'

'I will admit to reading the reports and to hearing that Lieutenant Spencer was sent on a mission to Rajmahal, but where Mr Nash is concerned, my meeting with Mr Bellamy must be very conditional. You cannot expect me to say anything against my husband.'

'Indeed, I do not. I understand your dilemma.'

After a journey of about half an hour, we arrived at the high street in Whitechapel. It was bathed in a pungent scent that reeked of tanneries and breweries. We drew up outside a brick building of three storeys that stood next to a dishevelled coaching inn. As I disembarked from the cab, I nearly stepped on a grubber, scratching around in the street for items dropped by heedless passers-by. I stood on the broken pavement, looking up at the sun-blinded windows of the rotation house, while Martenson paid the driver.

I followed Martenson into the hall of the house and glimpsed through an open door a knot of low-looking people. I supposed that they were reporting crimes and activities they believed to be suspicious. It was a new system of justice. If the magistrate of the house judged that there was a charge to answer, he would dispatch an officer to gather information about the felony and bring in the suspects. An emaciated boy was on his knees at the end of the hall, sweeping something into a pan. Martenson gave him a penny and told him to announce the arrival of Dr Martenson and Mrs Nash to Mr Bellamy. The boy flew up a flight of stairs and we began to ascend in his wake. To Martenson's evident surprise, the boy reappeared promptly with the instruction that we should wait downstairs until we could be called. Martenson took in this direction with a steely expression. He waved the boy down the stairs and seemed to consider the unexpected rebuff for several seconds. Then, beckoning me to follow him, he reached for the door and opened it.

The three gentlemen in the room looked up, startled in attitudes that seemed braced for action, as we entered. The office was crammed with tables and cabinets and had a papery smell and threadbare velvet drapery. The shortest of the men stepped forward with a strained look as Martenson greeted them. I recognised him as the man I had seen in the gardens at the museum.

'Mrs Nash,' Martenson said, 'may I introduce you to Mr Bellamy, who is the high constable of this house.'

Bellamy was perhaps thirty years of age, with pointed features beneath a thicket of coarse hair. I could see the terrier in him and imagined his leaping at the chance to go to India. For young men like him, on the edges of influence, the door to promotion at home must have been low and narrow, with a crowd of competitors trying to shove their way through. Martenson took it upon himself to invite me to sit down. I sat in discomfort on a badly sprung chair against the wall, while Bellamy half-sat, with folded arms, on the edge of a table.

Martenson said to me, 'And that is Mr Bellamy's clerk, Jarvis.'

A young man with a long pale face that was badly shaved sat at a desk with a quill poised in his hand. He wore a crumpled blue cotton coat. He began knocking the excess ink from his nib with a vigorous rapping, which added to the tension in the room. I must say, I had not expected that the meeting would be conducted in such a cold atmosphere.

'Who is this character?' the third man asked Bellamy. He, clearly, was at the apex of the trinity. He had that florid, well-fed look of the upper classes, and sandy hair pomaded into two stiff rolls above each ear. His watered silk coat showed up the mundane turnouts of Bellamy and Jarvis. A quizzing glass hung around his neck on a black velvet ribbon.

'This, actually, is Dr Martenson,' said Bellamy.

'Martenson, is it?' the silk coat said. He did not acknowledge me.

'Mr Shortland-Brown,' Bellamy said, by way of explanation.

I knew his name, of course. I recalled it from Nash's latest expostulation for *The Discoverer*. Shortland-Brown's mentor was the Marquess of Rockingham, one of the prime minister's sternest critics. He was implacably opposed to the American war – an enemy of Hayle's, in other words. I was taken aback to see a politician of his rank in such a dismal location. Martenson was surprised, too, I noted. Obviously he had expected our gathering to have quite a different character, because he shot Bellamy a significant look, which Bellamy evaded.

Martenson bowed and said, 'Allow me to have the honour of presenting Mrs Nash.'

Shortland-Brown offered me a slight incline of the head, then raised an irate eyebrow in Bellamy's direction, and drawled, 'Since he is here, we might as well bring everything into the open and conclude our business.'

Martenson said, 'We have come to add to the arsenal of information that Bellamy has about the Neela Company. Mrs Nash has read the reports in the dossier that her husband has apparently sold to Hayle. She will testify to their existence and that they carry the stamp of the East India Company. Mrs Nash had also spoken to a grenadier who went on detachment to Rajmahal. We think we are able to explain how the casualties at Rajmahal met their deaths.'

Shortland-Brown offered him a thin smile. 'I hear that you

have quite a disorderly record, Martenson. Refresh my memory, Bellamy.'

Bellamy said, in a slightly apologetic tone, 'Ah, Dr Martenson twice fought illegal duels in Madras and he was censured by the Company for making an unauthorised expedition to Bhutan.'

'That was years ago.' Martenson looked at Bellamy in surprise.

'Nevertheless,' Shortland-Brown said, 'you are not a solid character.'

Martenson said, 'What is afoot, Bellamy? Why is my honour in question?'

Shortland-Brown interrupted. 'It is disappointing that these reports cannot be produced, but in any case they have become extraneous to our undertakings.'

Martenson frowned. 'But you are planning to raise a Parliamentary committee of inquiry. How can any testimony concerning the dossier be immaterial?' He appealed to Bellamy. 'Aren't we to discuss the results of your inquiries into the others who witnessed the subaltern's difficulties at Dinapore – the assistant surgeon, Dr Nugent, and the sergeant who was with me when Kinch was taken ill?'

Bellamy cleared his throat and rubbed at his nose with the knuckle of his index finger. He said, 'Neither of those gentlemen is alive, according to our findings.'

I could sense how infuriated Martenson was by the want of urgency in the room and the sense of obstruction. 'What of the magistrate who signed the reports?' I asked.

'He has no recollection of them,' Bellamy replied. 'Thank you, by the way, for coming forward, Mrs Nash.' He turned to Shortland-Brown. 'Mrs Nash is the daughter of Daniel Ravine.'

I exhaled a deep sigh, my emotions a mix of relief and sadness. Here was confirmation concerning the existence of my father, but it did not lessen my confusion.

Shortland-Brown turned an eye of icy interest on me.

I said, 'Dr Martenson tells me that Mr Ravine's expenses are paid by Sir Rollo.'

'That is correct,' Bellamy replied. 'Ravine has indicated that he has no intention of cooperating with any investigation into Sir Rollo's affairs, nor can we bring a prosecution against him while he remains in Bengal.'

Shortland-Brown said, 'I should like to hear what Mrs Nash knows of the relations between Hayle and Ravine – and her husband, too.'

'What do you mean?' I was greatly startled by the question. I caught Martenson's eye and he seemed to communicate his disappointment at the manner in which the meeting was proceeding. 'I know nothing of them. It is many years since I have had any contact with my father. As for my husband, I cannot speak for him.'

Martenson said, 'Mr Bellamy, the nature of our meeting seems quite altered and I do not know the reason. I wonder why it is that Mr Shortland-Brown should be in your office in a rotation house in Whitechapel. It is not his usual territory.'

Bellamy's gaze flicked to Shortland-Brown, who returned a barely perceptible nod, and Bellamy said, 'Events have hurried forward, Martenson. At dawn today, my men and I visited the counting house in the City where Hayle and Gifford have their operations and removed numbers of documents. Jarvis is interpreting them for us.'

Jarvis said, 'They concern the conduits that brought money to the Neela Company. It was paid through a warren of holding companies before nesting in the bank accounts that belong to Lord Casserly, Sir Rollo Hayle and Mr Gifford.'

Shortland-Brown said with satisfaction, 'Hayle's political career will be destroyed before it has properly begun.'

'And the Neela Company's lethal manufactures will be brought to an end,' Martenson said. 'Have you seized the account book from the Board of Ordnance?'

No one made a reply.

Martenson appealed to Bellamy. 'You know that a separate account book is maintained for the board's secret-service work and all of the names in the Neela network are mentioned there. You told me so yourself, man.'

Then Bellamy said, 'It was an assumption, Martenson. We have not been able to ascertain the account book's existence. By the way, thank you for bringing Mrs Nash to see us. It is an opportune moment to speak to her.' He smiled at me with his little terrier teeth. 'Your husband has made illegal investments in companies belonging to his masters, Mrs Nash. He has used information given to him by Gifford to purchase and sell stocks under an alias. If he will give us evidence of what he knows against Hayle, he will avoid prosecution. One of my fellow auditors is visiting Mr Nash, as we speak, to convey this message to him. It will reinforce our persuasion if you urge your husband to do as we ask. Otherwise, he is in danger of arrest.'

A feeling of alarm came over me. I had expected to hear that Sir Rollo Hayle had been brought down by Bellamy's investigation, but now it seemed that Nash was to be their victim.

Martenson said, 'But Oliver Nash is a completely tangential figure in this business.'

'Nevertheless,' said Bellamy, 'Mr Nash is in over his head. His boosting of Sir Rollo Hayle has proved a liability to him.'

Martenson said, 'It is the Neela Company you are supposed to denounce, not a small propagandist who has dipped his hand into the till. Won't the director of revenue and customs bring a prosecution against the Neela Company on grounds of fraud? Cannot we start there? God forbid, it is too much to hope that a prosecution may proceed on ethical grounds. The Neela Company will sell its materials to other nations. There are no regulations for such trade, but there ought to be. It is easy enough for ships supplying British garrisons to avoid declaring their cargoes. Don't you care that our enemies may use the blue agent to make a weapon that might be turned on us one day?'

Shortland-Brown said, 'I hardly think there is any danger of that.'

'You are wrong, sir. The danger very much exists when you form a company that will sell its military secrets to the highest bidder.'

Shortland-Brown turned to Martenson. 'I do not require a lecture from you. I practise the politics of virtue, sir, and as such I intend to expose those delinquencies of Hayle's that ought to prevent him from taking a seat in Parliament.' He stretched his lips in an oily smile. 'Look, Martenson, we recognise your efforts. They have been a help to us, but circumstances have quickly shifted. I think we will see a change of government in the new year.'

'A change in government? Good God,' Martenson said, 'it's all about politicking, isn't it?' Shortland-Brown looked in the direction of the window as if to communicate that his attention had strayed elsewhere. 'Your aim is to sabotage Casserly and neutralise Hayle's political ambitions, because he would have voted against your faction. This investigation,' he turned to Bellamy, 'has nothing to do with the Neela Company.'

Bellamy drew a handkerchief from his pocket and pressed it to his brow.

'Actually,' Shortland-Brown said smoothly, 'Casserly has come over to our side. He is a man who sees which way the wind blows. He has made it known that his patronage is withdrawn from Hayle, who will not get his parliamentary seat. We are satisfied with that result, but it is necessary to ensure that Hayle's reputation is sufficiently smirched so that he never can entertain the idea of entering politics.' He drew a silver watch from his waistcoat and glanced at it. 'Time to press on, gentlemen,' he said briskly.

Martenson said, 'I am disgusted but not surprised to find that self-interest has vanquished the common good in this case.'

'Look here, man, the government does appreciate your interest in this case.' Bellamy's eyes shifted as he addressed Martenson. 'As a token of its thanks, you are given leave to take up a contract once more for the East India Company. You may thank the influence of Mr Shortland-Brown, who has recently been elected to the board of the Company. But your advocating to raise a narcotic crop is not well liked. It bucks against the general plan, which is, as you know, to turn Bengal over wholly to opium.'

Martenson said, 'The hybrids I have raised have medicinal value, especially in regard to malaria. The medical board in Calcutta has indicated that it will welcome them for a series of assays if I can bring them to fruition again.'

Jarvis cleared his throat. 'Dr Martenson, I am afraid it was an error, apparently, of the medical board to permit you to run a trial in the first place. Your proposal for a Bengal dispensatory and associated trials are not condoned by the Company.'

Shortland-Brown said, 'I think we can agree that there is no need to draw on native plants when British medicines and British science already exist to answer the needs of the military and civil services. Frankly, Dr Martenson, you have swerved from the researches asked of you by the Company and there is a feeling that you are not absolutely on our side. But you are, aren't you? You are very attached to your work, everyone knows that, but you won't want to be out in the cold, where you can do no good at all. You won't want to have your marching orders, will you, and see your career go to waste. You may have your contract, but you will cultivate what it pleases the horticulture committee to assign you. And you must make up your mind about it sharpish.'

Bellamy said, 'The captain of the *Walter Raleigh* will receive his dispatches from the East India Company today and will sail from Deptford on the midnight tide tomorrow. You may choose to take passage with him or not, but the fact is you will never obtain another Company contract if you reject this opportunity.' He turned, next, to me. 'In regard to the conversation that you will have with your husband imminently: you might let him know that the East India Company is prepared to extend a pension to you both. It is small, but rather more than people in your position have a right to expect. In return, we will rely on you to live quietly and never speak of this affair.'

Shortland-Brown said, 'We certainly do not expect to see Mr Nash exposing his opinions in the town's news sheets.'

'I do not understand your meaning,' I said.

'Oh, come now, Mrs Nash, one notices your husband in the gallery at the House of Commons and sees him out and about, hobnobbing with Hayle and Gifford. It does not take a genius to guess that he writes as Nemesis.' Ah, I thought, Mr Shortland-Brown does not take kindly to the appellation

Nemesis has bestowed on him of 'Shiteland-Brown'. He eyed us balefully. 'So, there you have our offer – a passage for Martenson and a pension for the Nashes and, in return, you will leave this business alone. You may send your answers to Mr Bellamy before five tomorrow afternoon. I bid you all good morning.' Shortland-Brown could not get away quickly enough now that he was concluded. Jarvis rushed to the door to show the politician out.

Martenson stared at Bellamy, who shrugged. There would be no inquiry, I realised. Perhaps the investigation had started out as something robust and moral, then gradually it had broken down until it took the form of a stratagem to force a move from Casserly. But once Casserly, the pragmatist, had abandoned Sir Rollo and joined with the incoming coterie, I could understand that Bellamy's masters saw no point in making a commotion about the Neela Company and the immorality of its blue agent. Shortland-Brown would exploit the scandal to undermine the administration of the current Prime Minister, Lord North, and his political rivals. Martenson, Nash and I were pawns in the game.

Martenson was white with fury. 'This is a shabby outcome, man. You were to amass evidence to expose the Neela Company and to launch an inquiry!'

Bellamy said, 'I must be politic, Martenson. Shortland-Brown is a rising star in Parliament. He has the potential to hold high office and to advance or to hinder my calling. I must think of the greater good that I may do in the future.'

'I'll be hanged, but you have switched sides too, just like

Casserly. You were one of Lord North's investigators. Now you seek to please Lord Rockingham's faction.'

Bellamy gave Martenson a resentful stare. 'Look at this house, Martenson. It is practically derelict. We are trying to do things with a new method here, to reform the way in which crime is investigated, but we need patronage. We need someone to put money in our coffers so that we may do our jobs. I would be a fool not to consider the entirety of my life, as would you. I urge you to take the long view.'

'I believed in you. I asked Mrs Nash to believe in you. How could you become such a turncoat?'

Bellamy sighed. 'Let me tell you, Dr Martenson. After my return from India, I was employed by the secret service to work at the office of the Exchequer of Pleas. Ostensibly I was to scour the archives for tax defaulters. My actual task was to gather intelligence from records of tax and disbursements, which might show links between the Board of Ordnance and officials in the Exchequer's office. In other words, evidence that a covert mission had existed within the Exchequer's office to fund military research for the Board of Ordnance. Money is sometimes filtered through that office instead of through the Treasury, you know. We suspected that an insular commissioning body existed either in the Ordnance office or in the Exchequer's office. That would have been the conduit by which money flowed from Westminster to the cantonment at Dinapore and then to Hayle and Gifford.

'I was enthused about the work. I was convinced that your suspicions were correct, that a lethal compound had emerged from Sir Rollo Hayle's station in Bengal, and that it had not been subject to the usual checks and balances. I know very well that no moral compass was brought to bear on the productions that arose from Casserly's cabal. Nothing is out of bounds to these people. They do not hesitate to eliminate those whom they consider to be obstructions, or otherwise destroy their lives, as they did with your crop in Bankipore. I do not know how the prime minister came to hear of this malignant group, but he decided it must be rooted out and destroyed, and its members indicted.'

'And yet nothing is to be done.'

Bellamy flinched. 'It never occurred to me that the prime minister's own secret service was not above unprincipled interests. Its members saw that their political survival was tending away from the prime minister and towards Shortland-Brown and his cronies, and so the investigation was exploited for a political gain. I understand your anger, doctor, I feel it myself – and I will not give up.

Bellamy made a helpless gesture with upturned palms. 'The truth is that the roaring despots of the world always get their way and idealists end up hamstrung by their principles.'

I said, 'I cannot accept an attitude which vanquishes our best impulses. It makes my blood boil to think of it.'

'My advice to you, Mrs Nash, is to simmer down and take the pension that Shortland-Brown has offered you. Live quietly. It is dangerous to do otherwise.'

I deigned no reply to Bellamy except by a look.

Chapter 17

The Sign of the Blue Anchor

August the 24th, 1776

Martenson and I were silent as we left the Whitechapel rotation house. As we set off along the high street in the direction of Houndsditch, past stalls selling messes, we were aware of the simmering gaze of shapeless people in rags, who congregrated at the entrances of desperate dwelling houses. I think Martenson and I had a shared feeling of foolishness as well as outrage at the naïvety of our idealism. After a while, Martenson said, 'I very much regret the way this business has unfurled. I dragged you into it in a stupidly high-minded and tub-thumping manner and it has turned out to be a squalid, small thing.'

'I came into it of my own accord in the end.'

I thought of the time I had first laid eyes on Martenson at Hillier's and how the sword he wore showed him to be out of his element in a place where weapons are either decorative or concealed. Martenson's weapon was out in the open and its purpose was sincere. It marked him as a man apart.

'I suppose that your reports are destroyed,' I said.

'Without question.'

'Will you take the passage from Deptford tomorrow night?'

'Yes. One must go on with a fierce devotion to something. I will continue my work as best I can, and that includes exposing the existence of the blue agent. What about you, Mrs Nash? Will you seek to take the Company's pension?'

'I do not see how we can and then live in a way that is inimical to our characters. How to survive, though? Nash and I must set an altered course, but not in London, perhaps. We have already made plans to go away for a few weeks in France. It will be an opportunity to consider our future.'

At the junction of Bishopsgate Street, we reached a stand of hackney coaches and I realised that Martenson and I were about to part ways. The prospect of it aroused great sadness in me. Then I was struck by inspiration. 'Arthur Wheeler,' I exclaimed.

'I beg your pardon.'

'The printer I once mentioned to you. Before you leave, you must put to him a proposal to print your dispensatory. I am sure he would do it – and your work would not languish unseen. It is just the kind of subject that interests Wheeler. Let us go there now!'

Martenson's eyes lit up at my suggestion and in a flurry of motivation we hired a hackney and set off for Ink Yard. He became gradually more preoccupied, however, as we proceeded towards the river. After a while, he said, 'I can imagine how Lieutenant Spencer must have felt after his sortie to Rajmahal with his lethal rockets. A proud grenadier goes to war on the right flank, you know, and faces the enemy in his regimental colours. He does not go sneaking about like a common murderer. If Lieutenant Spencer's assignment was to poison men unawares, he would have deemed it unworthy of proper soldiery. It is a shrivelling feeling to be disappointed in oneself.'

'Dr Martenson,' I said, 'you have done everything you can to expose the wickedness of the Neela Company.'

'I ought to do more.'

'But you cannot act alone in this case, without the support of agencies.'

'I could publish a pamphlet with my findings.'

'With no one to back you up, you will be arrested and jailed for slander. Your findings cannot be proved. They are only speculations. I believe in them and in you, but you must admit that Bellamy has hung you out to dry. If Shortland-Brown is now on the board of the East India Company, you can be sure that he would not hesitate to destroy your livelihood and probably your reputation, too. If you languish in prison, then you are no good to anyone. You may hate to hear me say so, but in one respect, Mr Bellamy is right. You must live to fight another day. Please, I implore you, publish your Bengal catalogue.'

The coach seemed to arrive in a flash at the sign of the Blue Anchor and I felt another flush of disappointment at the looming end to Martenson's companionship. I had come to think of him as a friend and the hours that I had spent with him had shown me, I realised at that moment, an altered way of being. Sharing his mission to expose the Neela Company had made me feel alive and less full of myself. Miss

Wheeler caught sight of me through one of the shop windows. She waved and I waved back and showed Martenson into the bookshop.

'Good afternoon, Mrs Nash.' Miss Wheeler curtsied. 'How may I assist you?'

'Is your father at leave to speak with me for a few minutes?'

She went to fetch him. Martenson stood with his hands clasped behind his back, scanning the titles of the books on the shelves. When Mr Wheeler appeared in his apron and cap, I introduced the two men and explained to the printer that Dr Martenson might have a manuscript of interest that was very much congruent with the tastes we had discussed several weeks before. Mr Wheeler excused himself to conclude a task and said that he would soon speak with Dr Martenson. After Mr Wheeler had returned to his presses, Dr Martenson thanked me for the introduction.

He said, 'What may I do for you in return? I wonder whether you would like me to carry a note to your father.'

I was surprised by my hesitation.

'It is none of my concern,' Martenson said gently, with his eyes on mine, 'but I should not like to see you hurt.'

I thanked him for his courtesy and said I thought that I might lack the courage to invite further rejection from my father. 'At the same time,' I added, 'I still long to see him.'

'Perhaps you will come to Bengal in due course,' Martenson said.

'If only I could!' I cried. 'But I doubt that Mr Nash would agree to it.'

'Of course,' Martenson said. Two spots of colour appeared on his cheeks and he seemed uncharacteristically embarrassed. 'I did not mean to suggest that you might undertake such a voyage alone. In any case, I must not keep you, Mrs Nash. Time presses upon us both.'

Two or three more customers had come into the shop while Martenson and I were there and I felt self-conscious about saying farewell to him in their presence. Martenson must have interpreted the expression on my face, because he invited me to step outside. We stood awkwardly at the head of the lane that led into Ink Yard. After exchanging a few civilities, I wished Martenson a *bon voyage* on the morrow. He responded with a rather formal inclination, and I said, 'Sir, adieu.' At that, Martenson held out his palm to me and I placed my hand in his. There wasn't a breath of air and all of the sounds of the street seemed to have stopped. A trickle of sweat ran down my temple. I looked into his face. He smiled and said, 'Do not concern yourself about my fate, Mrs Nash. I know who I am and that will keep me steady. I will not fear for you for the same reason.'

'I certainly would enjoy a lifting of unease,' I said.

'Then that is our parting gift to one another – confidence in our futures.' He smiled. He raised my hand and briefly touched the knuckles with his lips. The gallant gesture scarcely lasted a second, but it gave me a kind of shock. Without saying anything more, I hastened away.

As I walked to Hood Street, I was overwhelmed by the volume of my thoughts – of what I would say to Nash; of what I would say in a putative letter to my father. To venture into the subject of Papa's desertion was to plunge into a snarled and thorny undergrowth, where I was likely to find myself hopelessly snagged on implications and too impeded to break free. I prevented my thoughts from turning to Martenson. What would be the point, since it is unlikely I will ever see him again? In addition, despite my assertion that I would not brood on his fate, it was troubling to think of the feelings he had nearly aroused in me.

A rich smell of fat, with an undercurrent of hops, greeted me as I arrived home. I found Ned was at the kitchen table, bent over a glistening sausage like a miser with his hoard. A foaming tankard told me that he had helped himself to the keg. He looked at me with startled guilt, then rose hastily to his feet, wiping his greasy mouth on a sleeve. I noted the blackened frying pan sitting on the hob and the dirty plates piled on the draining board, next to the sink.

'We 'ave 'ad a bite of dinner, missus.' Ned was standing in a manner that obscured the culpable tankard.

This exchange dispirited me terribly, for some reason. It was the furtive atmosphere and the expectation of blame.

I said, 'Sit down, Ned, and have a drink.'

Nash was divesting himself of his coat as I entered his office. He swung around and exclaimed, 'There she is, my wife the stranger. Where have you been?'

'I might ask you the same.'

'Why, I have been out earning our keep and damn thirsty

work it is, too. Would you care for *un coup de rouge*? I know I would.' There was an open bottle of claret on his desk and he splashed wine into two tumblers. He raised his glass to me in what could only be an ironic gesture and offered me a quizzical smile. 'What is your news, my pretty? You look as though you have some.'

A great many thoughts were racing through my mind. I picked up the wine Nash had poured me and acknowledged his toast with a clink against his glass.

'How delightful it is to see you again,' Nash said, as if we were acquaintances who had run into one another at a pleasure garden. What a complex character my husband is, always juggling a multiplicity of situations and covering for himself with a wit that is constantly at work. There is never any rest for him. His eyes were exhausted and there was a faint tremor in the hand that held his glass, yet I felt the old libidinous attraction flare between us.

I stepped to the window and twitched at the gauze curtain. The light was dull outside. Nash came up behind me and stroked the side of my neck. His hand strayed to my breast and he hooked his thumb inside my shift. There was a glow of desire in my belly. I could have turned to him then and let him take me. When we had slaked our pleasure, we would have finished the wine and drunk more until we fell into oblivion, our senses satiated.

Instead, I said, 'I went to see Bellamy this morning.' Nash fell back from me and muttered, 'Ah, Carey, you fool.' It saddened me to douse the flame that flickered between us, but how could we look at our situation coolly otherwise? I turned to face Nash. 'Your masters' schemes are broken and Casserly has betrayed Hayle. But perhaps you already know it. It must be the talk of Westminster already.'

Nash reached for the bottle and topped up his drink.

I said, 'I expect that someone came to see you.'

Nash made a fist and pressed his knuckles against his eye, as if to staunch his emotions. It struck me that he was putting on a performance and I felt overcome with bewilderment, and a hint of despair, at what to make of him. I said, 'I wish you would explain how everything started. Why you took that dossier from the courthouse at the Company Bagh to begin with.'

Nash laughed in a hollow way. 'What is there left to tell you, my sweet? You seem to be comprehensively informed.'

'Oh, Nash, do not be tricky. Please, enlighten me.'

He slumped on to the divan and I came and sat at his feet. He said, 'Of course, I knew that Rollo Hayle was a rum devil, even before I arrived at Patna.' He gazed at the ceiling as he spoke. 'I was sent up there by my firm in Calcutta. We were one step ahead of the auditors that the government had sailed out from London to scrutinise the Company's transactions in Bengal. It was my task to make good the conveyancing documents in regard to Hayle's estate, Lalatola, which were somewhat irregular. The estate had been purchased illegally from a native landowner.' Nash sat up and swung his feet to the floor. He rested his chin in the palm of his hand and his gaze swivelled towards me. 'If you can forbear nagging me about it, I will admit that I fell in with old Spencer again in Dinapore. The place was insufferably tedious and the soldiers a low set of fellows, but it gave me a fillip to see a face I knew, especially one that had always held me in regard. Spencer introduced me to the drinking shops of the cantonment. He had become quite the souse, I am sorry to say.'

That would have been after Lieutenant Spencer had returned from Rajmahal, I knew.

'One night, when the men were in their cups, someone raised a sentimental toast to a gunner from his company, who had met his death a year or two before in odd circumstances.'

'James Kinch.'

Nash raised his eyebrows by way of acknowledgement. 'As the night wore on, and Spencer grew more plastered, he muttered something to me about Rollo Hayle having poisoned Kinch at the army hospital. Naturally, anything to do with my employer was of interest to me, but I could hardly take such lurid gossip seriously. Felix was roaring drunk and, in fact, the same night, he ran amok in the camp and was cashiered not long afterwards. I asked around a little, discreetly, about the business with Kinch. For a small consideration, one of the clerks at the archive confirmed that a report had been written on the subject, in accordance with the Company's procedures, and that Rollo Hayle had been rather exercised over the report's aspersions – there was some dispute with its author that ran very high. I refer to your admirer, Dr Martenson, of course.' Nash arched an eyebrow and I could not help but colour. 'Hayle considered Martenson to have borne false witness to the incident at Dinapore Hospital.'

'Don't be absurd, Nash. Martenson is hardly my admirer.'

Nash laughed and refilled his glass. 'You might not be astonished to hear that I was in need of funds at the time . . .'

'A gambling obligation.'

'How well you know me, my love. An all-night whist party at Colonel Flegg's in Calcutta had resulted in the laying at my feet of a sudden and inconvenient debt and I thought it best to absent myself *tout de suite*. A colleague of mine had been supposed to travel to Patna to undertake the work for Hayle, but I offered to go in his place. I instructed my valet to pack trunks for me and told my steward to inform callers that I would be gone for three or four months – and away I went. I trusted that during the time I was cooling my heels at Patna, some scheme or solution might present itself to me by which I could obtain the two hundred and twenty pounds that I owed the colonel.'

'And the reports on the poisonings proved to be such a solution.'

'Having found how attentive Hayle was to their existence, I knew they must be worth something to him and the more I sniffed around, the more it seemed there was something fishy about the poisonings that might embarrass Hayle. My valet, Prasad Mukherji, found out for me, by speaking with his ilk, that Hayle had paid one of Martenson's servants to steal the copy Martenson kept of his reports. I had learned, by this time, that the assiduous doctor had also reported on a poisoning at Rajmahal. Since Martenson's servant had looted his employer, the only reports extant were the originals in the archive at the courthouse. The clerk had told me that the usual copies had not been dispersed to Calcutta and London, as one would expect. I suppose that Hayle used his influence with the magistrate to prevent other copies being made. I imagine he would have inveigled the magistrate into turning over the originals, too, if I had not got to them first. I had no idea what the reports signified, by the way. That is the truth. And so, I picked the lock in the archive with my penknife and removed the dossier.'

I fixed Nash with my gaze. 'And during the course of your inquiries into Hayle's affairs, you never heard mention of Daniel Ravine.'

Nash sat up straighter and replied firmly, 'I did not. As we now know, my love, Hayle had settled Ravine on an estate far from Patna. Didn't you tell me so yourself?'

I felt chagrined, then, for having doubted Nash on the point and urged myself to leave the subject of my father alone. I said, 'Did Lieutenant Spencer speak to you about the sortie to Rajmahal?'

'I believe he might have bleated something about wickedness in the jungle, but I was hardly disposed to pay attention to the ramblings of a drunkard.'

'What happened when you offered Hayle the dossier?'

'Alas, my campaign never got under way. I pondered my approach for a few days, while I considered the repercussions, for I knew that inciting Hayle's ire in Bengal could be a dangerous thing, but I delayed too long. Hayle went out from Patna to enjoy the hospitality of the Nawab of Bengal and I returned to Calcutta. You know what took place then – I fell out with my firm and was struck off the roll. I was glad to take passage for England, not least to escape Flegg's debt. The next time I saw Hayle was that night at the Mango Tree – and I knew that my moment had come. A day or two afterwards, I met with him and suggested he might like to make me an offer for the dossier. He was very unperturbed and said that it was of no interest to him. However, he was amused at my gall and over an excellent dinner, he proposed that I might perhaps work for his partner, Gifford, writing in their interest. Obviously, it was a ploy to keep me close and under scrutiny, but the position was also to my advantage.'

'And then Martenson turned up.'

'If I had had any doubts that the dossier was worth anything, they were dispelled by Martenson's arrival. Of course, I took the precaution then of putting the dossier in a safe-deposit box.'

'At Packham's Bank?'

'Of course not. Packham is one of Casserly's cronies. I put it in safe keeping elsewhere and, once it was clear that Sir Rollo was planning a colossal political career, I offered him the dossier again. And he capitulated. You understand I could not tell you any of this until I had got what I wanted, but we have money now to keep us afloat.'

'How much money?'

'Enough, my little inquisitor.'

'But you are in trouble on another front. Mr Shortland-Brown intends to have you arrested for the illegal trading of stocks.'

Nash looked surprised. 'Old Shiteland has taken you into his confidence, has he?'

'He was at Bellamy's rotation house. He is the victor in this affair. Nobody cares what Sir Rollo did in Bengal, but Shortland-Brown is a name in the Rockingham faction, which is determined to destroy Sir Rollo's political ambitions. You are at the House of Commons every day, aren't you? You must know who is in and who is out. And I am sure you must also know that the East India Company has offered to buy our silence with a pension.'

Nash laughed uproariously. 'Yes, the lure of a miserable pension was dangled before me in the interview I had this morning. A *pension*.' He spat the word. 'Are we to live like mice, in hiding?'

'We could alter our course, though. You might even risk becoming an authentic critic of corruption and injustice.' I remembered the printer that I had noticed in the rookery by Drury Lane when I was fleeing from poor Lieutenant Spencer. It would not be difficult to find radical printers to set Nash's work if he turned his hand in that direction – if he really were to inhabit the guise of Nemesis.

But then, with the lazy wolfish smile that had always turned my head, Nash said, 'Not my style, lovely.'

★

I realise that I have learned something during the course of this turbulent summer. What is a marriage if not a journey across the shifting sands of compromise? It takes a steady hand on the reins to avoid the pitfalls and come through safely. The follies of my husband have crept between us, but I am no less flawed than he, and one of us, at least, must try not to let passion run away with the senses. In the aftermath of Nash's revelations about the role he has played in the drama of the dossier, I felt in regard to him a medley of emotions — disappointment and resentment among them. Perhaps, in the past, I might have been disposed to luxuriate in such feelings in order to shore up my righteousness, but now I have become impatient with such indulgence. Oliver Nash is my husband and I must live with him in friendship and esteem in whatever way I can. It was refreshing, actually, to hear him speak the truth of what has occurred and I slept last night with more ease than I have done for some time.

This morning, we breakfasted together, our conversation light and smooth as we made our plans for the day. No further mention was made of the people and events that have preoccupied us throughout the summer. There is an understanding that we are to put it all behind us. We are to take the stage to Dover in a little over a week and Nash has urged me to make haste with my preparations. After breakfast, he went to his bootmaker in Jermyn Street and I attended the mantua maker in Beak Street to be measured for a riding coat and sundry other items of apparel to take abroad. Afterwards, I strolled to Golden Square and knocked at Selina's door. I had not seen her since our altercation at the Soma Ball and I feared that our friendship might have soured. I waited for five minutes, but no one came at all to the door, not even a servant. On my return home, I wrote a lengthy letter, asking Selina to have supper with me before Nash and I left for our tour, and I renewed my declarations of affection and regard. I went across to the Eclipse and paid a boy to take the letter to Golden Square. As I crossed the street again to the house, I felt my footsteps slow and I thought of the night that Nash and I had given the supper-party at the tavern. I saw again Martenson's face, looking up at me, as he waited in the street, biding his time. He would have left already for Deptford, I surmised. In that moment, I missed him intensely. I thought that the ship he was embarking on was fortunate. His fellow passengers would be glad that such a capable gentleman – and one that put the wants of others before his own – was travelling with them.

I entered the house and made my way to the parlour. I had just taken off my hat when I remembered that Selina had mentioned, ages before, that she intended to take the waters at Bath with the tottery Newington and I felt a fool for dramatising her silence. She was out of town, of course, that was all there was to it. I spent the remainder of the afternoon in the parlour with the account book and receipts and invoices, making a list of monies owed in order to balance the household ledger before our departure. As soon as that was done, I began to compose another list, this time of essential items to pack into the trunks that were due to be delivered at the end of the week.

Nash arrived home surprisingly early and surveyed the list of creditors I had made and reassured me that they would be paid. After supper, we played ombre together in the drawing room until just before midnight like an old married couple – and the quietness and calmness of the evening greatly pleased me. It was restful, a quality that was usually foreign to our undertakings. Before he extinguished the candle at the bedside, Nash kissed me on the forehead and settled down to sleep. I thought that he remained awake for some time, but I did not remark on it. I preferred not to chatter.

I woke in the night to hear a squall rattling the windows and moaning in the chimneys. I pictured Martenson out on the open sea and hoped that his ship would not have to labour too dreadfully in the bad weather, but in my heart I was certain that he would be all right. However, I could not extend this reassurance to other matters. I was finding it more difficult than I had imagined to consign scruples as well as events to the past. As I waited for sleep, I tried not to dwell on the knowledge that the money funding our future had been obtained by deception and fraud. Oh, where was the light and easy mood that had attended me at breakfast? It seemed that the not-worrying trick might not work where something not-moral was concerned.

The next morning, I proceeded to Long Acre, to Hall's Grand Tourist bookshop to buy a guide to Paris and its environs and spent the day devising an itinerary for Nash and me. As the hours went on, I felt increasingly restless, pierced by feelings that I did not recognise, and afterwards, when I had cleaned my nib and closed my ink pot, a dull anxiety lodged in me. Nash arrived home just as the clock in the parlour chimed eight o'clock. He appeared in the doorway and glanced in, as if surprised to see me. I went to kiss him on the lips, but he turned his face away slightly so that I kissed his cheek instead.

I said, 'I have made an itinerary, if you would like to look at it.'

We seemed to stand in the doorway for a long moment and then Nash said, 'By God, I am famished. Have you dined at all?'

'I scrambled an egg.'

'Let us go across to the Eclipse. I cannot think on an empty stomach.'

We sat upstairs, in the dining room, the lamps glowing warmly, the hum of conversation all around. The alewife was pleased to see us. Nash made some humorous observation that I missed, but it set her roaring, her hands on her hips, the globes of her breasts bursting above her stays. She said she had two pieces of a good rabbit pie left, and we ordered them along with a bottle of claret. We settled ourselves on high-backed benches and faced each other across the narrow planked table. The windows were open and we could hear a ballad-seller singing in the street. '*My true love hath left me, I know not why. Left me and my baby in sorrow to cry . . .*'

The wine arrived and Nash held the bottle to a lamp to consider its clarity. There were other snatches of song outside now. It was that lovely moment when twilight gently shakes its veil over the sky, the light a soft rose-pink, and there is the promise of the evening's escapades to come. We drank a mouthful of our wine. Nash leaned forward and said, 'I hope you know that I have not set out to be a cad or to prefer myself to others. It is the fault of vexing circumstances that have forced me to be less candid, less virtuous, than I should like.'

I touched his hand. We drank a little more, the wine already making me feel giddy. 'Let us go on the run, Nash,' I laughed, 'and live on our wits.'

He grinned and leaned back in his seat and the lamplight softened his features, but his thoughts were elsewhere. He drained his glass and smoothed the lapels of his coat. There was a raucous party at my back and Nash had to lean into my ear to make himself heard. He said, 'Will you excuse me for five minutes, my dear? I saw Nick Foster downstairs on the way in. I must have a quick word in his ear. Let him know I am an agent for hire once more.'

I nodded, trying to think who Foster was. Nash almost collided with the serving girl, who had arrived with our slices of pie. Nash filled my glass and said, 'Please do start, my dear,' and then he was gone.

I was famished and so I did embark on the pie. I chewed on a mouthful, trying to chase down something – I knew it was quite a small thing – that bothered me. I laid down the fork, preferring to wait for Nash. I drank more wine. Yes, that was it! It was odd the way Nash had called me 'my dear'.

Had he said it more than once? *My dear.* It was unlike him to use such a pallid term of affection. I was always his beauty or his lovely. The diminishment saddened me a little. I ate another mouthful or two of the pie, then worked my way through a second glass of claret. Heavens, Nash was taking his time. The serving girl returned – I remembered her name, Patsy – and asked if she might remove my plate. She complimented my earrings and we fell into a discussion of gemstones, about which neither of us knew much. I drew out the conversation so as not to seem a lady rather obviously alone in the dining room, but eventually Patsy was obliged to attend to her tasks and she went away. I regarded Nash's untouched meal, which had transformed itself into a still life representing abandonment. I noticed the alewife standing at a table in the corner with a tankard in her fist, laughing at some observation of a customer's. I might ask her to find Nash for me and tell him to make haste. I half-rose, then sat down again. I was sorely vexed. How long had I been waiting, for heaven's sake? I reached out a finger and poked at Nash's slice of pie. It was quite cold.

As I got to my feet, I realised I was rather woozy. I signalled Patsy. I pointed at Nash's pie as if it were a culprit, and said, 'You may dispose of that. And please,' I made a stirring motion, 'put this on the account for Mr Nash.'

She curtsied and I left the dining room. I made my way carefully down the stairs, holding up my skirts very tautly, as if they were on tenterhooks. The ground floor was packed and smoky. Even if Nash were concealed among the throng,

I had not the inclination to search him out. I thought it a miracle that I had brought my house key with me, but then I remembered that Nash had insisted on it.

Into bed I went, tipsy, tired and Nashless. It was just like old times. I woke too early with a headache and dry eyelids. What a beast Nash was for leaving me in the lurch like that. He was probably staggering out of a gaming room at that moment, with the suit of clothes off his back in hock, or sleeping it off at one of the nighthouses he favours, the Whippet or the Cockpit. What a couple of shameful recidivists we were. I fell back on the pillow and dozed, listening to the wind whistle in the chimney.

At last, I levered myself out of bed. I noticed then that one of my pot plants was lying on the floor. It had fallen from the stage. The pot was cracked and soil was spilled on the floor. Perhaps I had clumsily tried to water the plant the night before and knocked it over. It was one of the woundworts, too, that was just coming into bloom. I tried to scrape the soil back into the broken pot, but gave it up. As I was washing my hands in the basin, I heard voices in the street. I looked out of the window and saw Jane and Ned come around the side of the house and walk off. Ruth was probably still at the green stalls in Covent Garden. I realised, as I watched Jane and Ned make their way down the street, that Ned was wearing one of Nash's old coats. It had distinctive crimson pockets on a blue ground. Was it the thought of Nash's clothes that made me think of his closet? I looked down at the empty space on the plant theatre where the woundwort had stood. That is where Nash usually kept the key to his locking box.

I opened the door of his closet and stood motionless with shock as I took in the evidence before my eyes. Nash's things were gone. Not everything, but many of his articles of clothing. The locking box had been wheeled out from under the coats. The key was still in the lock. I pushed up the lid and with trembling hands rifled through the contents of the box. I could not find Nash's passport or his credentials or his jewellery cases. My stomach turned over and a feeling of nausea passed through me. I tried to tell myself that a thief had struck, but even before I opened the door of my closet, I knew I would find that the items belonging to me would be in place. I ran downstairs. In Nash's office, his pipe lay on a plate in a mess of ashes and droppings of tobacco. His newspapers were strewed on the divan. A cushion had fallen to the floor. It was difficult to identify if anything was missing. I found myself wringing my hands. Had he been abducted from the Eclipse and arrested by one of those secret-service men Bellamy had mentioned, or by someone from the Rockingham faction? Had he sold personal effects to pay yet another gambling debt? My spirits lifted a little at that possibility, because it was so very likely. But in my heart I knew that it was not true.

Chapter 18

Nemesis

September, 1776

In desperate need of counsel, I ran most of the way to Golden Square, hoping that Selina might have returned. My persistent banging at the door brought an irate servant from the rooms on the ground floor, but he would not admit me and the door was slammed in my face. I retreated a few steps, shaded my eyes with a crooked arm and looked upwards. The curtains of my friend's apartment were drawn. Utterly bereft at Selina's absence, my hopes of sympathy dashed, I was not sure what course of action to take next. I hurried back to Hood Street in case Nash had returned in the meantime, but there was no one at home, not even the servants. I found a few shillings and put them into my pocket and went out to hail a hackney. It took me to the rotation house at Whitechapel. I asked to be announced to Mr Bellamy, but I was told he was not there. I waited in the crush of complainants in the room beneath Bellamy's office until a clerk was free to attend to my inquiry. As far as he could say, the house had not issued an arrest warrant against Oliver Nash. Once more, I came home, and now the silence and emptiness of the house had an absolute quality that frightened me. I changed my clothes, putting on a more opulent gown and bonnet and my best cloak, and left the house again. I walked westwards until I reached the quarter of St James's. In the season, it would flock with fops and witlings, but there were only a few insignificants on the streets, rigged out in fine ensembles above their station. A few minutes later, I arrived at my destination – a discreetly elegant former townhouse that belonged to Packham's Bank.

A footman showed me into a vestibule; its large squares of black and white marble gave it an implacable air. The tellers' room was lofty, panelled, with enrichments picked out in gold. An absurdly handsome clerk in a snowy wig responded to my introduction with a smile. To my tremendous surprise, he said, 'Ah, Mrs Nash, I know what you have come for.' He held up a finger to indicate that I should wait and went away and returned. 'You have missed this article,' he said with a bow. He proffered one of the cream lace gloves that I had given to Selina for her birthday.

I took the glove from the clerk with a roaring in my ears. I heard the creaking and grinding of the cogs and springs of my mind as they turned over very slowly, moving towards a terrible realisation.

Nash and Selina.

'Are you in order, madam?' the clerk asked.

I mumbled that it was only the heat that had made me feel faint. I pressed a hand to my face in an attempt to suppress the muscles that were twitching in my cheeks. I had the appalling feeling that I was about to be seized by a spasm of terrifying laughter and that it would go on, convulsively, until I was unable to draw a breath; at the same time, tears had started in my eyes and my legs were turning to jelly. I asked if I might sit down. The clerk made an effort to overcome his exasperation at having to play the nursemaid and directed me to the nearest chair, which stood before a teller's table. I sank on to the seat and closed my eyes until I managed to compose myself. When I opened them, the teller who sat mutely opposite offered a tentative bow. I saw that he was as discomforted as the clerk had been by my display of female feebleness. I took a deep breath and asked if my husband had yet closed his account.

'You know,' I said, making a guess, 'that Mr Nash and I are about to embark on our tour.'

The teller frowned and looked up at the clerk. 'It is Mrs Nash,' the clerk said. The teller coughed and frowned, weighing whether to respond to my question. Determined to have an answer, I fixed an unappeasable gaze on him. *Sapere aude*. Dare to know. Hadn't I written that swaggering phrase on the title page of my neglected commonplace book? God almighty, the vanity of it!

'Yes, the account is closed,' the teller replied at last, 'but you understand, don't you, madam –' his tone was kinder now, as if coaxing a child – 'that Mr Nash is in receipt of Packham's universal letter of credit.'

'Forgive me for being such an idiot, but will you remind me again how the letter of credit works?'

Thanks to the teller's thorough explanation, I learned that

Packham's universal letter of credit is a novel way of transporting money, devised to assist, in particular, those who are bound for the Grand Tour. Only yesterday, it seems, Nash had converted his considerable funds – the money he had made trading illegally on the stock exchange as well as Casserly's payment for the reports – into something called circular notes that any bank on the Continent will exchange. It is a method that allows a traveller to take all of his money with him, without the risk of carrying it in hard cash.

'It is a mighty convenience for the tourist,' the teller beamed.

Crafty Nash; he had sequestered his assets. He and Selina had gone off marvellously well provisioned.

I heaved myself to my feet like some creature on its last legs, still clutching the glove. As I turned to go, the bank clerk wished me *arrivederci* and a pleasant tour of Italy.

I blundered into the street, squinting against the sun. I managed to reach one of the shaded alleys near the entrance of St James's Park before the hot tears began to overflow. I collapsed on to a bench with my fingers pressed into the sockets of my eyes, wracked by sobs. I sat there for an age, lost in my heartache, until my weeping began to subside. I fumbled in my pocket for a handkerchief and blew my nose. I thought of Nash in the lamplight at the Eclipse, clinking his glass against mine. It had been our last supper. I thought of Selina, her eyes lowered, the lids stretched like silk, and the way she had smiled into her chocolate on that afternoon of her birthday and then stood up for Nash against me. I opened the palm of my hand and looked at the twisted glove. I couldn't bear to speculate about when their affair might have begun. I lacked the fortitude for that degree of torment.

I dropped the glove at my feet and rose, leaving it there.

I did call at Golden Square again, but this time when a ground-floor servant answered my knock, I heard that Mrs Colden had gone abroad. I walked home from St James's in a dazed, wandering way. As I opened the front door of the house, I struck my shoulder violently against the door jamb. Later, I would find a large purple bruise and struggle to recall what had caused it. Nash's office smelled of tobacco and stale smoke. The traces of him brought tears to my eyes. I wiped them with the heel of my hand and picked up a cushion that was lying on the floor and tucked it into place at a corner of the divan. I poured a glass of brandy, but its taste was harsh and I left it undrunk. The house itself seemed to have stopped breathing, as if in shock at the catastrophe that had taken place. I dabbed at my face and pulled myself together and went downstairs to speak to the servants. They were all three at table, drinking beer and eating pies in a very free manner. I asked if they had seen the master – it was not an unusual question – but they shook their heads with great indifference and bent to their dinner. I asked for a pitcher of water and, when I had it, I bade them goodnight.

In our – my – chamber, I sat down on the unmade bed, with thoughts of Nash and Selina operating upon my mind. My mood continued dark and cold as the hours went by and

I revisited scenes that insisted on showing themselves to me in a new, infernal light. I could see Nash, the morning after our party at the Eclipse, waking up in his office. I remember thinking that he looked rather fresh for a man who had been out all night drinking with Doyle, as he had claimed. But, of course, he had been tucked up with Selina in Golden Square. No doubt it was true of all those nights I had spent alone, while he was supposedly out carousing. Had he tumbled with Selina at the masquerade as well? A burst of wild laughter sounded in the street. I got up and looked through the window. A trio of merry women, arms linked, was passing by the house.

I fell asleep in my clothes and then woke to a watchman shouting the midnight hour. The tapers were nearly spent and the air was rancid with their smell. My head felt heavy, my heart was a stone and there was a flat, offensive taste in my mouth. I washed my face, brushed my teeth and my hair, threw off my gown and stays and went back to bed in my shift, and stared at the ceiling.

Not long after I had first met Selina, she had told me a trick she knew to get a guinea. When you are in the company of a gentleman and you gauge that your charms have put him at his ease, and he is feeling pleased with himself, suggest to the gentleman that you and he might toss up a guinea for entertainment and call heads or tails. If you should win, then you may take the guinea. If you should lose, promise him that you will pay the debt at another time. By the laws of chance, you are bound to come away from this ruse with at least one guinea in hand, without having risked anything yourself. It was a trick I would never have brought myself to play. It seems obvious, doesn't it, that the world can be divided neatly into two kinds of person: those who are clever enough to come away with a guinea in the hand, and those who are not.

I was drawn to Selina at the outset because she understood that survival is the invariable of life. When I told her how I rued my capitulation to the merchant at Chelsea, she remarked, 'You did what was necessary.' Her recognition had consoled me. She always knew how to prevail and she was clear about our work. 'You learn to see what a gentleman wants and you give it to him.' Nash must have been drawn to that strength in her too. If Selina has a guinea, she will keep it. If I have a guinea, I will spend it or otherwise lose it.

Nash has spent me. He has taught me the lesson of what love is not and then cut me from him. I do not know if I can bypass this pain. What can I do? Where can I go?

After ten days, it became apparent to me that I must quit the house at Hood Street. I made my way to Whitechapel again and, this time, I succeeded in seeing Mr Bellamy. He confirmed that Nash had not been arrested. I asked if it were possible to take up the offer of the pension that he had mooted, although the deadline had passed; but I discovered that the lack of a husband invalidated the offer. 'You understand, I am sure –' Bellamy smiled – 'it is the kind of settlement that can only be made with the head of a household.'

As I was about to leave, I asked if there were any hope of Sir Rollo being brought to account. Of Gifford, too, I had heard nothing, although I wondered if *The Discoverer* might have suspended publication.

'A mighty battle is about to begin between the respective lawyers of Hayle and Gifford,' Bellamy said. 'Hayle has dissolved his partnership with Gifford and is hurling an arsenal of blame at his former associate. As for his reaction to Casserly's betrayal, a man like Rollo Hayle is a predator and he has gone prowling about, looking for new prey, which he has fallen upon in the form of Lady Margaret Lanchester. She is a daughter of Earl Montgrise. Hayle has already announced he is to marry her. Of course, Hayle must have something over Montgrise to engineer such a match. She is only seventeen, the poor little pawn.' So, his schemes begin anew.

I am taking measures now to prevent myself from being thrown into a debtors' prison. What little I had went to the servants' wages; they have gone now. I have walked around to the printers, looking for work. Mr Wheeler might have something for me in a month, but I fear that will be too late. Stephen Norton at Pasternoster Row has several indecent titles that he has brought from France, but he is canny enough to have sensed my desperation and has lowered the price for a translation to almost nothing. Yesterday, furniture men came to take back the contents of the drawing room, which gave me a free space to lay out everything I owned that I could possibly sell. It is curious, but when I began to clean out the house, it was a shock to perceive the chaos beneath the surfaces. How had I never noticed before what a jumble there was in the cupboards and the drawers? The plants I may be able to sell to Hillier's. My clothes may go to the second-hand shops in Covent Garden. I opened my closet and dragged out the hats. The slippers I was wearing were a fine lemon-yellow kid. I thought I might be able to get a good price for them. I threw them on to the pile and returned to the closet. I was thinking, furiously, of many things – of men like Casserly and Hayle, who stood for havoc and trepidation and owned the machinery of ego and ambition to ride over mice like me, who really only wanted to be tucked away in their little holes, safe from the tyrants and their ever-expanding capacities.

All at once, I cried out in pain. I had trod, in my stockinged feet, on something sharp – a tack, perhaps. I lifted my foot. In the dimness of the closet, a tiny object winked at me. I stooped and picked it up. A diamond earring glittered in the palm of my hand. Sir Rollo Hayle's diamond. It must have lodged, after all, in the bodice of my masquerade costume and fallen out when I tore off that garb after returning from Underfall House. I sat down on that floor with my head bowed like someone accepting a benediction.

I paid three visits to Jacob Dezevedo's premises over the course of two days before he agreed to meet me at Hood Street. He has an office in the basement of a lacklustre building at Vine Hill, but he does most of his trading in the establishments of his clients. He arrived with his myrmidon, a soft-eyed bruiser of towering height, who sat almost primly on the divan in Nash's study. Divested of its papers and general mess, the room looked larger and altered, and reminded me less of Nash. I invited Mr Dezevedo to take a seat at the desk, an item of furniture, along with the divan, which I have managed to hold on to until Monday, when it will be returned to its warehouse home. Mr Dezevedo is a paunchy man with blue jowls, black ringlets and the affability of a salesman that instantly puts one on alert. His appearance was rumpled, sumptuous dark silks and a long fine gold necklace dangling from his neck. A diamond in a heavy gold setting flashed on one of his little fingers. He did not ask after Nash or why it was that I had offered only one earring of a pair for sale. He gently took the earring from me and placed it in a shallow velvet-lined tray, which he had extracted from his leather valise and set on the desk. The stone seemed instantly to become insignificant, so reduced it was hardly worth bothering with. Then Mr Dezevedo brought out a small magnifying glass from his valise and began his assessment. In the normal scheme of things, a neophyte such as myself would be no match at all for a gem trader, and certainly I did not know what the earring was worth; but it happened that I had a specific sum in mind that I should like the diamond to fetch, one that was incidental to the merit of the stone in my eyes. Anything less than that sum was of no use to me. It was all or nothing and I was unbudgeable. Acknowledging, at length, the intransigence of the amateur, Mr Dezevedo came to an agreement with me that suited us both. He purchased an excellent Indian stone, and I bought a new life.

As I dismantled my existence at Hood Street, the miscarriage of Martenson's quest preyed on my mind. When all of my possessions had been sold, I was left with a very few necessaries, which included my writing box. I gazed at the box. I felt like a paltry creature that has been let out of its cage and is frightened of its liberty. Over there lies a jungle; close to hand is the comfortable familiarity of the wheel behind the bars. I could lodge in a small room with wainscoting and a rug and a bed. I could make translations for Stephen Norton for shillings. I could manage to live in a meagre space and engage myself in small undertakings; meanwhile, Martenson's findings remained obscured with no one to expose the wickedness of the men behind the Neela Company. The Neela Company, which stood for all that was callous and life-denying in the world. As my thoughts turned on this subject, they gradually coalesced into an idea, although it was one that would require a sacrifice on my part. I was not sure if I possessed the kind of character that was courageous enough to abandon the last shreds of safety that were left to me. It was an idea that would require me to become alienated from my homeland for as long as I could foresee and to cast myself adrift on the world.

The rookery behind Drury Lane, where I had mistaken Lieutenant Spencer for a predator, remained as sinister as ever. I picked my way around the offal and feculence that strewed its lanes and tried not to breathe too deeply of the noisome air as I found my way to the court where the printer kept his press. I was dressed in the attire of a market girl – easily done, since I had sold my silks – with the brim of a straw bonnet obscuring my face. The refurbished stable was as I had remembered, the dark oilcloth hanging over the entrance giving the appearance of a horrible den. With my heart beating hard, I coughed at the doorway of the stable to gain attention. There was nothing about this place and the people living in it which could be trusted, yet I did not know where else I could find a printer to undertake a commission that was bound to be sued for libel, no matter how certain its truths. A dog began barking furiously and I heard a man shout at it. There was a thud and a clang, as if an object had been thrown, and the dog quietened. My mouth was dry and I could hardly swallow.

A swarthy man of about forty pushed aside the oilcloth.

'What do you want?' He wore a flat dun-coloured cap, a dirty buckram smock and a leather apron. His arms were folded across his chest. I said I wished to negotiate for a piece of work. A handbill. The printer scratched the side of his neck and stared at me, expressionless.

'A political handbill.' I cleared my throat. 'There is a risk of libel.'

He uttered a snort of contempt, though whether it was aimed at me or at the libel, I could not tell. He stood, staring at me, dead-eyed, then he said, 'My price will reflect the risk. How many words is it?'

I brought the pages out of my pocketbook and gave them to the printer. Since the present age is one of publicity, it is apt, I think, that Nemesis should draw attention to his departure with a shocking exposé. I had determined to push the case of the Neela Company into the open, although I knew I could be arrested for it.

The printer indicated that I should follow him. I hesitated, then squared my shoulders and entered the workshop. The space behind the curtain had been divided into the approximation of three rooms by means of discarded doors. Light beamed through a hole in the roof and illuminated a wooden press, stood in a corner. There was a small woman sitting on a stool near cases of type. She was nursing an infant.

'My wife,' the printer said. 'She is the typesetter.'

The woman gave me the faintest of nods. Her hair was cut off at the shoulders and I wondered if she had got it caught in the press. The printer said that he and his wife did all the work themselves and that payment must be made in advance. He would not accept a job on account. He noticed my gaze assessing the premises and said, 'I moved here from Grub Street and no doubt we will shift ourselves again before winter comes.'

As the printer began reading my pages, I mentally followed his progress: New Revelations From Nemesis. Secret Contracts. A Frightening Invention. Deaths Hushed-Up. A little-known fact that recent baronet and would-be parliamentarian, Sir Rollo Hayle, was once a chemist. Even less well known, he is the author of a paralysing vapour that can kill a human being in five minutes. Nemesis calls it the blue agent . . . research laboratory in Bengal . . . secret correspondence between Dinapore and Westminster . . . the Board of Ordnance that supplies the army's weapons. Lord Casserly, the board's provisional master . . . at stake: an enormously lucrative contract to furnish the army, clandestinely, with the toxic vapour . . . private communications between Sir Rollo and Lord Casserly . . . the establishment of an entity called the Neela Company to take commercial advantage of the blue agent . . . Encouraged and uplifted by Lord Casserly's interest, and bolstered by funds paid him through the Ordnance's secret account, Sir Rollo set out to test the deadly agent on human subjects – without their knowledge . . . Nemesis hears that there are plans to manufacture the blue agent on British soil, indeed manufacturing might even be underway. Perhaps that might account for recent payments made to the directors of the Neela Company . . . A secret account book kept by the Board of Ordnance . . . public funds have found their way into the fat accounts of Lord Casserly, Sir Rollo Hayle and newspaper proprietor, Fenton Gifford. Anyone who cares to check may find that the Neela Company has created false invoices and receipts to account for the cash. You may ask why Nemesis, who has so faithfully supported the interests of Casserly, Hayle and Gifford in the past, should turn on his former paragons now. It is because, my friends, when a line is crossed, there comes a time to make a stand. Must we purchase commodities, territories and victories at any cost, losing our humanity in the course of acquisition? It is in the interest of fulfilling a public service that Nemesis is compelled to expose the greed and disgracefulness of these villains. For, if we walk the path of dishonour, how may we hold ourselves up to the world as conquering heroes, when we are nothing but shams with our secret evasions? Are we really no better than our enemies?

The printer scratched at his neck again. 'I can jam this up on a broadside if it suits you.'

'I require it to be printed as soon as possible. If it could come upon the streets by the morning, I should be grateful.'

'Two hundred perfect sheets in two hours. Three guineas. But you can recoup that sum to yourself, if you charge for its sale.'

'No, I prefer the sheets to be *gratis*. Are you able to distribute them for me?'

The printer nodded. 'My boys will take them to print shops and coffee houses. I can even send them out into the counties. You must supply your own paper, though. For twelve shillings more, I can provide a ream.'

I gave him earnest money as a token and arranged to return, when the broadsides were printed, with the full reward. I had the coins ready. I had obtained them by selling my writing box. Now I owned nothing that was of value to me in any sense – having spent the money I had got from selling the diamond to Mr Dezevedo on a passage to India. Oh, and I have cut off my hair. I sold it for ten guineas to a wig maker. The printer did not look like a man one could trust, but he was as good as his word. The next day, the broadsides were everywhere.

As I rode in the wherry, bound for Gravesend, I could see an occasional bonfire burning on the banks of the Thames and hear traces of fiddlers and pipers striking up a tune. The fires were to celebrate our great victory in New York. Washington's troops have been routed in Brooklyn and chased back to Virginia. The wherryman turned to us as we set off and cried, 'New York in our pocket! Three cheers for our bold General Howe!' It was low tide and the water was choppy, slapping noisily at the hull of the boat. The watermen say that the restless souls of people who have drowned in the river cause the agitation of the waves. I do not know how people can believe such things. There is no living on after death, not even as a ghost. Reward and punishment and the proper expenditure of one's life only count in the here and now. I twisted around to look over my shoulder at the fading victory fires, and then, impatient to put to sea, I turned to face the future.

Chapter 19

Upriver

March, 1777

How very far, how madly far, I have come, and at what cost. The Indiaman had looked inviting enough at anchor in the mists of Gravesend, its rigging hung with lanterns and flags, and a little band on the wharf playing a jaunty air, but once on the high seas, the ship proved to be quite an incubator of disease. I had neither light nor air in my cabin. Hardly a week went by without a beshrouded cadaver chuting into the ocean. The dispatch always took place before breakfast and the dull, final splash of the remains brought back to me the loss of my little sisters. They have been very much in my thoughts, more than usual, since I embarked on this journey. On the ship, I seemed to feel them close by. It was an eerie sensation. I could hear that lisp of Jenny's and her slow way of speaking, as if she had all the time in the world. I recalled the sensation of carrying Maryanne on my hip as I busied myself in the seed loft at Durand Gardens, her heavy little body like a packet of oatmeal, and the smell of her, sour and sweet.

We stopped for less than twenty-four hours at Madeira to take in wines, and set sail again. The point of my journey, I continued to remind myself, was to renew the bond with my father and be restored to his good opinion. He was all that I had. The wind would vanish sometimes for days and we would flounder on the ocean, and at other times storms would pound the ship so hard I feared it would split asunder. Tremendous seas would break over the deck and carry things away. Sometimes, I would stop to converse to a fellow passenger as we walked on deck, but I never spoke of anything personal, only remarking on the seamen fishing or the flying fish skimming the waves.

I spent weeks thrashing over Nash's betrayal, but the further I sailed from England, the fainter the pain became and, at some point, I gave up my rancour just so that I did not have to badger myself with it any longer. The more distance there is between us, the more clearly I see Nash. It is in his nature to spring forth to the next adventure, pausing only to set on fire the bridge he has passed over. Yet I could not help but ask myself, as we approached Calcutta, if he had marvelled at it at first sight as I did now. It moved me to think that he had once looked on those fields of a fantastic green and the town strung out along its flat bank. But his name reminds me of past hopes sunk in disappointment and so I bring it less often to mind, except to wonder now and then if Selina will grow tired of him when the money runs out.

I did not stay long at Calcutta, passing only a fortnight in a boarding house while I arranged a passage upriver and accomplished the only endeavour that mattered to me in that city, which was to visit my mother's grave in the European cemetery. It was an oppressive place of coarse dank grass, and trees infested with carrion birds. I found the grave among a crowd of monumental stones, obelisks and pedestals bearing urns. The headstone had been carved with an oddly suggestive epitaph: *God takes the good, too good on earth to stay, and leaves the bad, too bad to take away.* My father, I assumed, had been its author.

While I was in Calcutta, I also wrote to Martenson care of the research station at Bankipore to announce my intention to visit Mr Ravine at his estate, Kaligar. I included in the letter a copy of the broadside I had written in the name of Nemesis. I was not confident that Martenson would ever receive the missive, since I had had no news of him and could not be sure if I would encounter him again. Perhaps I might travel on to Patna, eventually, but for the moment I was preoccupied with the prospect of visiting my father. He did not know I was on my way, and I was anxious about what I should find when I reached his estate. There are no rules of etiquette that I know for confronting the mystery of a parent who has made himself over into a stranger in order to exclude affection. I have learned to form a habit of independence, but it is fundamentally human to live in kinship and connection, I believe. Since my mission was to repair the past and to sew up the rent between my father and me, I kept thoughts of Dr Martenson at a distance.

It was very early in the morning when I departed Calcutta amid the clouds of crows and vultures that surrounded the *ghat*. The turbulence in the air quickened my blood. I and my fellow passengers were to travel the river in a stout two-masted vessel, about forty feet in length, called a pinnace. The accommodations were rudimentary – a covered part divided into cubicles where we slept, and a veranda – but it served well enough. We went in convoy on a strong tide, with a cookery boat and a barge that carried the livestock for our meals. The countryside was flat at first, dotted by palm trees and the cones of temples gleaming whitely. I was moved by the luxuriance of nature and the grandeur of the landscape – and I was shocked by the funeral pyres on the banks of the river and the occasional sight of mouldered corpses bobbing in the brown waters.

As we ascended the river, novel objects constantly presented themselves to my notice: temples and forests of shivering bamboo; I was transfixed by the sight of elephants, by the vast flocks of waterbirds flying over them, and banyan trees filled with screaming monkeys and green parrots. Perhaps it was that frame of mind, of being open to newness, that tilted my perceptions at a violent angle, because, as I ran through the story of Durand Gardens, something I had done countless times, its events presented themselves to me in a quite different light.

Grandfather would not accept the investments in the nursery that Papa had made. He would not go after new customers and, as a result, his business failed and my parents were compelled to leave in search of other opportunities. That was the tale of Durand Gardens. But how could I have accepted such a narrative unconditionally, when so many contradicting facts were known to me? Why did I never question the feasibility of a story that claimed my grandfather, a man who had run a business successfully for many years, had all at once lost the acumen that had sustained the Gardens ever since he was a young man? The plants of utility that he reared, the hedges and avenue trees, were stalwarts, bought for England's parks and estates in their thousands. He sold dependable plants, climbers and twiners, anything that covered walls and deformities and shut out the view of undesirable objects, and the kinds of evergreen perennials one uses to fill vacancies in borders during the winter months. Plants whose dependabilty reflected his patient and deliberate character. He had amassed customers everywhere, in Germany and the low countries and Scandinavia, as well as in Britain. I remember my mother remarking it, since she kept the order book and the cash book. He would travel to see his customers to settle up with them and leave the nursery in the hands of my parents. That is when Papa seized his chance. It must have cost a fortune to buy that modern stock of exotics – needy plants, expensive to rear out of their habitat – and to construct the pits and stoves and forcing houses that they required to coerce their growth. Papa used to say that people lose interest when they must wait years for a plant to mature. They want them full-blown at the outset. They want to be able to buy a punnet of strawberries in February.

In all these years, I had never let myself consider that it might have been my father's interests that had bankrupted the nursery and that it was he who had wrecked everything my grandfather had worked for.

Eight days after leaving Calcutta, we moored at the *ghat* that led the way to the city of Murshidabad. Here, I was to disembark. The estate of Kaligar was at Afzoulbang, about four miles from the city. I hung back, letting officers and their wives go ahead. There was a military cantonment near the city, I had learned. An hour passed by and still I did not shift from my spot. I looked out at the wooded hills beyond the riverbank. I had come to Bengal to find my father, but what I really wanted to find was that he was not a villain; that there had been a mistake in regard to his work for Sir Rollo Hayle; that there were mitigating factors that would let me, in all good conscience, continue to admire him, despite his criminal undertakings.

As I sat in that strange paralysis upon the deck of the pinnace, the drone of chanting and the din of bells and drums came to my ears and my gaze was drawn to a finger of land, running away from the bank, where a gathering had amassed. People dressed in rags were squatting on the ground, with their knees up around their ears, in devotion before a woman robed in white. I stood up and crossed to the railing to get a closer view of her. She sat on a cot, in a pose of swooning, open-palmed lassitude. As I gazed at her, she opened her eyes and raised her hands in a mystic gesture, then she turned her head in my direction, as if it were drawn on a string, and began to laugh. At that instant, a shaft of unexpected grief skewered my heart. The hairs stood up on the back of my neck as if something peculiar had happened. I was overcome by the revelation that I was at a crossroads in my life. On the one hand, truth; on the other, illusion – the illusion of my father. Oh, I can picture him so vividly, breezy and brazen, whistling through his teeth. Everything that he did was brilliant and correct, except when it was not. I knew, then, that my affection for him had grown as dead and cold as my feelings for Nash and I saw how deficient was my motivation to descend on him – for, actually, lurking beneath the desire to have my father properly own me was the need to shame him into remorse.

With a kind of horror, I realised that Daniel Ravine and Oliver Nash were cut from the same pattern. They were both reckless schemers, charming chancers, each hiding his self-serving nature behind a handsome veneer. It was blazingly clear to me now. I had chosen to make my life with a man who was a repeat of my father. Isn't it amazing how blind one can be to the colossal blunders of one's life? I had been a fool for Oliver Nash and a dissembler to myself.

I had been telling myself for weeks that I was reconciled to Nash's betrayal, but, of course, the opposite was true. Nash, my God, I loved you and yet I never knew you. Nash the vandaliser and falsifier. He had lied to me so very thoroughly and yet, although in my heart I must have suspected his sincerity, I could never get enough of him. I believe, now, that he did marry me only for the sake of those five hundred pounds. I was a liar, too, pretending to be something I am not and acting like a child who must have her sugar water and her toys to pacify her laments. I am astonished, and mortified, too, at how determined I was to rehearse a play whose plot was so familiar to me. I already knew very well how it was likely to end, and yet I was still surprised when Nash deserted me.

On the stone quay at the bottom of the *ghat*'s flight of stairs, our team of oarsmen was gathering. I resumed my place under the boat's veranda. I would not go to the house of my father. That would be to return to the past – and to disappear from view as completely as a woman sequestered in a seraglio.

I had travelled upriver on a rising tide of insights – and the most breathtaking of them struck me now. I had come to Bengal in search of Adam Martenson. The revelation felt like rain falling on land that had been parched for years. How stupidly hard it had been to admit the ascendancy Dr Martenson had gained over my mind and feelings. Even if he were gone from Patna, I intended to find him.

Our convoy proceeded upriver at a laborious pace. The waters were exceedingly low, awaiting the onset of the rains, and the oarsmen were frequently obliged to attach ropes to the pinnace and tow it along the banks. Sometimes, if the boat came near enough to shore, children and women would swim out to beg from us and we passengers would drop coins into their outstretched hands. Often, in the evening, there was lightning and thunder, the sky lit up as if by fireworks. When the storm had passed, fireflies glowed in the blackness and, overhead, the sky was thick with stars. However, my appreciation of the beauty of these scenes was mingled with frustration at the slowness of our progress. Three weeks passed before I caught my first glimpse of Patna. The sun was rising as the boat came into berth, staining the walls of the town a limpid pink. Ancient buildings clung to massive old revetments above the turbid waters and I stared up at them, excited by the undeflectable urge that had brought me to the place. As I leaned over the railing, a gust of wind lifted my light straw hat and flung it on to the waters. I pressed my hands to my hair, searching for the pin that had come astray. There was no advantage to losing my defence against the sun, and yet an odd feeling of pleasure stole through me as I watched the hat whirl lazily on an eddy.

The freshness of the dawn gave way rapidly to waves of heat and I soon regretted the economising that had led me to take an ox-cart from the *ghat* instead of accepting a carriage ride with my fellow passengers, who were subalterns bound for the cantonment. I had nothing with me but a valise. The cart passed through a city gate carved from blocks of basalt and lurched on to a wide and frantic high road, choked by traffic. The town within the walls was closely built, the houses stepped down to the street, with each storey standing on the roof of the veranda below. Patna, it seemed, was all about front. The flower-bedecked terraces and ornamental balconies were only visible to those approaching from the river. The grandeur that showed itself from a distance was undermined at close quarters by the presence of crumbling masonry, invading creepers and flimsy bamboo roofs that were anchored with stones to prevent them from blowing away.

The cart was a plodding, dusty experience and the powdery earth that coated the back of my throat forced me into a fit of coughing. I was not sure if the driver had understood my instructions to go to the Company Bagh at Bankipore, where I intended to ask after the whereabouts of Dr Martenson. The driver made no effort to hurry and eventually we came to a halt altogether in a *mêlée* of men and animals, and he indicated that I had reached my destination. I looked around with uncertainty at the crowded quadrangle. 'Company Bagh?' I asked. 'The English Factory?'

Surely this was not the Bagh; nevertheless, I noted on the far side of the quadrangle a substantial building that looked promising. A sign above a veranda proclaimed the *Bankipore Warehouse, European Articles*. A carpenters' workshop and a blacksmithery stood adjacent. A large tamarind tree shaded the warehouse's veranda. Perspiration poured from my skin and I felt that I could not spend another minute out in the sun. I paid the driver, stepped down from the cart into the confusion of buffalo and bullocks and creaking conveyances, and stumbled with my valise across the quadrangle on weak legs. I flailed through a curtain formed of strings of beads that hung in the doorway of the shop and put down my bag in the mercifully dim interior. I was aware of figures gliding about in white shifts and of a medley of merchandise – stationery, dinner services, hats, candlesticks, birdcages, and European clothes displayed on wicker mannequins. As my fingertips brushed the sprigged muslin of a deliciously light-looking gown, I caught sight of myself in a looking glass. My face was ghastly with a sort of haunted gaze and my short hair made me look like some creature from an asylum.

'Madam?' The clerk's tone carried something of a challenge in it. He was a bluff, tow-headed lad, who looked like he came from generations of cheesemakers. A violent shiver ran through my body as I tried to speak and I leaned on the counter for support. The clerk, who had been staring at me open-mouthed, suddenly snapped to attention.

'Will you serve this lady's needs or must we wait all day?'

My head turned slowly, wondering if I had conjured an apparition. But there he was: Adam Martenson. I was terribly affected by the sight of him and I fought to control my emotions.

'Have you a hat, Mrs Nash?' he asked.

He looked different. He was darker and more sinewy to my drooping gaze.

I said, 'It is fearfully hot, isn't it? Even my bones feel as if they are on fire. That is why I rid myself of my sleeves, you know. They were intolerable.' I held up my arms and looked at them as if I had never seen such things before.

'You were wise to travel lightly,' Martenson said, 'but you might take the hat with you. You will need it.'

A bonnet had appeared on the counter. 'Is this mine?' I asked.

'It is now.'

I groped for the hat and let Dr Martenson steer me from the shop. As we came out on to the veranda, I gave a cry. A little painted elephant with bells tinkling at its ankles was being led on a crimson halter by a boy across the quadrangle. I thought the elephant the most beautiful thing I had ever seen and a wave of euphoria passed over me.

Dr Martenson handed me up on to the seat of a buggy, beside a driver wearing a yellow turban and the mark of his caste on his forehead. I felt so weak it took a great effort even to turn my head to take in my surroundings. We passed a long wall of the kind that encloses an estate and I saw sepoys stationed at a gatehouse. Was this the Company Bagh, where factors and civil servants worked in mysterious ways? But we did not stop there. The buggy bumped onwards beneath shade trees that grew along the roadside. They were hung with pendulous mangoes. I caught a glimpse of ominous shapes heaving in the shadows beneath the trees. They might have been buffalo searching for forage or chimeras of my imagination – the further we went into the flat, open country-side, the worse I felt. My body shook with chills – how could that be, under such a fierce sun? – and my stomach churned. I hardly noticed that we had left the road until I saw, swimming up ahead in the waves of heat, a grassy com-pound and a low, pale house with a thatched roof. There were white spectres moving about on a wide veranda supported by slim poles. I closed my eyes and straight away had the sensation of toppling.

I woke in the night in a silence that seethed with croakings and rustlings. I could not think where I was. My ears strained to detect the carousers of Hood Street, the carts rumbling over cobbles, the sounding of the watch, the inordinately early church bells. An agonised howl sounded from very far away. Whatever creature had uttered it, I knew it could not harm me and I slipped back into sleep. It was light when I next opened my eyes. I lay on a hard cot, blinking at the open-raftered ceiling, summoning the strength to sit up. My flesh seemed to have turned to gauze and my bones to glass. My stomach ached as if it had been punched. Suddenly, a strong hand slid beneath my shoulders and pulled me upright against a plumped-up cushion. It was a woman, her head wrapped in a turban from which a muslin mouth-cloth dangled. She tipped water from a ewer into a bowl, her bangles clinking, and swabbed my hands and face with a towel. Then she passed me a cup and said, 'Medicine. Doctor giving.'

I sniffed at the tincture. It was milky with an insistent mossy smell, the flavour, one of cucumber or melon. I swallowed another mouthful and the attendant, satisfied, pushed aside the mat that hung over the doorway and left me alone. I drained the remainder of the physic and lay in a tranquil state, watching a couple of small, translucent lizards run up the wall next to my cot. They seemed almost to glow, or was it a trick of the light? The sun shining through the blind filled the room with mysterious raked shadows. How warm and rosy I felt. I heard myself laugh, and I said out loud, 'Things are well, just as they are.'

I fell asleep again, which seemed to last for hours, but when I awoke, feeling refreshed, I thought that perhaps very little time had passed, after all. The attendant, whose name was Amira, accompanied me to the bathing room. It was a dim chamber in a partitioned corner of the veranda, with a draining board on the flagged floor. Under her direction, I sat on a low stool in my shift and used a dipper to splash water over my head from a tank. The water ran out through a hole in the bottom of the tub, into a cesspool. Amira rubbed a paste into my hair that smelled of bergamot and then sluiced me with water. When I had donned my clean shift, she unstoppered a bottle and massaged sweet-smelling oil into my skin. I thrust my arms into a wrapping gown and tied it at the waist. As I combed through my damp hair with my fingers, I noticed a smell of mildew in the air and a sense of waiting.

I emerged from the bathing room feeling weak but relieved, as though I had purged a lifetime's worth of pestilence, and wandered along the veranda. Night had fallen and the inky sky was scattered with stars. I gazed out across a silvered expanse of lawn towards a grove of fat-trunked palms. The rising moon had made a glamorous silhouette of their crowns. A few yards further along the veranda, faint yellow light fanned from a doorway. I approached the door and saw that Martenson was working at a desk in a wide room with mismatched tables and chairs. I noticed a gun case and a plank table neatly laid with various horticultural objects. I recognised a herbarium press and budding knives. He looked up and, seeing me, got to his feet. He was wearing a light, white shirt that looked comfortable in the heat.

'Good evening, Mrs Nash,' he said. 'I hope you are improved.'

I allowed that I was feeling better.

'I am relieved to hear it. These fevers come on very quickly in India and they can be fatal.' The moment stretched itself out and then he said, 'But, please, do come in.'

Dr Martenson stepped forward and I offered him my hand. As he bowed over it, a pandemonium of emotions started up in my breast. It was extraordinary to be in his proximity so many thousands of miles from London, but I was sorry to find that his manner was rather unfathomable. He had the politeness not to remark on the abbreviation of my hair, for which I was grateful, not because I cared about the appearance of my chopped locks – travel and illness have a way of dissolving vanity, I have discovered – but because I did not wish to divulge the reason they had been shorn. I asked how long I had been under his care.

'Four days,' he replied.

I was astounded that so much time had slid by.

Martenson pinched at his mouth with thumb and forefinger. He said, 'I . . . Well, as you can imagine, I am astonished to see you. But I suppose you have been at Kaligar in the company of your father and thought to look me up.'

I shook my head. 'I did not see him. It was my intention

to do so, but when the boat reached Murshidabad, I could not seem to make a move. I had come all that way and, yet, when the moment came to disembark – well, I knew it would be pointless. My feelings about Mr Ravine, I realised, are cold and dead, just as his are in regard to me.'

'I appreciate that it must have been a difficult decision.'

How remote Martenson sounded. 'It was, but I ... I ...'

I wished to be the new, unartificed woman who had thrown off her past downriver, but as I gazed at Dr Martenson, I felt my courage fail me. I had told myself that I would risk declaring my feelings to him in a frank manner that would admit no doubt about their authenticity. If he did not respond with an equal fervour, I would gracefully retreat, knowing that I had at least tried to open myself to a different experience of love. But my sangfroid had deserted me completely now that Dr Martenson stood before me. He was such a good person, so deep and anchored, I could hardly bear to think what I should lose if he rejected me.

'Please do sit down, Mrs Nash,' he said. 'You do not look well.'

I collapsed on to a stool. Dr Martenson went to the door and called something in a native language and shortly Amira appeared. He spoke to her – I could not understand what was expressed – and then said, 'Amira will return you to your room. You must rest. And I must get on with this paperwork. I have a great deal to organise.'

I had a rushing sensation in my veins as if all the blood were leaving my body. 'Are you going away?' I asked faintly.

'Perhaps. The contract I have here obliges me to help raise new strains of opium and that is not where my interest lies; at least, I do not wish to undertake an activity that must be purchased at the cost of one that is more useful.'

'And what is that? Raising your hemp hybrids?'

'Yes, and searching for plants of a medicinal nature. Do not concern yourself, Mrs Nash. I will make every effort to ensure that your stay is as comfortable as possible. When you are feeling up to it, we will discuss what you shall need and where you should like to go.' He was already at his desk and was half-turned away from me. I was glad that he could not see the dismay – no, that is not accurate – the *anguish* that was stamped on my face at the prospect of his departure. I stood up and stumbled towards Amira. I turned, hesitated. Seeing him again had caused my sentiments to overrun and I could not think how to contain them.

Chapter 20

The Cloudburst

April, 1777

I sat on the veranda with paper and a pencil to my hand. Dr Martenson had supplied me with the materials after I had expressed a desire to record impressions of my journey to Patna, then he had gone to the Company Bagh to meet a plant hunter. It was late in the morning, but I had no idea of the exact time. I sighed and tucked up my legs on the squeaking divan. It was hardly more than a string cot with a couple of cotton carpets stretched over the ropes. Its makeshift nature was typical of the house in general, I had observed. There was a provisional quality to the cloth ceilings, the unglazed windows and the reed partitions and hangings, which served instead of doors and hallways to divide space within the dwelling. The effect very much appealed to me. One felt to be living in a tent, untied to the normal routines of domesticity. I looked at the paper on my lap. I had spread it on top of a book of Bengali grammar for a writing surface. I had thought to compose an account in a random way — actually, I did not know how else to order my observations; I depended on a structure to emerge in the fullness of time from an outpouring — but I had yet to write anything at all.

I could not help but think of the empty commonplace book that had sat untouched in my parlour at Hood Street.

The atmosphere was somnolent, the only sounds the rasp of a sweeper's broom on the stretch of beaten earth that surrounded the house and the secretive rustle of the sugar palms and the tamarind tree. I do not know how long I sat there in a dream-like state, but presently, I heard the sound of hoof-beats and saw in the distance Dr Martenson returning along the driveway on a big horse. A boy ran out from somewhere and caught the reins as his master dismounted. Dr Martenson clapped the horse on the shoulder in approval, before it was led away; then he caught sight of me and offered a rather stiff bow.

As he approached me, I said, 'Your horse looks a robust beast.'

'That is Junu. He is an old cavalry mount, toughened by years of travelling over rough ground. He has served me well.' He removed his hat and struck it a blow to dislodge the dust. Then he said, 'How are you, Mrs Nash?'

'I am perfectly well,' I said, as coolly as I could. I was determined to steel myself to parting from him.

He nodded and looked around as if he were trying to decide which of many tasks he would embark on next. He stepped up onto the veranda. There was a dreadful awkwardness between us.

I said suddenly, 'I suppose I should tell you that I am no longer Mrs Nash. I have returned to my original name. It is Carey Ravine.'

He widened his eyes in surprise. 'Have you separated from your husband?'

'He has separated from me.' Then I added, 'And I am glad of it.'

Dr Martenson waved away another of the servants, who had darted out onto the veranda and salaamed before him. He sat down in a basket chair next to the divan and looked at me with concern. I said, 'He went off with the money he got from Casserly for your reports, and with my friend, Selina Colden, too.'

'I am very sorry.'

I threw the paper and the book to one side and toyed with the pencil.

Dr Martenson said, 'I hate to think of you being hurt.' After a pause he cleared his throat, and added, 'Will you like to tell me about it?'

'No, I will not. All there is to say is that it is over between Nash and me.'

I looked at him and this time he held my gaze. I had a yearning to stretch out next to him on the narrow little day bed he kept in his office, hardly daring to breathe, while he was asleep, and to bask, with a deep, abiding love, in his presence.

All of a sudden, he rose to his feet and said, 'You really do seem stronger today, Miss Ravine. I am very glad of it.'

'So I am. I am a great deal better.'

He said, 'Perhaps you might like to test your vigour by coming out to ride this afternoon?'

★

I felt perfectly comfortable as we set out, having borrowed a pair of Amira's trousers in order to ride astride and a veil of hers to wrap around my head against the dust. It occurred to me, as I was dressing, that it was the authentic version of the costume I had worn to the Soma Ball. Dr Martenson had found a docile Arabian mare for me, while he rode his cavalry horse, Junu. As we rode along an imperfect dirt road, my gaze followed the hawks that were swooping over the poppy fields. Protected by levees and fences of prickly pear, the fields stretched with determined monotony towards the horizon. Lines of women and children moved among the expanse of poppies, bleeding the capsules. Scattered here and there were clusters of mud huts with roofs carelessly thatched, and numbers of stringy men clad in loincloths, who sat motionless on their haunches as they watched us go by. Women in enveloping drapery of a dun colour looked up from the mortars, which they were pounding, as we passed. Although the sun was descending from its zenith, the temperature was like a furnace, and yet my enthusiasm for the vitality of the surroundings did not lessen.

Presently, a village came into view and we rested under the shade cast by a blessedly large tree with feathery leaves, and Dr Martenson bought coconut water from a woman to quench our thirst. The tree seemed to be the only handsome feature of the settlement, which otherwise was little more than a collection of flimsy dwellings, but even in this neglected setting I had no yearning for London. The fops in their chocolate houses, the gamesters in their laced coats, the damsels and their *billets-doux* – they had all faded along with their chatter. Now I heard only birdsong, the soft thud of the horses' hooves and the shouts that flew up from time to time from the labourers in the opium fields.

After leaving the village, Dr Martenson led us to a field that was bound by a tract of forest and it was here that we dismounted. We brought the horses to drink from a large tank that stood in the field, then tethered them and made our way into an enormous grove of bamboo. Its graceful arches formed a cool, shady vault. The bamboo gave way to a clearing surrounded by an abundance of large trees, which the sun penetrated at odd angles, casting exaggerated shadows. Malevolent-looking monkeys squatted in their branches and shrieked at us. Dr Martenson drew my attention to a mossy wall on the far side of the clearing and I realised that we were standing before the ruins of a mansion. Where the walls remained, the stucco had fallen, revealing rotten bricks beneath. We picked our way over a collapsed flight of steps and entered the shell of a great hall. Trees had broken through the mosaic floor and breached what was left of the roof. They bathed the space in a greenish light. The effect of the scene was both eerie and somehow moving – the disintegrating structure was a testament to the relentless operation of time on human endeavours. I remarked on the sense of erasure and melancholy at the site and I saw that Dr Martenson felt it too.

At the sound of a sudden rustling in the undergrowth, I swung around to determine its cause. Dr Martenson quickly reassured me that it was only a monkey. 'There are no tigers or elephants here,' he said. In fact, I was not afraid. At home I was a jumpy creature at the beck and call of nerves and feelings and yet here, where more material threats were present, I felt quite equable and capable of confronting them without panic. The fascination that the surroundings held for me neutralised any apprehension.

As we turned and clambered back over the jumble of broken steps, Dr Martenson reached out his hand to assist me. I took it, although I hardly needed to, since I was almost more nimble than he. I was sorry when he let go of my hand.

We retraced our footsteps through the grove of bamboo and it was at that moment I chose to tell Dr Martenson about my final act in London. I said, 'My arrival here has overtaken a letter I sent you from Calcutta. It includes copies of a broadside that I published under the name of Nemesis the day that I took passage for India. It revealed everything that you and I learned about Hayle and the blue agent. I found a man willing to print it and distribute it around the town.'

Dr Martenson stopped in his tracks and stared at me in amazement. 'How brave of you,' he cried. 'And you waited so long to tell me.'

'It had seemed to me, at the time, little enough to do, in the end, against such prevailing men as Casserly and Hayle. Whether it had any effect on the public, I do not know. I have a copy with me. Should you like to read it?'

We returned to the field and sat down on the ground under the protection of the tree. I brought out the broadside from my pocket and Dr Martenson unfolded the paper and held it flat on his knee with his fingertips. As he absorbed the columns of print, I felt a sort of effervescence light up my face. Had there ever been an accomplishment in my life that had caused me as much satisfaction as the publication of the broadside? I had not known so, until I saw Dr Martenson reading it. I had underestimated the value of an act that is bigger than oneself.

He put the paper to one side and aimed at me such a look of admiration, I thought my heart would burst. 'What a wonder you are, Miss Ravine.'

'I wish you would call me Carey.'

'Carey,' he repeated, uttering my name thoughtfully. The sound of it in his mouth thrilled me.

'I will call you Adam. We are friends, aren't we, after all?'

He said, 'There are few people whose estimation means very much to me, but you are one of them.' After a pause, he added, 'I am glad you did not go to Kaligar.'

'I believe that I told you, when we parted in London, that I lacked the courage to be shunned anew by my father. So it proved.'

'It is my guess that your father would have frustrated your intention. Men like Ravine and Hayle can never acknowledge their errors. The affront to themselves is too great. You possess more than courage enough, Carey. Publishing this statement has come at a great cost to your liberty, hasn't it?'

I nodded. It was true that I risked arrest for libel should I return to London, but I did not care – and said so.

All at once a flock of teal rose up screeching from the tank as a dust-devil came spinning across the field. It dashed grit into our faces and we got to our feet, rubbing at our eyes. When the gust had dissipated, it left behind an atmosphere of heavy stillness; there was something apprehensive in it. I followed the direction of Dr Martenson's – Adam's – gaze and saw that a towering cloud had appeared on the horizon.

He said, 'Usually the monsoon comes later, but these are signs of an early burst. It will make headway difficult on the trails.'

'You are going to work for the plant hunter, then.'

'Yes. His name is McLeod. An old colleague of mine from Edinburgh commended me to him. He is adept at raising money for private expeditions and mountain hemp is among the species he is after. I can return to Bhutan on his patrons' coin, without being bound to the East India Company. McLeod has also offered me a contract to procure plants of interest in Venezuela and Cuba. Perhaps I will do so. I haven't decided. But I would certainly like to add to my dispensatory. Your friend Mr Wheeler was very helpful to me and he is interested in publishing it. Perhaps you will write something for him while you are here?'

'I do not know if I have anything to say. My mind, you see, is fast emptying itself of many ideas that I have held dear. I am swirling around in something of a void.'

He smiled at me. 'Sometimes, just to be alive is worthy of note. In any case, please know that I will not depart without making sure that you are well taken care of.'

I said, 'Adam ...'

His smile grew warmer and I thought that perhaps he liked as much as I did the shift in closeness that the use of our Christian names signified. I said, then, 'Take me with you.'

The colour drained from his face. It was not the reaction I was expecting. 'Carey . . .' he said, after a pause, his voice husky.

I repeated, with a quickening pulse, 'Wherever it is that you are going, take me with you. You can teach me things, practical things. I do not wish to write down thoughts and impressions in a pretty notebook and sit at tea while servants rush about me. I want to be useful.'

Still he did not say anything.

'Perhaps you will think that I will not be able to manage in far outposts,' I said, my tone urgent, 'and that I will miss having a female coterie, but I do not care about that. Please, do not underestimate me.'

'I have never underestimated you,' he said. 'I have revered you from the moment that I laid eyes on you and it has taken all my resolve to keep my feelings from you.'

I felt dizzy with ardour at his declaration, but there was also a reserve in his face that dimmed my smile.

He said, 'I have never told you that I was once married. Lucy was her name. I pressed my way of life on her and, as a result, I rendered her deeply unhappy and lonely. Our living together came to be attended by mutual sorrow. She arrived at her death, here in Patna, in a tragic accident that torments me still. Had I not brought her out to India, had I not asserted my own preference on a woman, she would still be alive. The experience altered me and I have felt for a very long time that I am not fit for affection.'

I seized his hand. I said, 'I am very sorry to hear about your poor wife, God rest her soul, but, if you will only allow me to, I will risk your defective affections. My own can hardly be less faulty. Despite my feelings for you, I fear a situation where the foundation of my happiness is bound up in another. I am afraid to lay myself open to you and yet I do – because I believe you are not a man who would try to turn me from a course of action that is important to me. That is, I mean to live differently. I do not know how, but I think you could help me to find the way – and I would love you for it.'

He gave me a burning look and kissed my hand. A fit of shivering overtook me and he said, 'Carey, we must make haste. The character of the day has altered.'

While we had been speaking, the towering cloud had covered the sun and washed the air in a cold, violet light. We sprang to our horses, then, and followed the road to Bankipore under the darkening skies. There was a sense of urgency about the people we passed, the drovers goading starved-looking bullocks, and scurrying women holding on to the baskets on their heads. As we neared the house, tongues of lightning began to flicker among swollen clouds. Then came the sound of a deafening thunderclap. We could see the station's servants and labourers milling about in the compound, amid barking dogs, shouting in anticipation.

As Adam and I left the stables, a few fat drops of rain fell with slight puffs in the dust and a cry went up from the people. Suddenly, the downpour sluiced out of the clouds and we ran for the veranda. We dashed under its eaves and turned to watch the rain come hissing across the clearing in front of the house. The people in the compound lifted their faces to it in exultation. Within minutes, our clothes were soaked and my feet were squelching in my shoes. I looked up through the dripping strands of my hair at Adam in his wet shirtsleeves. He was laughing with an expression of delight that I found heart-rendingly boyish. We both turned our gazes upward, like saints looking towards heaven, as the torrent pounded the roof with the noise of falling stones. Then Adam directed his attention to me and a quiver passed through my body as he fixed his eyes on mine. The blood flowed to my cheeks and heat flooded the pit of my belly. At that instant, a gust of wind shook the house and the tamarind tree overhead began to hurl its limbs around. The air was filled with the confetti of its tiny scarlet petals tumbled by the rods of rain.

It is dawn and the six bearers have assembled in the compound. I am waiting with my horse on its lead for the man of my heart to conclude his address to the cortège, before we sally out on our journey north. We hope to manage a march of eight or nine hours before the afternoon deluge descends. There will be few resthouses upon the road. We shall travel with two sets of tents, the one proceeding ahead for our reception, while we make use of the other. When we reach the great mountains, we shall leave the tents and travel light and in disguise as Asiatics – that is our plan, at any rate. I am advised that the journey will be arduous and the roads heavy and steep and hazardous to our safety. We must forego ordinary comforts and accommodations and content ourselves with whatever cookery we can find. But the life I have lived up until this moment has prepared me for the undertaking and I approach it eagerly. I have achieved a sufficient hardness and my mind is estranged from all that is sham and prone to deceiving sentiment. Adam has shown me how to prepare ox bladders for the preservation and transport of plant specimens and I have learned the use of our portable bearing compass, for we have no map to follow once we enter the chain of mountains. We must be our own field engineers, taking the bearings of the unknown road, and depend on our wits, our instincts and the will to preserve ourselves from destruction in order to reach the wonderful elevation that we seek.

Adam has approached me now with his soulful smile and begins to explain the best way of putting the strap around my waist and fastening it to the crupper of the saddle, so that if my horse should stumble, I will not fall. For it is a precious, short life we have, is it not?

**Keep reading for some exclusive material about
Debra Daley's first historical novel:**

Turning the Stones

Georgian England, mid-eighteenth century.

As a foundling the young Em Smith is brought to
the Cheshire country home of the ambitious Waterland
family, where she serves as a companion to their daughter,
Eliza. But as they grow up, Em's position becomes
uncertain and she is increasingly troubled by the mystery
of her birth. When Eliza goes in pursuit of a husband
and a fortune in London, Em finds herself implicated in
a horrific crime and must flee for her life.

Her frantic escape takes her across country and
onto the high seas, where she is at the mercy of the
enigmatic smuggler, Captain McDonagh. But there
is a more potent force drawing Emily on: a spirit whose
presence she has felt all her life, and whose irresistible
design - be it malicious or benevolent - will force her
onwards to a distant shore. There she will confront the
astonishing secret of her origins.

My approach to the supernatural in *Turning the Stones*

By Debra Daley

I love a good ghost story, and I'm always fascinated by occasions of mind over matter, but in *Turning the Stones* I was more interested in the psychology behind my characters' experience of the supernatural rather than have them wrangle with actual wraiths and weird entities.

We are all wired to look for meaning in the world and that's an impulse that can encourage some extreme ideas when you're under intense emotional stress. It's possible to have the experience of anomalistic things happening without anything paranormal necessarily taking place – it's called magical thinking – and that's a state of mind I played with in *Turning the Stones*.

There are characters in my book who respond to trauma by seeing things that aren't really there and by attributing a pattern to events that are in fact brutally arbitrary. Personal investment in ritual objects like wishing wells and Irish cursing stones – which are the kind of stones referred to in the title of my book – is an extension of this need to give ourselves the illusion of control. We all do this to some degree when we automatically say things like 'fingers crossed' or 'knock on wood', as if these little invocations could actually influence the operations of the world. It's very human to want to believe that there is a moral order at work in the universe, instead of having to face the reality that bad things can happen randomly to good people.

Ghost stories present phenomena that are generally regarded as impossible, whereas I tried in *Turning the Stones* to place my supernatural elements in a context in which they could be plausible. Hidden memories, for example, triggered by a sense perception such as a smell or a voice – or visions and other intense perceptual experiences that could arise from hunger or exhaustion or mental disorder.

I saw the supernatural elements in my book as expressions of the subconscious mind as well as indicators of the mysteries of the mind. As my heroine Em says, 'Perhaps you might think as I do that there is more to the world than meets the eye. I will even go so far as to say that the human mind has a capacity for communication that has not yet been entirely revealed to us'. That possibility excites me.

About Irish Cursing Stones

A cursing stone tends to be found in a distinctive cup-shaped hollow, called a *bullaun*, in the bed of a larger stone – which is known as a *bullaun stone*. Stones accommodated in a *bullaun* can be turned like a pestle in a mortar in order to do their work of cursing or curing.

The stones are turned clockwise to make a cure or anti-clockwise to put a spell or a curse on someone. The original purpose of *bullaun* stones has never been established, although archaeologists have suggested that they may have been used for grinding grains or crushing iron ore. But a ritual/religious interpretation of the stones has in general held sway, even if unproved.

They were likely sites of pagan nature worship at one time as were other celebrated stones in Ireland such as standing stones, dolmens, kissing stones, wishing stones, rocking stones and speaking stones. Supernatural powers — even sentience — have been ascribed to many of the stones. These powers are usually accessed by uttering charms and undertaking a ritual performance such as circling the stone or turning the stone or crawling through a hole in it.

Whatever the class of stone, it was an entity that commanded respect. A curse on a stone was not to be undertaken lightly. It was said to rebound on the curser if there were no just cause for it.

There don't seem to have been any forgiveness stones.

Debra Daley's *Turning the Stones* is available online or from any good bookshop.